QUANTUM CRYSTAL SKULL

Book I of The Emagication Trilogy

by Gare Martin

© 2016 Gare Martin

All Rights Reserved.

No part of this publication may be reproduced, stored in a retrieval system, or transmitted, in any form or by any means, electronic, mechanical, photocopying, recording, or otherwise, without the written permission of the author.

First published by Dog Ear Publishing
4011 Vincennes Rd
Indianapolis, IN 46268
www.dogearpublishing.net

ISBN: 978-1-4575-4844-4

This book is printed on acid-free paper.

This book is a work of fiction. Places, events, and situations in this book are purely fictional and any resemblance to actual persons, living or dead, is coincidental.

Printed in the United States of America

CONTENTS

PROLOGUE v

PART ONE   1927: PRISMS OF DESTINY

Chapter One   Fights For Life 3

Chapter Two   Survival In Stinks 9

Chapter Three   Lights Above, Lights Below 15

Chapter Four   Prophecy And Secrecy 21

Chapter Five   The Smell of Inspiration and Hope 29

Chapter Six   Skullarly Opinions 38

Chapter Seven   Sound Investment 45

Chapter Eight   Crystal Unclear Fate 52

Chapter Nine   We: A Sacred Dimension 62

PART TWO   1939-1975: PRISM SHADOWS

Chapter One   Unexplained Skies 72

Chapter Two	Crystal Skull Spies	79
Chapter Three	Left From Boston, Right To Telepathy	87
Chapter Four	A New Life In A Cold World	96
Chapter Five	Mark Of Family, Mark Of War	104
Chapter Six	Crystal Clear Overseas Connections	111
Chapter Seven	Denial Denied	124
Chapter Eight	Skull Mates In Prism	126
Chapter Nine	A Path Of Progress, A Street Of Tragedy	139
Chapter Ten	Run From The Past, Trip Into Fear	150
Chapter Eleven	Alone Trail Of Freedom	161
Chapter Twelve	Grace Balls Of Fire!	166
Chapter Thirteen	Rekindled Kindred	179
Chapter Fourteen	Jinxed, Of Curse	185
Chapter Fifteen	Reimagining Heredity	191
Chapter Sixteen	Scrambling Destiny's Egg	203
Chapter Seventeen	Out of Prism for Bad Behavior	218

PROLOGUE

BEWARE OF THE MIRROR
AT THE EDGE OF THE UNIVERSE

"Oh...I'm so sorry!" Tessa grabbed the now empty plastic cup from the cola saturated man's lap. She dabbed soda pop from the middle aged man's neck before giving the remainder of the her napkins to him and hurrying to her seat.

"He didn't recognize me. Anyway, the plan has been activated."
"Give him more," suggested a different voice inside of her head.
"Not yet," reasoned her more familiar personal voice.
"But he is the one."
"For what?" But the question did not linger in Tessa's mind.

PART ONE

1927

PRISMS OF DESTINY

CHAPTER ONE

FIGHTS FOR LIFE

Spokane, Washington
March 1927

BAM! Amanda awoke immediately at the sound of a door slamming somewhere in the house. She heard loud noises and shouting as she grabbed her robe and pulled it over her eight month pregnant body. "It's Lenny! Get up! They're here!" Amanda woke her husband with her command while in the same instant attempting with growing success to escape her dream world and blend in with reality for everyone else.

"No, no!" her three year old son Lenny yelled, seemingly arguing yet alone in his room.

As Amanda made her way out of her bedroom doorway, she heard the sound of something glass breaking and something else hitting the wall and then the door. She could turn the door handle but the door was jammed or blocked. A prismic flare of light glowed under the door, curiously stirring memories of her late grandfather Strong Eagle. "Jason! Lenny! Jason!"

Jason was already in his robe and in the hall. "What in hell is that kid doing?" The next loud crash against the door startled them both. "What is happening in there?"

"No, no! You get away from me!" Lenny's young voice bellowed from behind the door.

SLAM! "That's the play room door!" Amanda began beating on the bedroom door, agressively but not in panic, while Jason banged his shoulder into it with no results. He tried the door handle once again and was startled as the door seemingly pulled itself open. "What the...Where is he?"

"He's in the play room. What a mess!"

"Go away!" the toddler screamed in pure fury.

"It's just a nightmare, Lenny!" Amanda begged. "Come on, come out of there!"

The screaming and yelling by their son ceased. Jason twice tried to push open the door but failed. "Get away from the door, son."

"You leave!" The command from the three year old was calm and decisive.

Both parents pushed against the door and both were relieved how easily it opened.

"Mommy! Daddy!" Lenny stood trembling and began crying as they entered the room.

"What happened in here?" Amanda asked her son as she dropped to one knee to hug him.

"The devil was here!" Lenny responded, hugging his mother.

"How could you block the door?" Jason inquired as he joined in comforting his son. "It was just a nightmare. You'll be fine."

Amanda carried Lenny to his bedroom. "You already look calm and sleepy."

Jason Michael Galvin had little use for religion. "The tale of the devil coming to Spokane tonight is not one I will likely share with many people," he said when he returned to bed. "He spoke so candidly about the devil. Where did he get that idea?"

* * *

"You have been working at the telephone company for a year now but you spend just as much time fixing up the boat," remarked Amanda. "I thought you were trying to change it into an arc."

"You talked me into it!" Jason joked, but he wasted little time completing the repairs on the cabin cruiser. By the end of March it was declared fit for sailing. "I would like to spend a night on the new boat sometime soon. We can go to Lake Couer d'Alene. After that we'll be on new baby time."

Jason took his son with him to the lake several times before the family outing on the boat. "Lenny seems to be learning the boating rules very well,"

Amanda commented to her husband as they both watched their son watch a boat slowly leaving the docks while walking along the wooden dock.

"Lenny, let's go. It's time to shove off!" Amanda called to her young son. She was not watching when Lenny slipped on the wet dock and fell into the 40 inch deep water without much splash.

The boy did not panic, nor did he fight to find his way to the surface. Natural instinct or perhaps previous experience in the bathtub made him hold his breath. "Look at the fish!" Lenny thought, gazing underwater at the rainbow trout under the dock. He wanted to smile but instead remembered to keep his mouth closed. He watched the rays of light refracting through the water from the surface, and something else. "What is it?"

As Amanda began to move the pace of the world, in her reality, became slower. Her mind instantly registered the ripples in the water indicating Lenny's location. Her instincts told her to move quickly within the warped time. It took the nearly nine months pregnant woman some seven seconds to yell to Jason, make her way past the gear on the floor of the boat, get up on the side and jump onto the dock. The sheer velocity of her jump and the extra weight of her pregnant body made the dock displace a great deal of water. As the top of Lenny's head momentarily became visible, Amanda dropped to her knees, reached into the water and snatched her son by the shoulders.

"I've got him! He's safe!"

Amidst all of the fuss and the towels and the wrapping of the young boy in a blanket, Lenny remained calm. He was cold and wet and unaware of doing anything wrong. "I'm okay. What's wrong mom?"

"You could have drowned!"

"What's dwown?" Lenny responded. "I'm okay. The angel in the water was there too."

In the coming weeks, Lenny heard his parents recall the story to their friends. The image of the nine-month pregnant Amanda and the "gawoosh" of the dock giving way to her jump produced a laugh by the listeners every time as did the continued image of her yanking her son out of the water like a bear snagging a fish.

Lenny's memory was different. "I saw the fish, and the light, and the angel."

* * *

When Margaret Louise Galvin was born on May 6, 1927, Lenny had a new source of fascination. "Mom, why is she so little?"

"Everyone is that small when they are babies. They need bigger people to take care of them."

"I can help gooder than anyone."

"I saw you helping the neighbors today," acknowledged his mother.

"Tommy got to throw stuff on the big fire but I need to get older first."

During early March, groundbreaking for a house had commenced on the abutting lot to the south. Several weeks after Margaret's birth the neighbors moved into the dwelling but the two families became friends well before that time. Patricia was a librarian and Ed was the princial at the same elementary school. The Tonning family had older children but they knew no other children in the sparsely populated valley. Sometimes twelve year old Shelley or ten year old Tommy would babysit Lenny while other times the neighbor kids would stay with the Galvin family.

"Is Lenny giving you any trouble when he visits?" Jason asked Ed.

"Mostly he seems interested in whatever we are doing at the time. He has different activities with each of us."

"Well, don't let him get too much in the way. How much is yet to be finished on the house?"

"Finishing the basement is a project for a later time with later funds but we still need to finish the stairwell walls."

One weekend in May Ed was working on a project in his new basement while Patricia was preparing supper. Tommy and Lenny were playing in the living room when Tommy broke one of his toys. "My dad can fix it. I'm going to ask him."

Tommy opened the door to the basement stairway and headed down the stairs. Lenny followed for three or four steps but then missed the next step, falling sideways and downward.

"Lenny!"

Ed heard the sickening sound across the unfinished basement after Tommy yelled. He turned abruptly and could see Lenny through the framed two by fours, lying motionless on the floor. "Oh heavenly God!" He ran to the young boy with no notion of what to expect. The sight far exceeded his fears.

"I don't know what happened! I didn't know he followed me down the stairs until he fell," Tommy moaned.

The inertia of the young boy's body was no match for the concrete floor. There was little blood but immediate swelling on Lenny's head, which was fractured, swollen and mushy on the right side.

Ed charged up the stairs and through the door with the unconscious child. "What happened? Oh my God!" Pat briefly sank to one knee in shock.

"I am taking him to the hospital. Go tell Amanda! Round everyone up and drive to the hospital!" As he left his previously peaceful domicile, he turned for one last instruction. "Somebody call Jason! He can meet us there!"

The drive to Deaconess Hospital was fourteen miles. Jason worked only two miles from the hospital and he arrived shortly after Lenny was admitted to emergency where he received immediate attention. After being told he would not be able to see his son until the doctors were finished, Jason approached his badly shaken friend. "What happened?"

"I'm not sure. He followed Tommy down the stairs and he went off the side. It was the worst sound I've ever heard. Lenny was a mess when I got to him. His head was already badly swollen."

Jason's hazel eyes squinted while contemplating the image. He paced momentarily, several times running his fingers through his well groomed brown hair. Ed slumped into a chair.

"Thank you, Ed," Jason managed, fighting back tears. "Thank you for your quick actions."

"I've seen a number of hurt children at the school but the sound and the sight of this will haunt me."

Amanda, Patricia, and the three children arrived shortly. "No news yet," Jason informed them. Ed took the children to eat at a nearby cafe after taking food orders for his spouse and friends.

At 9:30, Amanda motioned to Jason to meet her in the hallway. "I'd better get Margaret home," she said with a sigh. "I'll be back in the morning."

"I will call right away if there are any changes," Jason said, placing his hands upon his wife's shoulders and then pulling her to him.

"It is his destiny to live," Amanda whispered. "I can feel my son fighting for his soul somehow. It is some kind of struggle for the prophecy of Strong Eagle, my grandfather."

"What if the prophecy is for Margaret instead? The doctors have never seen a case like this and they are very uncertain our son will live."

Amanda pondered the notion briefly, her dark brown eyes appearing to focus on a distant vision. "He will live. To fulfill a destiny, miracles must be expected."

After Amanda left, Jason paced in the hallway. "Am I being punished? Is my son injured because of my big secret sin? That isn't fair but neither is life."

At 10 o'clock the next morning, Ed and Amanda arrived again at the hospital. Lenny had yet to awaken. "I am glad it is Saturday so you don't have to worry about work," Amanda said. "You need some rest."

"I do. I am going to sleep in the car for a couple of hours." Later, after waking up, he purchased a sandwich at a café and ate it on the way back into the hospital.

"Still no word," was Amanda's initial response when Jason entered the waiting room.

Sunday afternoon brought a change in the waiting relay. "I came prepared. Margaret and I both can
stay for awhile," Amanda told her husband. "You need to rest and you definitely could use a bath."

Later that evening, Amanda was returning to Lenny's room with the baby after using the telephone when she noticed a stream of light shining out of the bottom of the door. "It's like the warming flare of a campfire but it reminds me of a rainbow." Opening the door, she stood puzzled at the lack of anything in the room that could cause such a glow.

Amanda sat in the chair near the hospital bed alternately looking at her injured son and her infant daughter. "Strong Eagle, my grandfather, my son is in limbo. Was the crystal light part of the healing?"

Jason was back at the hospital shortly before Lenny reached his 50th hour of being unconscious. With each passing hour, hope diminished. After 72 hours, very little hope remained.

CHAPTER TWO

SURVIVAL IN STINKS

Leningrad, Soviet Union
April 1927

Fumbling a pair of wool socks as Alexiev pulled them out of his dresser, he watched helplessly as a small framed photograph of his late wife crashed to the floor. He carefully replaced the picture on the dresser and then chuckled at his effort. "I will never see this again," he thought, mindful it was dangerous to speak those words.

"I'm glad I decided to wear several layers of clothes so I won't have to carry them," Alexiev thought, stuffing his coat pockets with socks. His luggage consisted of one bag, the smallest one he owned. "Time is of the essence."

It was growing dark outside. It would be completely dark in less than an hour. In 70 minutes Alexiev would meet his friend Nicholas, who would then drive him out of the city. Alexiev could not wait in his flat for his friend. It was too dangerous.

"Wearing the extra layers was a good idea," Alexiev thought as he stepped outside. He had some difficulty buttoning up his overcoat. "I look fatter."

Alexiev considered buying an apple for a quick snack but reconsidered. "No recognition…no tracks," he said to himself and kept walking. When he neared his destination point, Alexiev found a darkly shadowed spot in an otherwise dark alley. He could see most of the area in his environment and he would easily be able to spot the automobile that Nicholas would be driving. He lit his last cigarette. When he finished it he realized, "That might be my last cigarette in Russia."

Finally Nicholas arrived. It seemed an eternity but actually his friend was several minutes early. Acting out what he had rehearsed in his mind, Alexiev casually strolled to the vehicle. He opened the car door. "Hello comrade."

"My old friend!" Alexiev loudly proclaimed. "I seem to have missed my ride. Can you drive me home?" Alexiev stood smiling, "Perhaps I could buy you a vodka?" He laughed in a jolly manner.

"I could use a drink my friend," Nicholas responded, instantly recognizing the act.

"I thought you would be wearing your fake beard. It is a good time of day to drive you out of the city," declared Nicholas after Alexiev closed the car door. "I offer again to drive you where you need to go. Just say the word."

"Thank you my friend but I fear danger in my near future. It will be much better if you are not seen by anyone while driving me to meet the train. Soviet authorities might try to intercept us."

After parting with Nicholas, the transition into disguise and onto the train went smoothly. As the train accelerated into the dark rural countryside, Alexiev faintly smiled at his reflection in the window. "This phony beard used to make me look older," reflecting upon his brief attempt at acting prior to the revolution. "Now it fits my age of 32."

He flinched and cringed at the sound of something dropped onto the railcar floor. "That scared the hell out of me!" He quickly regained his composure. "I do not want to invite conversation." Alexiev used his acting skills to overcome his anxiety and paranoia but pretending to be asleep was not an option. "I will wait for almost everyone else to fall asleep, then I will rest briefly."

As the train advanced toward Alexiev's unknown destination, he thought about Nicholas. "I am thankful he is not leaving the Soviet Union with me. Things are under control for the present time, but who knows what the future holds? I cannot imagine Nicholas in a different country, a different culture. I can't imagine myself in another country either but I'm on my way. I will lose myself in Prague and then again in Paris. After that, I don't have a plan. I'll figure it out then."

Previously, Nicholas had watched Alexiev's train pull away from his parked position about a block and a half from the station. He left simultaneously with the train although headed in a different direction. It took him approximately two hours to drive home. Despite being early April, a snowstorm made visibility very limited for nearly the first 20 miles of the trip. The remainder of the drive was rainy. "It's a relief to be home. I am exhausted and I am tired of trying to figure out the big mystery of Alexiev."

After opening his apartment door, Nicholas flipped on the light. He had less than three seconds to wonder who his assailant was before two bullets killed him.

* * *

Alexiev awoke in a startled manner as he felt the train losing speed. He had dozed longer than anticipated and was surprised to see the early shades of daylight outside the window. "Soviet vehicles!"Alexiev screamed in his thoughts, "maybe 1500 meters away. The train is going slow enough to jump."

Calmly, Alexiev stretched, collected himself and straightened his clothing before getting up and walking out of the passenger car. Within seconds he bolted from the train.

"Don't be so paranoid," Alexiev advised himself. "Those government cars may have nothing to do with me." Nonetheless he instinctively realized that his survival required constant focus. "Staying out of sight when possible is sound strategy."

Being in disguise was distressful. "This fake beard is driving me crazy. I must force myself to leave it alone. Even in this dark alley, fooling too much with the beard is revealing."

A bottle went skittering along the cobblestones as though it had been accidentally kicked. Alexiev sank deeper into the shadows when he easily recognized two Soviet goons talking.

"I am out of cigarettes and I want to go home."

"You complain too much!" Alexiev held his breath during the following momentary silence. "In only a couple of more hours we can go."

"I wish someone would catch the bastard and get it over with."

"They aren't waking Yuri until daylight. When he tracks with the dogs, our Comrade Alexiev will not be difficult to find."

Fortunately the two men continued walking down the street. "Up until now I actually thought those Soviet thugs were after someone else. Now I have to come up with a plan to save myself within the next few hours."

He knew the search would be thorough. He knew about the hunting dogs, "all expertly trained in the pursuit of humans. Trotsky never liked the dogs. There were times when he wanted someone with him when the dogs were anywhere near and many times it was me. I respected him. I will miss him."

For weeks before his escape attempt, Alexiev grew increasingly uncertain about the status of Trotsky in the ongoing Soviet political power struggle. There were rumors of a potential expulsion from the Communist Party. While not intentionally eavesdropping, Alexiev heard his boss discussing Stalin with one of the Soviet brass. "Stalin ordered the execution of several loyal party members. He must be stopped."

The staff member was much closer to the Stalin camp than Trotsky realized and subsequently Alexiev was advised by inside sources to escape Leningrad. "As Trotsky's automobile driver you are a marked man."

Alexiev kept walking toward the hills. "Yes, I know the dogs. Those dogs will remember me only to well if they catch me."

Before 8 o'clock, Alexiev was in a wooded area. The hillside as well as the trees and rocks were good cover. "I need to keep moving. I need to cover some ground before worrying about finding a way to mislead my scent to the tracking dogs. I can't believe I'm not hungry. That's a blessing."

Finally, at about three in the afternoon, Alexiev felt himself tiring and needing some rest and perhaps some nourishment. It was only moments later that Alexiev heard the distant sound of the dogs for the first time. "Their sound will be getting louder very soon."

Alexiev quickly surveyed the valley area he was crossing. The vegetation and trees indicated a stream or creek some half mile across a small hill. Alexiev walked in a southwesterly direction, not getting any closer to the creek until finally reaching an angle to see a cabin. "Maybe there is some food."

Although the sound of the dogs was still distant, Alexiev began running toward the cabin. "Whatever I find, I'll need to eat in a hurry. I won't be able to carry any food with me. Will this be my last supper?"

In the first place he looked in the cabin, Alexiev found two homemade canned jars of peaches and pears. After opening the jars, he went from one to the other while he searched the remainder of the kitchen cabinets.

After finishing, Alexiev went outside and circled the cabin several times, looking for somewhere to hide the empty jars. "Since it is only a matter of life or death, you might want to think of something quickly," Alexiev reminded himself sarcastically. "The dogs are getting closer and there is no time for burying garbage." He spotted an outhouse and trotted over to it. Lifting the seat, he tossed the jars into the abyss. Judging by the splash in the darkness below the seat, the drop was about four feet to sewage. It also sounded like there was water seeping into the pit. "There has to be. The cabin probably has not been used in months. Even a family of bears would not pee that much."

Alexiev tried not to think of the image of when the dogs could be seen by him and not just heard. He considered a scenario where he would surrender to his pursuers but it was not at all a practical notion. "They will never bring me back alive." His words were intended to reinforce his necessity to think and act quickly and decisively but with each passing moment the scenario became more bleak. "My chances are somewhere between not even slim and very none."

"What will throw off the dogs?" Alexiev sat on a boulder, contemplating his environment. He certainly was not an expert on hunting dogs but he had to at least try something. "Death by dog bite is worse than death by a bullet and it looms as a very real possibility." He was aware that his scent had thus far traveled into the cabin as well as around it several times. He also knew his scent led to the outhouse. "My scent leading away from the site will easily be tracked by the dogs. I wonder if the canines are actually closer than they sound. Well, Mr. Escapee," Alexiev said to himself, you better think of something real soon."

In his anxiety Alexiev had a bizarre and discomforting sensation of every hair on his body growing. Almost instinctively he rose to his feet and started walking, soon circling the cabin as he previously had done. Suddenly his gray eyes widened. "That's what I'll do!" Alexiev immediately ran roughly 100 meters from the cabin and then proceeded to run in circles around the cabin site. The circles were uneven as there were natural obstacles as well as the general topography to alter his course. Each circle became smaller, closing in on the cabin. As he ran Alexiev said several prayers out loud. "I wish I was better at praying, like my parents were. It's been a long time since I have tried."

After seven orbits of the cabin site, Alexiev settled into a walk. He occasionally veered off the circular course momentarily for the purpose of misdirection. He maintained this course until the sound of the dogs was uncomfortable, nearly unbearable.

"It's do or die now," Alexiev said aloud. With a blend of chagrin and resolve, Alexiev lowered himself into the polluted quagmire under the outhouse seat.

"Either destiny will rescue me or my family line ends here. Am I really a villain?"

CHAPTER THREE

LIGHTS ABOVE, LIGHTS BELOW

Boston
May 1927

"Hey! YOU OLD FAT MAN! YOU'VE GOT MORE CHINS THAN A CHINESE PHONEBOOK!"

"Do you think Ty Cobb can hear you?" Emily inquired of Pete.

"He probably has rabbit ears. IS THAT YOUR BELT OR IS THAT THE EQUATOR?"

"Pete is counting on it," Clayton added, his blue eyes squinting beneath the brim of his Red Sox hat. "It is about 375 feet from these right field seats to home plate."

"Which is why I am LOUD! HEY! ONLY ONE PLAYER TO A UNIFORM!" Pete yelled.

"Please don't lose your singing voice," Clayton requested. "We have a party to play tomorrow night."

"Very true Mr. Piano Man. I'll try to be my most obnoxious self when Cobb is playing right field. He is probably too fat in that Athletics uniform to hear anything from home plate anyway."

"Indeed, he begins the season old and overweight, but Cobb does have more hits than anyone else in the history of baseball," stated Emily. "I think he is playing this last season with Philadelphia to be the first player to get 4000 hits."

"I am impressed," praised Clayton. "You know your stuff."

"He has shite for character," Pete responded.

"He also has the most money of any player," Emily continued. Her fingers gathered her bobbed flapper style dirty blonde hair out of the breeze

"More than Babe?" asked Clayton.

"Even more than your favorite player, Babe Ruth. His investments in Georgia have paid off in a big way," stated Emily.

"Yeh, the Georgia Rotten Peach," interrupted Pete.

"Actually Pete, he's made a lot of money from your favorite drink. Coca-Cola has made him a very rich man," Emily informed them.

Clayton reflected momentarily on his meager savings account. "I need to find a great investment. I wonder what Emily's father thinks about the idea of his daughter falling for a musician."

At the end of the inning Clayton and Pete left for the restroom. "What was that? It sounded like something I heard but it was inside my head." Emily's attention was drawn to something in the sky. "Is that some kind of airplane? It isn't moving much. The light from it is so strange, like a rainbow or prism or tiny blimp or something." Emily quickly looked at the patrons of the game surrounding her. "Maybe nobody else sees it but somehow it seems familiar to me. Does it see me?" She returned her gaze to the airborne object, only to see it rapidly streak southeastward and disappear, leaving a momentary trail of prism colors.

"What is dad's explanation for that going to be?" she asked herself. During her question an illogical impulse came to mind. "Something is going to happen. My intuition tells me something is going on. Or maybe I am just crazy. After all, a lingering and then speeding crystal prism in the sky is not a normal sight. It probably was just a reflection of something, maybe something that was moved very quickly."

Clayton returned to his seat, smiling at Emily as she gathered her body on her seat to let him pass. Emily felt her insides churn but in a happy way. "I like that guy. I just realized how much I really do like him. I wasn't so sure until today. Somehow I feel we share some mysterious destiny." She pressed her hand briefly upon Clayton's hand before allowing him to pass to his seat.

"I just talked to a guy who thinks the Sox are going to take last place because of the curse of Babe Ruth supposedly put on the team," reported Pete.

"Why would people believe in something so illogical?" asked Emily. "A curse can be no more than a coincidence."

"I'm not sure I agree with that," conceded Clayton. "People do believe in them."

"Who cares what people think?" Emily paused momentarily to gather her thoughts. "It is hard for me to believe something as unscientific as a curse. Besides, it only matters if the team believes it is cursed."

"The curse has nothing to do with the regular season. The curse is about the Red Sox never winning the World Series again," noted Clayton. "It all started when Babe Ruth was traded to the Yankees for the 1920 season."

"And so now you have a Yankee for a favorite player," complained Pete. "Maybe that's a curse."

"I admit it is weird," acknowledged Clayton, "because I actually hate the Yankees."

"Yet another illogical way of thinking," teased Emily.

In the last two innings, the Athletics rallied to take the lead by one run. The hopes of the Red Sox fans were stimulated in the bottom of the ninth with a single. With one out and a right-handed line drive hitter at the plate, Ty Cobb moved abnormally shallow in right field. After the first pitch, he moved in again, almost a shadow of the first baseman.

"Look where Cobb is!" Clayton said quietly, as though the player might hear him. "This park has been open for 15 years and I bet no right fielder has ever played that shallow here. If a ball gets by him it is a tie game."

Cobb moved ever closer before the next pitch was swung at and lined over the first baseman's head. Moving with the pitch, Cobb caught the ball on a full run. He kept running and reached first base before the base runner could retreat there for an unassisted double play to end the game.

Most of the crowd became dead silent, except Pete. "SHITE! I'M NEVER BUYING ANOTHER COCA COLA AS LONG AS I LIVE!"

* * *

Later that evening following the afternoon game, Clayton worked at a movie house playing piano. The score was not very challenging but the crowd was large and enthusiastic. It was nearly eleven o'clock before he left the theater.

"The city sure is dead on Sunday night," Clayton remarked to the empty street, "but it really is nice tonight." Looking up at the stars in the sky and combing the brown waves of his hair with his fingers he realized, "I'm in no hurry. It is a nice night for a stroll on the pier."

Clayton tried to envision the infamous Boston Tea Party more than 150 years past. "Would I have been in it?" He answered his own question quickly. "No chance, I couldn't stand the war paint makeup of the Indian costumes."

"I wonder what Dr. Hiller would think if I came up with an investment scheme?" He envisioned Emily's father, a professor of physics at MIT, but no new ideas came to mind. The calm, lapping waves provided no answer either. "Maybe I should figure out some sort of business to begin, soon. How many times today have I said that?"

Gazing at the calm saltwater, Clayton's attention became focused upon a light reflecting on the water nearly a quarter-mile away. He viewed the dark horizon casually but his mind was drawn back to the reflected light. "Boy, boy, come away," a voice whispered.

He twisted around, scanning his environment while trying to solve the mystery. "Am I hearing things. It sounded like a whisper, or maybe it was inside my head. Am I going crazy? That is an odd place for a reflection. Almost everything is dark and it can't be a street reflection where it is located. Is it a submarine?"

"They want me or maybe my future kids. Why did I think that? Who is they? This seems like a moon or planet thing but the lights came from under the water."

When he turned back to again view the strange light in the water, Clayton noticed it getting brighter. "What is that?"

Suddenly, without any great splash of water, the light emerged from the water and began rising. The shape of the object was difficult to distinguish as it hovered above the water. "Boy, boy, come away with us."

"Holy shite! What the hell? That voice was inside my head, I swear."

When the object reached a height of perhaps 50 feet it slowly began moving away from the city. After several seconds the light accelerated and within the next few seconds it streaked out of sight.

Clayton felt absorbed by something outside himself. "I feel like a big spotlight is pointed on me but there is no light." His attention never wavered during the event yet he struggled back from being infinitely and mysteriously overwhelmed. "I feel like I am regaining my body."

He was stunned with fear, drowning in a feeling of helpless ignorance. "Talk about your optical illusions." Clayton did not believe his own words. "Nothing can fly that fast, not even my imagination."

After a brief interlude of stunned silence, Clayton left the pier. "I sure would like to hear Dr. Hiller's opinion of whatever that was." He quickly changed his mind. "I can't risk giving him a lunatic impression. I can talk to Bucky about all of this soon enough though."

Thoughts about what he saw dominated his mind. After walking several blocks, Clayton looked at the starry sky. "Lord God, was I supposed to be there? Was I supposed to see what I saw for a reason? Actually Lord, I feel somehow blessed as a chosen one, but I do not understand anything. Is this some kind of destiny? Who, or what, asked me to go away with them?"

Clayton continued walking, steeped in contemplation of a newly comprehended future. Feelings for Emily flooded through his being as if she were nearby. "She is part of it, isn't she?" he asked the sky. "She is going to be part of some destiny of mine, I can feel it. But I cannot explain it. No offense Dr. Hiller but science surely is incomplete. No science I ever heard of has come up with anything as wild as what I saw."

When he reached his destination, Clayton stopped to send a brief thought toward the heavens intended for his late mother. "I hope this ain't the end of the world ma and I sure wish you were here."

Suddenly taking note of the sky becoming lighter, Clayton pulled out his pocket watch. "Four thirty-five? It hasn't taken that long to walk three miles, has it?"

* * *

Sifting through the mail, Emily briefly perused a letter postmarked from British Honduras. "It's from Anna! What is she up to this time?" The letter was brief and Emily read it again. "I don't have time to explain and I wouldn't try anyway. It is an amazing find from our archeological trip. Hopefully you and Dr. Hiller can visit us while we are in Toronto before we leave for London."

Emily pondered the letter momentarily. "Very mysterious but then again so is the life of Mr. Mitchell-Hedges. I wonder if Clayton can go?"

Emily sprang to her feet after hearing the knock on the door and quickly looked at the makeup surrounding her hazel eyes in the mirror and primped her medium blonde hair without actually changing anything. "Just in time, dinner is waiting on the table," she declared, hustling toward the door.

"So, Dr. Hiller is out of town?" asked Clayton.

"He was invited to New York with other MIT faculty to see a new invention, the television."

"Which is?"

"It is something like a radio but it receives moving pictures. My father told me the television was first demonstrated this spring when Commerce Secretary Herbert Hoover gave a speech to some bankers. The people at AT&T think it will be a household appliance someday."

"There will probably be broadcast studios for television. Maybe we should invent the first one."

"There are only three things wrong with that idea. You and me are two since we know nothing about a whole bunch, and we have little money. And no demand, which makes four things."

"Say, Emily, this blackened salmon is really good. You always tell everyone you can't cook."

"I can fake a few things pretty well but I'm not a good cook. The house cook is away at a wedding. You should have seen my omelet yesterday. It looked like factory waste, but I am persistent."

Several minutes later Emily suddenly remembered the letter from Anna. "Oh my, Clayton, I forgot to invite you to Toronto."

"You didn't invite me to Mexico City either!" Clayton exclaimed, his blue eyes revealing his jest.

"Father and I were invited to Toronto, but he will probably be going at a later time than when I can go. I was hoping you could go with me."

Clayton momentarily considered the proposed timeline of their trip. "I can go and I want to go. I have never been to Canada. What are we doing in Toronto besides seeing your friends?"

"We are going to see a crystal skull."

"It might be as hard headed as you are."

CHAPTER FOUR

PROPHECY AND SECRECY

Spokane, Washington
May 1927

"Hey!"

Amanda jerked to attention in the hospital room chair.

"How can I get out?" There was her young son, standing in the hospital crib, tugging at the netting over the top of it.

"Lenny!" Amanda sprang to her feet, pent up emotions gushing forth. Momentarily speechless, she adeptly began removing the netting, all the while thinking, "I should have sought medical assistance first. Too late now."

"I'm hungry."

Amanda wiped tears leaping from her eyes. "I'll bet you are son," she said through a wet smile, at the same time walking toward the door. In the hallway, Amanda spotted a nurse. "Please find Dr. Dickson. My son is awake and hungry." Before Amanda closed the door she saw the middle aged nurse wordlessly run towards the third floor main desk.

"My little miracle, I can't wait to get you home." A brief feeling of life force energy surged through her as she held her son, momentarily making her cognizant of the possibility of fainting.

"I went far away. I know how to get out of my bed at my house."

"But you are with me now."

"I'm hungry, I didn't eat when I was gone. They didn't have any food there."

"Where did you go?"

"I don't know. I went to where it didn't hurt and came back."

"And you are supposed to be with your family, it is your destiny."

"What is detsindy? Is there cake?"

In the weeks after leaving the hospital, Lenny resumed his energetic pace towards all activities. "Mom, can I help with 'Maw-get'?"

Amanda smiled at her son's innocent mispronunciation of the name of his sister. "Yes, you can take the baby blanket on the floor to the bathroom. She spit up on it."

Jason moved away from the doorway so Lenny could pass. "That looks disgusting!"

"It sure does!" Lenny agreed enthusiastically, pausing to scratch his bandaged head.

"Guess what's in the newspaper?" Jason asked his wife.

"Headlines, sentences and paragraphs?"

Jason blinked indifference to her response. "Bing Crosby and Al Rinker made their own recording, with that other guy too."

"Harry Barris?"

"Yeh, that's the guy. I'll buy the record if I can find it."

"They have come a long way since we first saw them a couple of years ago at the dance hall in Dishman. I love that up-tempo jazz."

"'The Musicaladers' were a six piece band then," recalled Jason. "Ed, have you heard my Bing and Al tale? It's one of my favorite stories to tell. In the spring of 1926, my friend Ralph decided to join the service in a rather abrupt manner. He asked me to sell his car for him, a 1918 Model T Ford. As luck would have it, none other than Bing Crosby and Al Rinker came to see the vehicle. We made a deal for $30. The two musicians drove that jalopy to Los Angeles to try to make it in show business."

"I see stories in The Spokesman Review regularly about those two singers."

"We went to their show at the Casino Theater when they returned to Spokane last November. That was before they headed to Chicago to play with the 30 piece Paul Whiteman Orchestra."

"One of these days I bet Bing makes a record of his own," stated Amanda.

"He certainly has the voice for it," agreed Ed.

"Maybe, but he has never been very interested in singing solo but you're right, there is no doubt that he has the voice for it."

"Someday the right song will come along and it will happen."

"It is probably as likely as a white Christmas. I have no reason to doubt you," confirmed Jason. "After all, you are the psychic in the family."

"And don't you forget it or I predict I will make you remember it in the future."

Their conversation was interrupted by a telephone call. "It's Mary," Lenny announced before Amanda
could reach the still ringing telephone.

"Hello," answered Amanda. With a look of surprise on her face, she turned to her husband before again speaking. "Oh, how are you Mary?" She briefly covered the telephone transmitter. After her brief conversation, she professed, "Maybe there are two psychics in the family."

"But you are a 'psychic medicine woman'," reminded Jason.

"His comment was not meant to be mean," Amanda advised Ed. "I am one-half Spokane Indian.
Our tribe primarily lived and hunted northwest of Spokane. My grandfather, Strong Eagle, was a "medicine man" shaman. He has been gone for about ten years and I still miss him very much."

"Amanda uses herbal cures for various ailments, which prompted the term 'medicine woman' from me," Jason conveyed. "Your herbal cures usually work great so why should I question them?"

"I have respect for conventional medical practices also. There is no conflict between traditional medicine and my herbal ways. I just figure modern science has yet to test many of the old remedies."

"Then old ways can be new ways."

"One old way of a different kind always bothered me. Nobody knows how old grandfather was when he died. How can that be?"

"Even among pioneers of the northwest a generation or two ago who could read and write, age was sometimes still a guess," Jason explained. "But there still are people who change the reported dates of birth of their children to avoid a military draft or other duty. How important was someone's age to natives?"

"I guess I don't know. Still, it is so odd that people would know their birthday in terms of month and day but not the year."

"At least you know about some of your ancestors. Everyone in my father's family except my dad died of cholera when he was four years old. Some of the neighbors adopted him."

"Strong Eagle often told me that I look nearly identical to my grandmother, Spirit Feather," Amanda told Jason.

"I don't look like anyone except hopefully our kids."

"Amanda, you told me before that your dad was from Bellingham," inquired Ed. "What did your father do there?"

"By the time Washington became a state in 1889 my father completed school and worked at several jobs, eventually finding steady work with the Bellingham Bay and British Columbia Railroad that connected with the Canadian Pacific Railway."

"It is a good thing he moved or we would not have met."

"Unless it is our mutual destiny," noted Amanda. "We both might have done things differently to rise to our destiny. My grandfather liked California but he did not want to return. His parents expected Bellingham to be another San Francisco anyway."

"What made him leave Bellingham?" queried Ed.

"He always hated the rain and mud and there came a day when he decided it was time to leave. George, my father, and his father by adoption Leroy Webster had traveled north towards Lynden on Guide Meridian Road to purchase farm produce. The mud was difficult after a real heavy week of rain. The Nooksack River flooded several miles south of Lynden and George actually saw a salmon swim across the road."

"The salmon was trying to spawn uproad, huh?"

Amanda didn't get Jason's joke until she responded, "Do you mean upstream?" She giggled mildly and continued, "Anyway, later that night in Fairhaven, my father George became the unfortunate victim of mistaken identity by a character named Dirty Dan Harris. Dirty Dan had a reputation for drinking, fighting and going barefoot. He unexpectedly shoved my father up against a wood plank building, cursing and accusing him of theft. He had never been in a fight but he reacted instinctively, catching Dirty Dan with a surprise punch to the jaw. The fight was broken up by a man who knew George and the case of mistaken identity was explained to Dirty Dan, who simply said, 'Sorry kid. That was a good punch,' and left."

"It sounds like you were told that story a few times," added Ed.

"So your father developed an overnight reputation as the kid who decked Dirty Dan Harris," remarked Jason.

"Yes, but he made an overnight decision to make his way somewhere else. Accepting a gift for steamship and railroad fare from his father, my father took the boat to Seattle before eventually making his way to Spokane. He found employment working for a railroad. By the spring of 1890, he moved south to Pullman to work on the construction of Washington State College. He later became a hotel clerk and a supplier for gold miners."

"You never cease to amaze me about the details you know of your family. The parents who adopted my father hardly knew his real parents."

"My grandfather, Strong Eagle, wanted me to learn about and cherish my ancestors on both sides of my family and I have listened to many stories."

"I wish I knew more stories about my ancestors," agreed Ed. "Anyway, keep going."

"My grandfather, Strong Eagle, was a frequent guest at our 40 acre homestead. My father never knew his grandparents and he was thankful his children had one. What little he knew of his biological parents was that they were dedicated abolitionists who hated racism. My father hated the Indian wars in the late 19th century and it occurred to him that his parents would have embraced his interracial marriage. My grandfather was a wise man and my father appreciated his positive influence on us children."

"You turned out pretty good, lucky for me," Jason proclaimed. "Your parents were probably pretty smart people. Both kids graduated from high school."

"I graduated 32 days before Hank was shot and killed in Germany." Her memory of the incident caused Amanda to close her eyes briefly.

"Was Strong Eagle alive when your brother died?"

"He lived long enough to see Hank enlist in the Army and go off to war but not long enough to hear of his death. It was the first day of autumn in 1917, I will never forget it. He gathered my parents and I to sit with him in the shade to tell them about a vision he had the previous night."

"Soon I will take the journey, but I have had a vision of many things," he said. "Many things are to happen in the coming lifetimes."

"My family was not sure how to respond so I spoke first. 'Grandfather, you are healthy. You have much life ahead of you'."

"What kind of things will happen?" my father inquired.

"There will be other great wars. There will be great discoveries that will not end the age of separation."

"I do not understand," said my mother. "What kind of separation?"

"All tribes have been separate on all lands for many centuries, trying to be independent instead of learning together and living as a larger family. And nations of the world will desire separation and power. Material things blind the spiritual vision of many. It will be lifetimes before we have a better bond."

"Is that part of great wars?" I remember asking. "My grandfather held up his hand to end the questioning and we respected his desire to continue."

"Man will learn to look outward to the stars and inward beyond sight. Worlds both larger and smaller than our imagination will be discovered. We are made of the same stuff as the river and the earth and all are part of the same thought. But it will take lifetimes, I don't know how many, before all of humanity learns this. There need to be changes in the hearts of many people. Our family will help people to share their hearts."

"Grandfather looked into each of our eyes," Amanda continued. "None of us interrupted him."

"Inner and outer worlds, the spiritual and the physical, will unite from the power of great crystal. We will find creatures under the ground, under the oceans, and in the skies. Some will be like myths coming to life."

"Do you mean like the 'great ape of the hills?' I remember asking. My father was always on the lookout for one. Again my grandfather held up his hand as a signal that he wanted to continue."

"Someday there will be peace, when mankind has a reason to agree, when the great white moose returns with her albino calf sometime in the future. My vision tells me that I am an ancestor of someone who will help the world to agreement, to an understanding of natural harmony. We are all part of that energy yet to be understood. The ape-man will be with the Holy Ones. That is my vision."

"Again Strong Eagle remained silent, again looking into our eyes. For perhaps a full minute, no one spoke. My mother broke the silence by changing the subject."

"Father, there are probably many questions we have, but I would like to have my own thoughts first. May I begin supper now so that we may have time to think about what you said?"

Amanda reflected briefly before continuing. "A pine cone fell from a tree near us and grandfather reached out and caught it. 'I have always wanted to do that.' After making dinner, my mother went out on the porch to awaken him. He did not respond. Strong Eagle had taken the journey."

"I would have like to have known him," reflected Jason. "I know so little about my own past."

"Your adopted family had a big impact on you, just not your blood."

"Oh yes, there are many challenges in overcoming being a hick."

"What do you mean?" asked Ed.

"The Skagit valley, where I grew up, was a rough and tumble backwoods place. For instance, my dad's parents understood his logging occupation but they knew little about his lifestyle. They thought he sometimes was injured at work but instead it was from a drunken brawls."

"What changed him?"

"At age 27 he found himself without any kind of family for the first time. Both of the parents who adopted him died in the two years before that. He sold the farm and the livestock and decided to visit Seattle. He didn't like the big city lifestyle, although Seattle was hardly a big city then. But that's where he met my mother, Sarah Elizabeth McGrady."

"Your mother's parents were killed in a fire that swept through a portion of the wooden buildings of the city, right?" inquired his wife.

"She was passed from household to household, including time spent with two madams of brothels," Jason added. "Sarah was 21 years old and a recent widow when dad met her. It was destiny. Four days later, they were married."

"And people thought we rushed into marriage," Amanda commented, giving a playful kick to Jason's shoe. "It was your destiny to move to Spokane, go to college and then meet me."

"Jason, when did you come to Spokane?"

"I finished elementary school here and then learned enough at Otis Orchards High School to get into Washington State College for two years before leaving to fight in the Great War. Me and some of my friends enlisted in 1917."

"You seldom mention anything about the war," his wife said quietly.

"My first day in war was Halloween but the entire experience was a nightmare. Many of my friends fell during many battles. I never became conditioned to the killing. I just hoped for survival by taking my job as a soldier very seriously. Luck helped a lot."

"You usually have good luck."

"I'm lucky to be alive. The last action I saw in Europe was the most brutal. Slowly our troops retreated until we were surrounded. My troop and a platoon of black soldiers from Alabama were all killed except me and Bobby Joe Jefferson. We were back to back in a foxhole, expecting the worst. To our surprise the enemy fire stopped. For the next 42 hours we were alone. The color of our skin didn't matter."

"Not enough people think that way." Amanda hugged her husband. "At least your family story has a happy ending. You met me, your destiny."

"Some people say you must create your own destiny."

"That is one way. Sometimes destiny chooses you, like you chose me."

"And you chose me," Jason added.

"Destiny can be an unknown factor," declared Ed.

"A person may shape their entire life to fulfill a brief but significant destiny for something bigger than themselves," added Amanda, "but there are signposts along the way on how to get there."

"My ultimate destiny is a secret to everyone but me," thought Jason. "There is much after the war that I can never discuss with anyone. I wish I could tell Amanda, but I can't. Revealing my secret is not going to help anyone. It is my burden alone. It is my ultimate destiny to go to hell because of it."

CHAPTER FIVE

THE SMELL OF INSPIRATION AND HOPE

Soviet Union
May 1927

"What a bunch of shit!" Alexiev announced with a laugh while viewing his clothing after emerging from under the outhouse seat. "The Soviet soldiers are gone and I am happy rotten foul."

"Some men's clothing! I can't believe that I could find any kind of wardrobe change in here. What's it been, 21 hours in the outhouse waste? Even now it is difficult to be convinced the last of the Soviet soldiers have left. My attempt to bathe in the creek really was disappointing. I need to get in the creek again, only this time naked."

After a quick and very cold second dip in the creek, Alexiev returned to the cabin to get dressed.

"These pants are too short," Alexiev observed. He pulled on the jacket. "And this is too big." At 6 feet 3 inches and 180 pounds he was much thinner than the previous owner of the clothes. "But I am grateful." He began his journey to western Europe with as much positive energy as he could muster.

Whenever Alexiev came upon a village, he kept a low profile and purchased meals without conspicuous spending. Every week or so he purchased a change of clothes. He also varied his hair length and facial hair. Several times Alexiev encountered soldiers and once his fictional identification was examined. "Those particular soldiers were not looking for anyone specifically so they had no cause to be suspicious of me. It scared the hell out of me but succeeding bolstered my confidence."

"Each day is a different adventure. I have no idea what will happen in my future or where that future will take place yet each day I am becoming more determined to create my own fate. I don't want to leave anything to be decided by the world around me. Just keep rolling with the punches."

"So far the plan is working," Alexiev stated supersticiously each day.

It was not until Alexiev reached Prague that he felt he could relax. His contacts were found without much trouble. Alexiev bathed, rested, exchanged currency, ate two meals, rested and bathed yet again before boarding a train. He had no set timetable but Paris was his destination. "It's a pleasure to know French. I am very grateful now to have learned French and English to communicate with foreign diplomatic passengers as part of my job as Trotsky's driver."

"Speaking French and English is necessary for my new plan. From France I will board a steamer to Canada and eventually go to Montréal. The French-speaking culture in Montréal will be the easiest place to adapt to North America. That is, until I learn more fluent English. Then I can figure out a way to make a living anywhere in Canada."

"You have been traveling under an assumed name?" his contact in Prague asked.

"My name changes with each location," Alexiev replied. "Only twice have I actually needed credentials and I have been on the road for almost two months."

"Here is your new identification and your railroad ticket. You should arrive in Paris on May 24th."

* * *

Checking into the hotel in Paris was uplifting. "This place is like a palace compared to some places I have been. I can't wait to take a bath, but first I need to call my contact."

There was no answer when he made the call. It was after the dinner hour so Alexiev tried phoning several more times during the evening. Still there was no answer. He quit calling at 11 o'clock and went to bed.

"Again there is no answer," he remarked after calling in the morning. I need to go to the apartment building where he lives."

A knock on the door at the contact's apartment produced no results. "Someone broke into his apartment and killed him two days ago," the building manager informed him. "Slit his throat. No one saw or heard anything. The couple in the apartment next door found his door ajar. They knocked, peeked inside and discovered the body."

Alexiev's mind raced. "Did the Soviets discover my contact? Is this a coincidence?" He listened to the manager in a stoic manner, trying to formulate an alternate plan. There was an awkward pause of silence as the manager anticipated questions but none were forthcoming.

The manager continued, "For some reason his phone has not been disconnected. I have heard it ring several times."

"Thank you," Alexiev said quietly. Smiling, he turned toward the door and left the builing.

Back at the hotel, Alexiev telephoned his secondary contact. "I have alternate identification and a passport for you. I was not prepared to have a steamship ticket to Canada but I will take care of it. Meet me at the airfield at 11 tonight."

Alexiev checked out of the hotel and found a restaurant close to the airfield. There was little time to do sightseeing in the world famous city but there was time to enjoy his best meal since leaving Russia.

At 9:50 Alexiev arrived at the airfield. "What is going on here?" To his dismay, there were thousands of people. "There are many thousands, with more arriving by the minute. Apparently I am early for something else."

Virtually everyone at the airfield was excited and animated. There was so much noise that Alexiev had trouble deciphering the rapidly speaking French people. "An airplane is soon to arrive? Why are so many people, mostly rather drunk, so charged with excitement? It must be some sort of celebrity or national hero."

Alexiev checked his watch. "I still have another 40 minutes. Did she know thousands of people were going to be here? Worrying won't help." Finding a place to loiter, he sat down to observe the throng of humanity.

An airplane arrived and circled the field. Alexiev's observation became participation in a matter of seconds. A tremendous roar of anticipation erupted and Alexiev stood up to see what was happening. The excited crowd began a mad rush in one direction, sweeping up Alexiev. He kept moving with the throng to avoid being crushed.

"What is happening?" Alexiev shouted to a Parisian during a momentary pause.

"An American has just flown across the Atlantic!" Involuntarily, and surprising himself, tears burst from Alexiev's eyes. The sudden emotion and rush of epiphany swelled into a moment of complete awe.

The crowd rushed toward "The Spirit of Saint Louis" after it landed and Alexiev went with them. He was nearly a hundred feet from the plane when the crowd saw a jubilant man holding a leather helmet in the air as he began to run. The crowd roared and followed him. But this time, Alexiev sidestepped the chaos and inched closer to see the historic airplane.

Then he saw a man… the pilot! "That's him!" The man with the helmet had merely grabbed the headgear and the masses incorrectly interpreted him as the pilot.

In a knee-jerk reaction, a massive portion of the crowd changed direction, heading back toward the plane. By this time Charles Lindbergh was hoisted into the air by the crowd. He was smiling broadly at the spectacle at first but soon wanted to be set down despite his exhaustion after the 33 hour flight. Lindbergh returned to the ground less than 5 feet away from Alexiev. Watching the pilot walk, he instinctively stuck out his hand. Amidst all of the chaos, Lindbergh stopped briefly and shook the hand of Alexiev. The pressure and force of the crowd pushed Lindbergh from behind and he was gone.

"He looked like he wanted a moment of peace in the middle of this surreal celebration. I wonder how many people are here? It reminds me of the eye of a tornado. Maybe he needed a moment of clarity in his exhaustion."

Finally Alexiev found his contact. The meeting went quickly and smoothly. He had a request for her that was spontaneous. "Please have my contact in Montréal arrange someone to help me improve my English."

The time table had changed. Alexiev now wanted to get to the United States as soon as he felt able to communicate effectively. "I don't know exactly what my future is, but after this experience, I feel that anything and everything are possible in America."

* * *

"I wonder how much my Russian accent is detectable in my speaking either French or English?" Alexiev wondered. "The voyage seems pretty safe but the less attention the better."

Crossing the Atlantic Ocean was a time of serenity for Alexiev. When he awoke in the morning he knew exactly where he would be that day. There were virtually no worries, no responsibilities, no fear. He spent hours at a time sitting or lounging on the deck.

Pulling out his new credentials, Alexiev examined them once again. "My new name is 'Al Sargent'," he reinforced himself. The name was supposedly generic with respect to national origin. Making sure no one could see his writing, "Al" practiced his signature on stationery he found in his cabin. "Until now, I didn't have a name long enough to practice a signature." When he finished, he crumpled the paper and sent it overboard into the ocean.

Alexiev nearly forgot his new name when he met a lady in the dining room the next day. They had a casual conversation, similar as any other conversation on the trip thus far until he discovered the woman, Deborah, was sometimes watching him. It seemed suspicious until her smile finally registered as flirting.

"I should flirt back." He was glad he did.

Certainly Al had previously not given romantic machinations any thought at all for this voyage but he became enamored with her black hair and curvaceous figure. "Those aqua green eyes seem to be looking for something inside me, or maybe something intended for me."

Despite becoming acquainted and spending time together, Al did not reveal anything about his escape but he did admit to formerly living in the Soviet Union. His plan was to learn by listening.

"I'm trying to be a feature writer for a newspaper or magazine," explained Deborah. "I wrote one story about a blonde haired giant roaming around Ontario and that story was syndicated to other papers. Finding good story ideas is my biggest concern."

"Maybe you could find a red haired giant."

"The story I wrote was as sarcastic as your comment."

"Are there plans for marriage and children for you?" Al inquired.

"I am only 24 years old so I still have plenty of time for a family. I hope to find writing work in Toronto. My hometown, where my parents live, is Nobel on Parry Sound of Lake Union. It's a pretty small town. We moved there in 1920."

Al found it difficult to not pour his heart out to Deborah about his life, or his former life. He resisted. "I wonder if I will ever tell anyone the truth about my past." He immediately began to feel his heart longing to go to Toronto. "I'm probably just afraid of being alone in my new world."

His conscience contradicted his sentiments. "Quit dreaming! Wasted planning is wasted energy. I am chasing a pipe dream even if I am denying my own feelings." Nonetheless, Al concentrated on the possible ways he could live in Toronto. "First, there is enough of a French-speaking community to get by while learning proficient English, which is already better than I had given myself credit for. Second, Deborah promised me a job working in her uncle's art studio and store plus the opportunity to translate books. Third, Deborah kissed me." He wanted to expect it but he was still surprised.

"The voyage ended too soon for me," Al admitted to Deborah and her aunt and uncle after arriving in Canada, "but I can't wait to see Toronto."

He could not help but think about the vastness of the changes in his life in the past three months. Alexiev had fled the Soviet Union, surviving every circumstance as it arose. He had visited Prague and Paris. He had witnessed the thrill of the historic, unique achievement of Lindbergh. And before he reached the shores of Canada, Al was on the gushing path towards love.

"This is a destiny I could not have guessed. I still cannot guess my destiny. To realize whatever my destiny is to be, I'll just do it first and learn how second."

* * *

"Part of the trip was in the dark but I still really enjoyed the train ride," Al informed Deborah when she met him at the grocery store at

Parry Sound ten days later. "Toronto was nice too." After Al's lips parted from Deborah's during their initial embrace, he whispered, "The trip was worth it for that kiss alone."

While driving her father's Cadillac to the family farm Deborah announced, " I'm glad you have your sea legs because we have a fishing trip planned for tomorrow morning."

"Excellent!" responded Al, inwardly delighted and relieved.

"My psychic side tells me that religion is generally outside of your experience. You were worried about going to church, weren't you?"

"You wouldn't need to go fishing to see a fish out of water. I probably would embarass everyone."

"Don't worry. The only person who is going to get embarassed is you, by me." Her grin gave away her charade.

After meeting Deborah's parents, Rollie and Ollie Holly, Al followed Deborah on a tour of the 54 acre blueberry farm. "You're a blueberry heiress. You must be blueberry blood nobility," teased Al.

"Maybe I should write stories with blueberry ink."

"That sounds like healthy writing. Tell me about finding the idea for your first story."

"I was outside of a police station in Toronto when I heard two men discussing 'Yellow Top', the ape-man. One man claimed to have seen it walk in front of his automobile. I interrupted the men with my seductive prowess and joined their conversation, introducing myself as free lance writer."

"Why would the parents of an ape-man name their kid 'Yellow Top'?"

"Very funny. Then I did more interviews in Cobalt, near Toronto."

"It sounds like a comedy play but only my dear Deborah was talented enough to make it a newspaper story."

"I tried to write a sarcastic story without making fun of anybody. I wrote it like a fish story and I implied that it was."

"So you sold your story to a Toronto paper before it was syndicated."

"That's right. It's a reputation. It's a resume."

On Sunday morning, Lake Huron was choppy for the first hour of the fishing trip. "I brought a friend of mine out here one time," explained Deborah's father. "He thought getting his sea legs was mind over matter. After he tossed his cookies, I told him it was more like 'vomit overboard'."

"So far, so good. Just don't ask me to do the 'Charleston'."

"Who caught the most fish?" asked Mrs. Holly when the three returned to the house.

"Deborah did, again," declared her husband.

"It is just a matter of thinking positive," revealed Deborah.

"It's not so positive for the fish," noted Rollie. "Besides, Al had the largest catch."

"Only if 'Moby Boot' counts," corrected Deborah.

"I'm not cooking it so it doesn't count."

Just after sunset, Deborah and Al found a seat on a fallen log. The blueberry fields were nearly dark but there was still a remaining sheen on the lake. A cool breeze was changing the hot and humid air of August. "In some ways you remain a mystery to me," admitted Deborah. "I seem to know about you but maybe I really don't."

"Isn't that better than a man of too much information?"

"People have their secrets but most of them really wouldn't hurt anybody."

"Especially if the secret is never told."

"Like all the history never written because those secrets were never told." Deborah turned into the moonlight and chuckled brieflly. "I should just stick to newspapers instead of trying to reinvent history."

Al's visual focus became distant. "Maybe you should write stories about catching fish. Wait! I saw something move over there, in the field."

"Oh my goodness!" Deborah stood up abruptly, catching the attention of the stranger. She began walking in his direction, resulting in his standing up, its yellowish hairy head rising well above the six foot tall bushes. The stranger then moved quickly away, vaguely revealing the back of its huge hair covered torso. Deborah ran toward the creature but there was no further sign of movement.

Paranoia ran rampant in Al's mind. "They're watching me. Oh don't be silly, I don't even know what it was. How could they be?"

When Deborah arrived at the creature's last seen location, she yelled, "I guess it is gone. There is no sign of it, not even footprints."

The couple made a hasty return to the house to discuss the experience with Deborah's parents, who had heard legends of creatures for many years. "But they are all a hoax. Do you have any jealous ex-boyfriends who might act out this way?" her mother asked.

"Maybe," conceded Deborah, "but they wouldn't have the ingenuity for such an elaborate outfit. Maybe the creature read my story and came to make fun of me. Think how silly it would look to write a story about this after my first story, especially if it turns out to be a hoax. At least I am glad someone else saw it."

Al managed a queasy smile. The entire ordeal eerily reminded him of the secret he took with him from the Soviet Union, the reason for his escape. "I am not familiar with the North American 'ape-man'. All I know I learned from Deborah."

"I think it is a big hoax!" Ollie was adamant. "Give me some proof."

"I agree," declared Hollie.

"Me too," remarked Al. It was easy politics to agree with Deborah's parents.

"Not me," returned Deborah. "If it is a hoax then I am fooled, but I'm still not going to write about it."

"Have you found any new topics?" her father inquired.

"I think so. Some adventurer brought a crystal 'skull of doom' to Toronto. It sounds like some good supersticious fun."

CHAPTER SIX

SKULLARLY OPINIONS

Boston, Massachusets
July 1927

C layton looked up from his newspaper and gazed out the train window at the boats on Lake Huron. "Mae West got in trouble again for her role in the play 'Sex'. She was fined $500. She must be getting paid very well."

"Would you like to see that play?" asked Emily.

"Sure, wouldn't you?" Clayton answered with exuberance. He then quickly slapped his hand over his mouth before saying, "I mean, no dear, I actually think it is a distasteful, vulgar show."

Emily gave him a mock stern look, her arms folded across her chest. "You said it is a distasteful, vulgar show. Have you seen it?"

"Okay, yes I have seen it, but only three times," Clayton falsely confessed.

"Let's change the subject. Are you still thinking about going back to Detroit in a few months to buy an automobile?"

"I am. Ford is coming out with the Model A when they cease making the Model T."

"Strange alphabet."

"The Model A will have shock absorbers and a speed meter. It should be a great car. Anyway, my mind is in Canada now. Where did your father meet Mitchell-Hedges?"

"They met fourteen years ago, probably for some academic reason. Their friendship is casual. Anna and I are closer. The only place I have ever seen them was in Boston. It has been about four years, since Anna was 15. Her nickname is 'Sammy' but I like her given name."

"How did you and Anna become so close?"

"I help her with female traumas like a big sister."

"Do you think Mitchell-Hedges will share a few adventure stories with us?"

"Maybe he will. He has been in some strange and dangerous places on his archeological hunts and big game fishing."

"You and your father are pretty gracious. Some people would consider it ludicrous to travel from Boston to Ontario to see one artifact. Have you given much thought to this crystal skull we are going to see?"

"I decided not to think about it and just wait to see what all the fuss is about. After all, it really is just a work of art."

After arriving where the Mitchell-Hedges were staying before they were to continue on to England, Emily and Clayton dined with their hosts. The crystal skull topic was not discussed during the meal. Finally, after dessert and tea, it was time for the unveiling. Everyone except Anna was silent.

"Nobody is sure how old it is, or how to make it, or if the Mayans made it. Some people think it could be evil but I don't. You should have seen the natives celebrate when we found it. My father believes it is all connected to the lost continent of Atlantis."

"Do you mean the story of Atlantis could be true?" inquired Clayton.

Emily's concentration remained fixed upon the crystal skull. "Why do I feel like the whole universe is looking at me?" Clayton put his arm around her and she seemed to return to common consciousness. "It drains my psychic energy," revealed Emily. "It feels like it wants me to communicate with it but that's impossible."

The viewing lasted less than 30 minutes. "A newspaper writer is coming tomorrow to see the skull. She is a skeptic. You can all take part. If you like we can also arrange private meetings with the skull and yourselves."

The following afternoon, Mike Mithchell-Hedges was delighted when Deborah Holly arrived on time, her shapely figure surrounded by a moderately flapper blue and white dress. The writer spent several minutes alone with the skull before Clayton arrived.

"Does the skull actually do anything?" she asked. "I guess my questions should be directed to Mr. Mitchell-Hedges. It kind of makes me feel weird, like it is communicating with my intuition."

"It seems like it can see right through me when actually I can see through it," contributed Clayton.

During the ensuing momentary pause of silence, an absorbing, overwhelming feeling came over Clayton of reclaiming his body. "I feel like my body left and my mind was somewhere else. It's like it knows about those mysterious lights in the harbor that night. I can feel my body becoming normal again. Is the skull recreating this odd sensation?"

"I found it," announced the voice of a third person.

"Are you Anna?" asked Deborah.

"Yes I am," Anna answered, stepping forward. "The jawbone was found a couple of months later."

"Why did the tribal people build an altar and celebrate when it was found?" inquired Clayton.

Deborah lauged. "I am supposed to be conducting the interview," she said, retaining her smile. She thought, "He makes me nervous but I feel like I should laugh. It's like I am absorbing someone else's happy energy."

"The local people believe the skull will help the world discover good things someday," stated Anna.

Emily entered the room and almost immediately her concentrated attention went to the crystal skull. "It's changing!" She widened her stance as if expecting a sudden collision of energy, her thoughts sifting the others out of her consciousness. "The skull is becoming pink and purplish. I feel like I am in a prism of colors, it reminds me of the prism I saw in the sky at Fenway."

"A halo?" Anna squinted at the crystal skull. "I've never seen a halo on the top before."

"Shhh!" commanded Clayton. "I can hear a sound, like a generator or some faint electrical frequency. Maybe it is some kind of sound and color frequency, a prism of sound."

"There is nothing to hear," thought Deborah. "But why doesn't someone say something about the red spot on the temple of the skull? It is pulsating and growing." She looked at the three others, all transfixed to the artifact. "Maybe they don't see what I see."

Mr. Mitchell-Hedges bumped into the door frame when entering the room, causing him to drop a book. The other three in the room were startled and when each turned back to the skull their individually observed phenomena was gone.

"Was that done purposely?" wondered Clayton.

Later at tea Deborah declared, "It hardly seems like a 'skull of doom'. I have a positive perspective, like my heart is telling me something."

"It was a little scary when it turned pink and purple and then prismic," contributed Emily.

"I did not see that," Deborah said with hesitation. "I saw a pulsating red spot."

"I saw a halo on the skull for the first time," volunteered Anna.

"Really? I didn't see anything except for some rainbow colors for awhile," said Clayton. "I heard some sort of pure electrical sound, but it wasn't a buzz."

"How do you plan to present the crystal skull in your article Deborah?" asked Mike Mitchell-Hedges.

"Certainly my article will not be sarcastic. I really don't have any story ideas yet but I'll come up with something."

"I feel smarter," Clayton proclaimed.

"Oh yeh," kidded Emily, "prove it."

"Easy," responded Clayton, "piece of perspicacious cake."

* * *

"I'm glad you are here Harley," acknowledged Mike Mitchell-Hedges to Dr. Hiller upon his arrival. "I have been anxious to hear a scientific opinion of the crystal skull since your daughter Emily was here a couple of weeks ago."

"It is sad the conquistadors destroyed so much knowledge of the perhaps advanced ways of Mayan civilization," commented Dr. Hiller. "Why do you suppose the skull was hidden?"

"It was likely used for religious ceremonies. Light shined up through the bottom gives the eyes quite a strange look."

"What kind of light? Surely a fire or candle would be difficult to conceal from people if you are trying to trick them."

"Personally I believe it is more than a ceremonial toy. I believe it has something to do with Atlantis."

"What is your line of reasoning?"

"Somehow I think it is some kind of ancient energy source or something from an advanced civilization. Sometimes I get the feeling the skull is broadcasting something that makes it hypnotic."

His comment caused Dr. Hiller to look away from the skull. "No inanimate object is going to hypnotize me," he thought, "particularly without any manipulation by a human being." Turning toward the skull owner, he suggested, "Maybe the crystal skull reacts to the energy field of the human body."

"Who can tell? To my knowledge, it has no effect on me. Maybe it does."

Dr. Hiller spent a solitary hour with the skull before leaving the following day. On the train back to Boston, the physics professor either thought about the crystal skull or slept. "Something about the skull bothers me. Something is different or has changed. What is it? Has someone been hurt?"

For hours he deliberated on his feelings, baffled by the notion of intuition. By the time the train arrived in Boston, Dr. Hiller began entertaining an alternative notion. "Perhaps I have changed."

Both Emily and Clayton were waiting for him when he arrived home. "I would like to bathe before dinner. I wouldn't mind a nap also but I know you are anxious to talk about the skull. I'll tell you the entire story after we eat. Let's talk about something else."

"Dad, Clayton is a follower of sports. I tried to tell him the story about your gym class in Springfield but I don't remember it that well."

"It was my junior year at Massachusets," Dr. Hiller began, obviously both happy and flattered to tell the tale . "The instructor of the class chose teams of four or five players for an indoor game he had just invented. We used an English football but the rules were nearly the opposite. A player could not kick it but could bounce it and throw it. A goal was scored by throwing the ball into a peach basket hung on the wall. After the first goal was scored, I was chosen to climb the ladder to retrieve the ball."

"And what did you tell the instructor?" asked Emily, baiting his response.

"I said, 'Dr. Naismith, I think the team who gave up the goal should have to get the ball out of the peach basket'. The inventor of the game agreed and thus the first rule of basketball etiquette was born."

"Was it fun?" asked Clayton. "Basketball must have been very different then."

"The game on the floor was not that bad, it's just that there were no boundaries. Once I was trampled as several players raced for a ball in the balcony. Another time I went face first on a stairway."

"And after all that you still like the game," said Emily.

"Basketball is much better with boundaries and without a ladder," noted Dr. Hiller sarcastically. "The open end net removed the ladder from basketball and the game is better for it."

"Now let's talk about the crystal skull," begged Emily. "I know you are tired from your trip father but I am really interested in hearing your crystal skull story."

"Oddly, I am still sorting out my thoughts on the matter. My scientific side tells me it is a work of art made out of a rock. The crystal could have inert energies similar to coal or a magnet, an energy you can't see. The unique experiences people report are astonishing. I wish I could see and feel what others do."

"The crystal skull somehow seems connected to destiny, the destiny of others and not necessarily mine," Emily added. "Not everyone has the same experience with the skull so a sense of destiny does not affect all. Father, do you suppose there is such a thing as destiny?"

"Oh, you have to believe in destiny, if nothing else but for the sake of hope. But I try to stick to physical and logical perspectives."

"Are you hinting that you are giving consideration to non-logical thinking?" Emily inquired.

"It may be psychological because I've heard stories about the skull, but something did seem different. It was like my own energy seemed to be enhanced and reflected back to me by the skull," claimed Dr. Hiller.

"It is possible that what you are describing could still be a physical occurrence," suggested Clayton.

"If it is physical, it is beyond our currernt knowledge of physics. If anything, it is somehow closer to quantum physics theory," responded Dr. Hiller.

"Oh, you mean like that E=MC squared stuff. By the way, let me know if you need the long version of that formula explained to you," Clayton joked.

"Then there is the simple physical skull itself. We have no technology to duplicate such an artifact. Making the crystal skull by hand would require decades, maybe centuries. Could ancient civilizations actually have been more advanced in some areas of science?" Dr. Hiller pondered.

"Which supports Mike's Atlantis theory," quipped Emily.

"It almost seems like the crystal material was liquid and was poured into a mold," remarked Clayton. "Or maybe it was a seed that grew into the skull shape."

The comment caused an immediate retreat into thought by Dr. Hiller. Emily broke the silence and changed the subject at the same time. "By the way dad, how was your trip?"

Later that night in her room, Emily's mind was dominated with thoughts of the skull. She made an entry in the journal she had begun several weeks before: "The crystal skull seems to have no race. Who is it based upon? If it reappears throughout time, who has kept it hidden? Why does it react differently with different people? Or is it the people who react to the skull? What was the world like when it was made? How is destiny tied up in this? The skull seems like it knows me."

CHAPTER SEVEN

SOUND INVESTMENT

Spokane, Washington
August 1927

"Look at this," remarked Amanda. "The ad for our new movie theater is next to a small story about the last Model T. It turns out it was old number 15,007,033. Isn't that your lucky number?"

"No," disagreed Jason, "my lucky number is 15,007,031."

"Why not 15,007,033?"

"I can't count that high."

"I can count many," announced Lenny, who had just entered the kitchen.

"Can you count as many as 15 million?" Amanda inquired of her four year old son.

"Is that more than 6?"

"I changed my favorite number," declared Jason. "Does anyone have any guesses?"

"Three!" shouted Lenny.

"It has a 3 in it, but the number is 435."

Amanda grinned broadly. "That's a great number. That's the seating capacity of the new theater."

"The 'Emerald Theater'," clarified Jason. "We are going to pack the place when the sound equipment arrives. 'Talkies' are a great investment. I am glad our little four person group bought it. There are many others across the country thinking the same way we are, but I like our location. Couer d'Alene is a great little town."

Watching Lenny trot out of the kitchen, Amanda chuckled. "Remember when we were considering building a theater. Lenny didn't get it."

"I know. I remember the day we stopped at that vacant lot and Lenny said, 'Can't have movies here'. Movies are in the dark'."

After a brief chuckle from her recollection of her young son's comment, Amanda's eyes widened at an advertisment in the Spokesman-Review. "The 'Rhythm Boys', Crosby and Rinker, are scheduled to have one performance in Spokane at the Liberty Theater before leaving for New York." She briefly scanned the remainder of the newspaper page. "I'll be back in awhile." Jason nodded as she grabbed the car keys.

When Amanda returned, she simply walked up to Jason and handed him two tickets to the Crosby and Rinker show. "Is it okay if we go to the show?"

"I can probably be bribed to go with sexual favors."

"Who the hell is 'Sexual Favors'? I want to go."

"Grammar isn't my strong suit. I'm glad we're going. And did you remember my excursion with Ben today?"

"What's he looking for again?"

"He wants to make a table out of a tree stump, so we are going to prowl around the foothills to see what we can find. I might make one too."

Jason joined Ben and his neighbor Rob in late afternoon. Three bottles of inexpensive bootleg wine were consumed as Ben drove the trio on logging roads in the heavily wooded area. Before the forest succumbed to darkness, several stumps had been gathered and placed in the back of the truck.

"We are done with the work and we are finished with the wine. Let's go home," declared Ben.

"I need to pee first," Jason informed his friends. Ben obliged and Jason jumped out of the truck and strode a short distance away to relieve himself.

"It is almost really cold and dark out here." His attention was drawn to movement directly in front of him, slightly uphill and no more than 15 feet away. An extremely large silhouette stood straight up from a crouched position, like a catcher in baseball. "A bear," thought Jason. "Be careful." He studied the outline of the being but could not discern any distinguishing features.

"It wanted me to see it. Did I just think that or did I somehow hear it in my head?" He consciously moved at a much slower pace than his mind was racing. The creature kept his ground, some 75 feet from the vehicle. While buckling his belt he noticed only two small red reflections where the bear had been. "They look like eyes." They faded from view and Jason moved quickly toward the automobile. Before getting back in the car, he peered up the slight slope into the dark woods but could not distinguish any specific shapes. "It didn't really have a bear shape," he thought curiously. "It didn't have shoulders like a bear and it seemed too tall and thin. Maybe it just seemed that way because it was a little bit uphill from me. Maybe I should get out of here before it decides to make a more violent appearance."

"Did you guys see the bear?"

"What bear?"

"Did he have toilet paper for you?"

"You were probably seeing things."

"It stood up while I was peeing."

"Was it pink?"

Jason momentarily pondered the question. "Maybe."

* * *

"Did you see the article about the man-ape yesterday?" Amanda briefly looked up from her bacon and eggs, awaiting an answer.

"Up in British Columbia…yes, I saw it. Your father used to say they were friendly."

"My grandfather said he knew of one, but sometimes I wonder if the ape of the woods is just folklore. Anyway, if there was a man-ape creature, my grandfather would not have shot at him."

"Good point."

"The funny thing is, I had a strange dream last night," revealed Amanda.

"When you say 'strange', do you mean stranger than normal for you?"

"Just because you hardly ever remember your dreams doesn't mean yours are not strange. Anyway, in my first dream, my grandfather and the man-ape were about ten feet apart. They were trying to communicate with thoughts and sometimes with hand gestures. A stranger showed up and the mountain ape disappeared."

"How can you picture a mountain ape in your dream when you have no idea what they look like?"

"If I had to guess, I am probably creating it mentally from information in the article, from grandfather's stories, and from your description."

"What I saw probably was a bear."

"Good point. Why did whatever it was want you to see it?"

"Whatever it was." The darkened outline of the rising creature came to his mind as it had so many times in the days following the sighting. "It stood up like a man. I think it had a different neck and shoulders than a bear."

"Anyway Jason, the mountain ape dream wasn't the strange dream I had. Do you remember the article about the new invention, television. We had one inside of a wooden box in my dream. I remember someone in my dream telling me that everyone had one."

"Why would everyone have one? It's not like there are television broadcasts like there are in radio."

"You don't think television is going to bypass movies in using sound, do you?"

"How many people are lining up to buy televisions? Most people don't know what it is. My guess is television will be a tool for business and government and not so much for entertainment," surmised Jason.

"It would have to take awhile to catch on. Besides, televisions would be expensive. Not all households have a radio. How could everyone afford a television?"

"You came up with a good answer to your own question. Television won't bypass movies in using sound because they would not be affordable to the general public. And you were right, your dream was strange," proclaimed Jason. "By the way, is there any chance of leaving in the next hour? I want to have some boating time at Priest Lake before we meet up with everyone at the potluck dinner at the resort. Pat and Ed and the kids already left."

"I need to pack a lunch before Margaret wakes up from her nap and then I'll be ready. It sure is nice to have the boat to sleep in instead of our old tent."

By late afternoon, Lenny and his neighbor friend Tommy were standing near the lake shoreline while Jason was putting the boat in the water. "Lenny! Look here! There's a fish!"

"Where is the fish?" Lenny inquired, peering closely at the water where Tommy was pointing.

Tommy suddenly threw a large rock he was concealing into the water, splashing water all over Lenny. Not fazed by the prank, Lenny simply wiped the water out of his face.

Several minutes later, Lenny tried the same prank on Tommy. "I see a fish!" The older boy was ready for the trick and tried to splash water on Lenny again but missed. Lenny stepped toward the shoreline again. "I see a fish! Look!"

Tommy crept up to the water, making sure to be in a position to easily move out of the way of a splash. Lenny then brought out his rock and wildly hurled it, striking Tommy on the shin. "Ouch! That hurt!"

Lenny quickly put his fingers to his lips. "Shhh! You'll scare the fish."

* * *

"We're going to the dump!" The excited children at the Priest Lake resort rushed to recruit parents to go. Lenny repeated what he heard other kids say. "We're going when it gets dark!" No one was sure who originated the dump idea but two families plus two other kids piled in the appropriate vehicles.

As expected, there were a number of black bears at the landfill sorting through the debris. "Aren't the two young cubs fun to watch?" Amanda asked Lenny.

From the safety of the automobiles the onlookers laughed and jeered at the action of the bears until one of the larger ones became curious and crawled up on the hood of a car belonging to someone else visiting the site. "That bear is not concerned at all about that guy starting his engine," Jason observed. The curious creature lost his balance when the vehicle was thrust into reverse but nonetheless landed upon the ground upright with a degree of grace.

"I guess we are going," commented Jason when Ed started his vehicle. He started the engine of his automobile, privately glad to be leaving.

"Anyway, the bear certainly could choose this vehicle as a perch." He followed his friend's truck along the dirt road, stopping when they stopped.

"Is something wrong?" Jason inquired.

"No, I just have to pee. I didn't want to jump out and pee with bears for an audience."

"That's a good idea. How about you Lenny?" His son was not interested so Jason found his own space in the dark about fifteen feet away.

"What was that?" Jason whispered to himself. He peered into the moonlit forest, cocking his head to hear any noises the environment might offer. "Something is moving in the woods." A very large yet undistinguishable shape moved diagonally away from Jason. "It moves differently than a bear. It walks like a man."

The notion seemed suddenly insane and he laughed, loud enough to surprise himself. "How come everything gets weird when I piss in the woods?" Everything went silent just after the door of his friend's truck slammed shut. He strained to see in the dark but with no more movement and no more sound, he walked back to his vehicle.

Shortly after he resumed driving, Amanda exclaimed with excitement, "Look, there is a bear moving through the woods!"

Jason stopped the truck when the bear stepped into the glare of the headlights. Standing on two legs at a distance of about 50 feet, the bear looked directly at the car. Then the bear seemed to voice a laugh! It caused Amanda to chuckle, but Jason recognized the brief guffaw. "His laugh is an imitation of my laugh a few minutes ago." The bear lowered onto all four legs and hustled into the darkness.

The laughing bear experience was not discussed during the remainder of the drive back to the boat. Only when the two retired for the evening, with both children asleep, did Amanda chuckle again about the bear laugh.

"It was imitating me," said Jason carefully.

"Imitation is a form of flattery."

"Seriously, I laughed that same laugh when I was peeing."

"Think of it from the perspective of the bear. How often does a bear see a chuckling man with his dick hanging out?"

"I love it when you speak French!" exclaimed Jason.

Amanda instinctively went along with the shift in direction of their conversation. In a joyous pun, as she felt his momentum growing larger, jammed onto her unclothed pelvic bone, she softly cried out, "Oui,oui…wheeeeeee!" as she grabbed his erection.

The following afternoon, Amanda turned the truck and trailer onto the highway for the three hour trip home. "Driving with the trailer behind bothered me at first but now I am comfortable with it."

Jason was joining the children in falling asleep. "You're a good driver. You were never meant to just be a passenger anyway, in anything in life."

"He detests not having a scientific explanation for things," she mused. "How do you explain the laughing bear, or 'Laughing Bear'?" She strained to remember any details of a laughing bear told to her by her long deceased grandfather. "I need to think about something else."

The kids were in bed within an hour after reaching home. Amanda poured a glass of lemonade and sat in a porch chair, gazing at the stars. Her thoughts focused upon 'Laughing Bear' and the first layer of memories came back to her. "Laughing Bear is very old, older than most trees. And he is good. Laughing Bear laughs because he is good. Is he a trickster? Strong Eagle, my grandfather, what am I to learn from this? Is this bear our friend?"

Jason joined his spouse on the porch. "I cannot escape the repetitive, monotous nature of my own thoughts about the laughing bear. My images of the ape of the woods and the laughing bear are beginning to be absurd. At first I thought the laughing bear was a great ape, which is a preposterous notion since we saw maybe nine bears in the prior fifteen minutes. Is my subconscious mind spooked? Some people would think I am damn crazy. I would."

"Just because you don't understand something doesn't make you crazy."

"Sometimes I think the moon speaks to me, like some silly persuasion from above."

"Remember to listen to both the moon and Mother Earth."

"Maybe the mountain devil I saw wasn't a devil but more like an angel from below?"

"Then we must be the balance between opposing forces."

"Are you suggesting opposing forces who aren't humans? The wisest action is to forget the whole thing. Sooner or later weird memories should fade." He thought about his words, unable to decide whether they were fact or fiction.

CHAPTER EIGHT

CRYSTAL UNCLEAR FATE

Toronto, Ontario
October 1927

"I don't feel like reading this." Al tossed the newspaper onto a table in his recently acquired apartment in Toronto. "I can practice reading in English later. What has changed with Deborah?"

He began pacing through his flat. "Maybe she really didn't want me to move to Toronto. Or maybe it is her menstrual cycle time of the month. Am I supposed to create a 'Plan B'?"

Al flopped onto the sofa, wondering what possible alternative plans he could develop. Within seconds he was back on his feet. "The crystal skull! This mood change of hers started when she saw the crystal skull! What can I do about this? At first, Deborah exhibited a great deal of exuberance in describing her skull experience, as if the skull released pent-up enthusiasm. That energy changed quickly from being about the crystal skull itself to how to write a story about it. Nearly all emotional response was sucked inward by her from that time onward."

He picked up the telephone but almost immediately put it back on the hook. "It has been two days since we spoke. She said she would call," he reminded himself again. "Maybe she found the angle she needs to write the story. It has been three weeks since she saw the skull."

Later in the day, Deborah did indeed telephone Al. "How is the story progressing? I can't wait to read it."

"Actually, I have let it go for now. Maybe I will be inspired if I just quit thinking about it for awhile. In the meantime, I got an assignment from a magazine which was easy. It is done already."

Their short uninspired telephone conversation was grinding to a finish when Al desperately tried to keep it going. "Is there any way I could see the crystal skull?" Realizing there was no logical explanation for his request to be honored by the skull owner, he added, "You could make up an excuse why you need to see it again, maybe to get better pictures or something."

The question caught Deborah off guard. "I had not thought about seeing the skull again." The thought startled her but her mind quickly overcame any resistance. "Yes, I would like to see the crystal skull again."

"Can I go with you. I might be helpful."

"You know, that is a pretty good idea. I don't really know why, but I don't want to lie or fib to Mr. Mitchell-Hedges. I will just ask if I can see it again and if I can take you along for an intellectual opinion."

"Now, describing my opinion as intellectual is already telling a fib."

A genuine laugh came forth from Deborah. It had been a long time coming.

* * *

"The crystal skull," thought Al, "is probably a fascinating piece of art with some myth of the Americas attached to it." Continuing his line of thinking, he turned to Deborah, who was driving them to their destination to see the skull. "What is a skull of doom supposed to be able to do to warrant such a description?"

"I have no idea although I have given it some thought. The skull has not doomed anyone the owners have known and you would think they would be doomed more than anyone else."

"Why do you say that?"

"Because the Mitchell-Hedges' moved it from its place of origin in the Mayan area. Anyway, it doesn't seem evil to me. It is more like it can somehow sense my thoughts and send them back to me with a slightly different outlook."

"Maybe it can turn positive thoughts into negative thoughts, a doomed thought process… for some people," Al reasoned, hoping his statement did not sound like a pronouncement of doom upon Deborah.

"Not with me." Immediately her mind scanned through the time after seeing the crystal skull, trying to confirm her statement to convince herself. "Except," she continued, "I still cannot find a good story angle on the crystal skull. I do not want to report it as a skull of doom."

"Maybe your story idea will materialize on this visit," Al said hopefully while at the same time dividing his nervous attention to the near miss of an automobile while Deborah was attempting to park the vehicle. Having been an automobile driver in the Soviet Union, he hoped to someday purchase a car of his own. "What does it take to get a drivers license around here anyway?"

"Thanks a lot!" Deborah protested, turning off the ignition.

"What?" Al asked, surprised. Then he recognized the ill timing of his question. "No, I was not thinking about your driving. It's just that I would like to get a car someday."

Deborah continued her suspicious look. "Maybe you should ask the skull."

Frederick Mitchell-Hedges welcomed his guests with tea before they were to view the crystal skull. "I have found that some people forget the questions they planned to ask in the presence of the skull. And of course some people simply think of more questions."

"That is not quite the case with me," revealed Deborah. "I just want to get to know it better."

"My question sir; how was the skull used?" Al asked.

"We cannot be certain, but it may have been used in some sort of tribal ritual, probably by shaman types."

Everyone pondered his comment momentarily and Al asked yet another question. "How old is it?"

"There is no way to know," replied Mr. Mitchell-Hedges.

"It is the same age as me... to me," blurted Anna, otherwise known as Sammy, the daughter of the Mr. Mitchell-Hedges. "I found it on my seventeenth birthday."

Deborah heard the story during her previous visit but she wanted to hear it again from Sammy.

"I saw something shining but I did not try to get it by myself. I was well aware from my father that it is best not to risk damage to other possible artifacts by charging in a hasty manner for one relic. They lowered me into a pit with a rope to grab it. The jawbone was found nearby a few months later."

Mr. Mitchell-Hedges patiently waited for his daughter to finish her well rehearsed story. Quickly, almost mysteriously, he changed the topic at the end of her tale.

Deborah had a fleeting memory of something similar happening during her first visit. "Perhaps Mr. Mitchell-Hedges does not want to discuss his role in the discovery and eventual relocation of the 'skull of doom'? Does he believe in a curse?"

As they entered the viewing room, Al posed the question, "How did the locals, the natives, react to the discovery of the crystal skull?"

"It was as if a festival happened," volunteered Sammy. "I didn't understand what was going on but it sure was a big fuss."

"The natives believe the skull has a purpose each time it surfaces throughout time. They believe it used to belong to a divine order and was lost. And other skulls are supposed to surface," explained Mr. Mitchell-Hedges.

"Do you know of any other skulls?" Al asked.

At that time the crystal skull was uncovered and placed upon a small table. The room became quiet.
Several seconds later Mr. Mitchell-Hedges answered the question. "There is one in London. It is not anywhere near this perfect."

"Stay as objective as I possibly can," Deborah counseled herself. "This experience is different." The color changes did not happpen. Clearly there was a different energy dynamic with the first group of viewers present when she saw the skull.

"Do you think your relationship or energy with the skull is evolving?" Deborah inquired of Mr. Mitchell-Hedges. "Does the energy level change around different people?"

Deborah looked at Al, who remained silent. He seemed entranced. "I probably looked just as intrigued at my first viewing of the skull."

"The skull is not anything like Deborah explained it," Al thought. "It is not changing. I'm not sure how the prism is projected from it. The prism seems spiritual, at least what I think spiritual is. For all I know it is a curse. The skull has an electrical energy but it doesn't seem positive or negative." There were visual images just the same. "And I have that odd hair growing feeling again," he thought, looking at his hands. "But nothing physical is happening to me."

Images from the Soviet Union were parading through Al's mind. "Why do I feel like the whole universe is looking at me? I'm just dreaming up some cosmic illusion to freedom but that is an illusion too." He envisioned soldiers removing the starving agricultural peasants, elderly people and protesters. "I recognize the process. They are being purged from society, from existence." A shudder of fear passed through him. "What if I get purged in North America?" He felt a mounting anxiety with guilt for leaving the Soviet Union and the fear of the unknown in North America. "I feel trapped in anxiety, trapped by the skull. What does it want from me?"

Deborah stepped in front of him briefly on her way to change vantage points, breaking Al's train of thought. "Shape positive thoughts. I am a survivor. I believe it because I proved it." He forced himself to smile and he just kept smiling. His intuition would let him know if it was the correct response.

Al sensed an image, the physical healing from a spiritual light. He felt an inner light, under which were no shadows. "The light is cleansing me," he thought. "Or is it tricking me?"

"Al?" Deborah was going to ask him a question, but she did a double take as she saw the grin on his face. She nudged him, "Al?"

The smile turned towards Deborah. She felt a momentary surge of energy from him, as though his energy was competing with the crystal skull. Quite suddenly the energy changed as did the expression on Al's face.

"That really is some kind of masterpiece," he exclaimed to the others in the room. "It has some powerful energy but it seems like it is reflective, like we are the mirror it is viewing. That could frighten someone into thinking about doom."

"That is a very interesting perception," responded the archaeologist. "Everyone seems to have a different reaction to the skull."

"Don't you wish you knew why it was made, and how and when?" Sammy asked the group.

"The amount of ancient knowledge that was destroyed when the conquistadors conquered the Central America area cannot even be guessed," stated Mr. Mitchell-Hedges. "The quality of that knowledge also cannot be guessed."

My father believes the crystal skull may be linked with Atlantis, the lost continent," declared Sammy.

He nodded in agreement but did not elaborate. He was expecting Deborah to pursue the Atlantis angle. "I would if I were the reporter."

Instead, Deborah said nothing. During the time the crystal skull was displayed, she listened and comprehended all the conversation but she scarcely contributed. "Why do I have so much anxiety? My mind is jumbled. I need to change this." Immediately Deborah began to get sleepy, the complete opposite physical dynamic compared to the rapid scramble of her mind and heart. The momentary collision of internal forces made Deborah feel faintly ill. She closed her eyes but she could still see the skull in her mind. As Deborah began to open her eyes, her left knee buckled and her balance was in jeopardy. Wordlessly Al caught her and physically maneuvered her back into standing balance. None of the group seemed surprised and none inquired about her condition.

"I swear that thing hypnotizes me," Deborah finally spoke. "But if I write that, people will think I am crazy."

"Another interesting perspective," remarked Mike Mitchell-Hedges. Everyone let out a chuckle, a laugh of relief it seemed.

An hour later, rolling down the passenger window of Deborah's automobile on the return trip to Toronto, sensory recognition registered in Al's brain. "I have gone without food all day."

"One of my favorite diners is nearby. A chicken dinner sounds real good."

"Just what exactly does a chicken dinner sound like? My guess is ragtime music."

"Yeh? Maybe your chicken dinner can do the Charleston? It could give you lessons."

While waiting for their food in the cafe, Deborah requested, "Tell me about your experience with the crystal skull." Seeing his puzzled look, she rephrased her question. "Well, what did you think?"

"I didn't see any of the things you mentioned that you saw the first time. It is powerful though. And it is real interesting that people have unique experiences."

Deborah moved a strand of black hair from her face. "What was your unique experience?"

Al was thoughtful for a moment, always aware of not wanting to reveal too much about the Soviet Union. The negative, sad images in his mind in the presence of the skull would reflect his past and his unspoken fears. "My unique experience, I guess, is the way it helped me recognize my inner strength. At the same time I had insights into those people less fortunate than I."

"That is better than I can describe," Deborah complained softly, "and I am supposed to write a story about it."

Finishing his last bite of apple pie, Al waited to speak. His mind briefly recalled the ape-man in the blueberry field he glimpsed with Deborah but his focus returned to the conversation. "This may sound strange and crazy, but maybe you should ask the skull what to write."

"I am not going back there again."

"No, I didn't mean that. I can still feel the energy of the crystal skull. You have been through it twice so you probably can still feel the energy like I do. Just ask the energy to work with you instead of against you in writing the story," said Al, not really sure of how his notion originated in his own mind.

"Ask who? Ask the energy?"

Al shrugged. "It was what came to mind."

Deborah shrugged in return and finished her coffee.

Later that evening, Al sat in a chair facing the window of his second-story apartment. "I seem to think more about the crystal skull as I get more fatigued. I wonder if Deborah is obsessed with her thoughts?" He took out a pen and paper and began doodling sketches of the crystal artifact.

"The imagery of the Soviet Union generated in the presence of the skull is surprisingly easy to recall, even in vivid detail." He recognized his own fear in the images of the purges. "I always hoped such things never really happened until it happened to my own family. It may be selfish, but I am glad to
have reinvented myself. The skull somehow validated my actions."

Al moved to the bed with a vague notion of sleep but he merely laid on the bed fully clothed. His mind turned to the images of war prompted by the skull. "The scale was too large. The tanks and bombs and airplanes in my imagination were not recognizable. Is it prophecy? Or destiny? Am I a bad guy? Seeing that monster in the blueberry patch was like looking into a strange mirror. Is the monster a bad guy? Is the crystal skull evil? I don't really think either one of them are evil but it seems like something must be. Maybe I'm not involved. I don't want to be involved."

He longed for someone to discuss the details of his true experience with the crystal skull or about his past in the Soviet Union but Deborah still could not be told about his true Russian life. "And I cannot explain the spiritual light even to myself. Somehow I hope the war thoughts fade away but I don't know if the spiritual light was actually real or just some odd perception. If it was real, I want to channel it toward a vibrant relationship with Deborah. What is my future?"

* * *

"Okay crystal skull," Deborah announced in her bedroom, "how about some insight into the story I am supposed to write?" She had been thinking about the skull since her first morning cup of coffee and she could easily visualize it.

While brushing her teeth an idea for the story popped into her head. "AGZAGUH!" She smiled. "AGZAGUH!" Deborah burst into laughter and toothpaste flew onto the mirror out of her mouth. She patiently rinsed out her mouth and looked at herself in the mirror. "As a girl!"

An outline for the story began to develop. "I will write the daughter's story about the crystal skull. Anna Mitchell-Hedges found it, on her birthday no less. Some of the strange tales about the skull can be explained through the eyes of a then seventeen-year-old girl."

Deborah began some housekeeping projects but she had trouble staying with a single task. "I enjoy the anxiety. I enjoy the anticipation." She prolonged her anticipation until she felt like a caged animal given its escape.

"It is time." Deborah went to her typewriter and began her crystal skull article. Her focus and concentration were easily bridled to the skull experience because it already dominated her thoughts. Later in the day she telephoned Al.

"Very well Deborah and I am very glad to hear your story is nearly finished. I'll talk with you tomorrow, good bye." Al hung up the receiver to the telephone in the hallway. "There is hope!"

He grabbed the book he was translating for a Toronto publishing firm and headed for the park down the street. While sitting in the shade on a park bench, Al worked on the translation of the third chapter from Russian into French. He was largely oblivious to the patrons of the public park until a man sat down on the other end of the bench. The visitor appeared to be getting ready to read a magazine. After a quick glance Al went back to his translation of the book.

"Alexiev."

The sound of his Russian name ripped at his heart. He tried not to show any surprise by ignoring the man.

"Alexiev." There was eye contact this time so the man continued. "People you do not want to know are aware of your presence here in Toronto."

Al lowered his head but the man knew he was listening.

"I am not one of those undesirable people. I am here to give you a different option since your 'unfriendlies' will be visiting you soon. I have managed to stay a half step ahead of them but time is of the essence. They are probably at your apartment right now."

"This is no coincidence or wild guess from this man. His words are specific to me," thought Al. "I do not believe we have met," he deadpanned.

"My name is Jim Jeffers," the stranger said, extending his hand. Al shook it and waited for the man to continue. "I am with the United States government. One of our people in Moscow notified us that you left Russia. We lost you until you made it to Prague."

"What do you want with me?" Al tried to portray a neutral, stoic demeanor.

"Some members of our government keep track of Soviets who defect. It is a sort of xenophobic hobby of some of our politicians."

"Your research brings you to Canada?"

"Not typically, but our government has a specific interest in you. That is why I represent a reasonable option for your future."

"And if I do not select your option?"

"No questions, no harm done, you are free to go. My opinion is that there is no 'free to go' place for you, not even with your girlfriend."

"Will they harm her?" Al asked wistfully.

"No, it is not their style. They don't need to risk unnecesary trouble and recognition. That is, not unless there is no other choice because of your actions."

"If I choose your option I will never see her again," said Al, the meaning of his words beginning to disturb him. There was no comment from Jeffers so Al assumed he was correct. He continued verbalizing thoughts, "And if I go to see her, I may no longer be an option for anything."

"The picture is beginning to focus."

"What happens if I go with your option?"

"You will get a new identity, a new vocation."

"That is what I thought I had here."

"Your plans have changed."

"Indeed they have. And what is my time frame?"

"Let me first tell you, if you want, one of our operatives will send a 'Dear Jane' postcard to your girlfriend with some lame reason why you had to leave. It really doesn't matter what it says, she will be surprised and disappointed. And you cannot see her again anyway."

Al contemplated the stranger's words in silence.

"Oh, and the time frame is now." A 1927 Pontiac pulled up and parked near them. "Our ride is here."

With no possessions other than the clothes on his back, his watch, and the money in his pocket, Al slid into the backseat of the waiting automobile. "So much for controlling my own destiny." A chill ran through him, causing the hair on his arms to stand with a sensation of growing. "The full moon is near," he thought, suddenly realizing the folly of his thoughts in the given circumstances.

"I am glad you chose safety."

"I don't know if I have succeeded or failed," thought Al as the car sped away. "How much do failure and circumstance contribute to destiny?"

"Two things," Jeffers announced. "Funds in a bank account will be secretly be signed over to you. Second, do you have a preference in a name?"

"Is 'Babe Ruth' taken?"

CHAPTER NINE

WE: A SACRED DIMENSION

Boston, Massachusets
November 1927

"Emily! That writer's story on the crystal skull is in our paper! 'GIRL FINDS MAYAN CRYSTAL SKULL'." Although Clayton had not finished reading the story, Emily snatched the newspaper away from him. "She did not depict it as a 'skull of doom' and there are no descriptions of any odd stuff. Deborah saw the skull a second time too." She cut out the article and placed it in one of her books.

"I thought she would write something whacky about the whole thing."

"Can you believe it? The article doesn't mention us at all," remarked Emily sarcastically.

"It should at least mention me."

Dr. Hiller entered through the front door and hung up his coat. "Clayton, I heard some good news today. Wall Street announced that General Motors will be declaring the largest dividend in American history."

"I should have bought more stock but who am I to spit into the wind of good news?"

"Ford is having their own fanfare this month," noted Emily. "The new Model A is a big success. It was very smart to buy stock in both automobile companies."

"Clayton, I have a confession to make," revealed Dr. Hiller. "I decided to invest money in the same stocks because or your ideas for investing in the stock market."

"The stock market does nothing but climb," stated Emily.

"But you still have to get lucky," added Dr. Hiller, somewhat amused about introducing the concept of luck. "Scientifically lucky I mean." Dr. Hiller excused himself and departed for the office in his home.

"What a year for you!" exclaimed Emily. "You absolutely guessed right on stocks, ole number 3 Babe Ruth hits a record 60 home runs and you have me in your life. I never would have guessed my eventual lover would have such great luck."

"I'm your eventual lover? And I thought you were already good in bed."

Emily placed Clayton's Red Sox hat on her head. "We better leave soon if we want to get to the 'Rhythm Boys' show on time."

"What a woman! Seeing you wear my hat makes my bat stand upright!"

"Put your equipment away," Emily scorned mockingly. "Where did you get this hat? It's not like you can buy one in a store or from a catalog."

Clayton gently removed his hat from Emily's head and put it on. "A friend of mine gave it to me...Bucky Fuller. He got it from some Red Sox vice president along with his fee for tutoring his kid."

"That's right, your mad scientist friend."

"He's just ahead of his time," clarified Clayton. "He was ahead of his time at Harvard too. The room I rent used to be his."

"It would be interesting to get dad and Bucky together."

"I'm having an early lunch with him tomorrow. He's leaving town soon for awhile and we hardly ever get to talk anymore. I love his theories and somehow I think he is fascinated with music, like he is trying to figure out some sound frequency for physics."

"Let's get going," reminded Emily. "I want to hear the sound frequencies of Crosby and Rinker."

The next morning, Clayton was expecting the clock to reveal an earlier time when he awoke. "Nine thirty?" He waited a few more minutes before announcing to his empty room, "Okay, I'm up. The furnace awaits me."

Clayton dressed to perform his duty of stoking the furnace with coal, which he did Monday, Wednesday and Friday mornings. He flinched at his reflection in the mirror. "My hair looks scared." He grabbed his Red Sox hat before departing.

Buckminster Fuller knocked on the room door less than two hours later and the two friends began walking toward their destination. As they walked past an undeveloped lot they were approached by three aggressive looking "toughs".

"It's up to you," one of the strangers began. "Give us your money with or without a fight."

Fuller, a small and wiry figure who recently had suffered the loss of a daughter, was not afraid but he nonetheless let Clayton do the talking. "That hardly seems fair, three against two. How about we think of something else?"

"Like what?"

"How about throwing rocks at that telephone pole over there." Clayton pointed at a pole some 60 feet away.

"We get three chances to your two?"

Clayton nodded his approval while Bucky stood stoically. "If we tie, we'll have a tiebreaker. You guys know baseball, I'm sure. Each team will explain what makes a curveball curve. Any Boston baseball fan should know that."

"If we lose we might just take your money anyway."

Bucky threw first and missed badly, skipping his rock off a sidewalk. He ignored the chuckles of their opponents. Clayton connected dead center with a resultant loud knock of the wood. The first two opponents narrowly missed but the repressed dignity of the trio was restored when the third rock grazed the pole. Next was the tiebreaker.

"You guys go first since we threw first," suggested Clayton.

"It's the grip on the ball."

"Continue," commanded Clayton.

There were looks among the toughs as if in search of more details. "It's in the snap of the wrist," came a second response.

The third opponent was calm and confident. "It's a trick pitch," he stated, but quickly added, "and it's a combination of all of our answers."

Clayton turned to Bucky. "Well pardner, win the contest for us."

"To verbally reconstruct the imagery and actual physical reaction of a spheroid object to be kinetically propelled in a curvilinear manner requires a basis in fact of both thermodynamics and wind resistance…"

Registering no comprehension of what was being said, the toughs were incredulous. They looked at Clayton, who was trying to keep a straight face. When Clayton laughed it became contagious. Bucky paid no attention and continued his lengthy monologue with his eyes closed. When he finished after more than a minute, he opened his eyes.

Clayton quickly pretended to regain a stoic manner and reached into his pocket. Now that's a fair fight. Here's 50 cents. You guys get yourselves a piece of pie somewhere."

As the three dumbfounded opponents left, one turned and remarked, "You guys are okay. Thanks for the laugh."

"Bucky," remarked Clayton while tugging at his friend's arm to continue walking, "it's always good to have new friends on the street."

"Clayton, you are a brilliant man."

Deflecting potentially violent situations came easy to Clayton. He had participated in his share of fights but never started one. "My most vivid memory of my father," explained Clayton, "is when he got beat up in front of our house. Some of the Irish guys on the block were sitting on the stoop drinking whiskey with my father when a bunch of other drunks from another neighborhood came by. I didn't understand the fuss, I was only seven. The next minute was like a riot. I don't remember him much. John Christopher O'Donnell, my father, was killed working at the railroad yard in 1909 when freight being loaded onto a flat car crashed into him."

"And both your parents were orphans?"

"My father escaped from an orphanage in Dublin. He met my mother, Elizabeth, before he enlisted in the Spanish-American War. She was a pious woman but she taught me to play piano. Little did my mother know I would make my living with music. And then came the curse."

"What do you mean?"

"Just after the fabled trade of Babe Ruth to the Yankees before the 1920 season, my mother contracted influenza. Just like millions of others around the world, her life was ended within weeks. Sometimes I wonder if the so-called curse of Babe Ruth was also accidentally put upon my mother. She loved the Sox. She vowed never to go to another Red Sox game until Babe Ruth retired but she died before he played another game."

* * *

Emily and Clayton stood hand in hand, gazing at the dancing sunlight reflected upon the Charles River. "I usually don't remember my dreams very well," revealed Emily. "I feel like I have had an awful dream that I cannot remember. I do remember my dreams last night real well though. One was pleasant."

"Tell me about the pleasant dream."

Lost in her thoughts, Emily displayed an expression of momentary confusion. "Okay, why not? Well, what I remember is you and I walking somewhere, like in woods and fields. You keep tripping and stumbling on things…branches, sticks, rocks. Then you asked, 'Where's the crystal skull when you need it?'"

"And that is a pleasant dream?"

"It is because the crystal skull showed up in the dream and began to warn you of potential dangers. You were real happy about it and started to talk with it. I couldn't hear what was being said," Emily chuckled, "but you sure were happy about it."

"Now don't you feel better?" Clayton asked in a mildly teasing manner. "The moral of the story is we end up on a happy path."

"I did wake up with a feeling of happiness and meaning." She pulled a Bible from the bookshelf. "This may seem a little out of character for me but I was wondering if we could pray together."

"The only time I've been to church in years has been for weddings," confessed Clayton. "I was raised Episcopalian but I haven't been there since mom died."

Both verbalized a short prayer. After its conclusion, Emily revealed, "I have been wanting to do that since we saw the crystal skull. Has anything been different with you since we saw it?"

"I'm smarter," boasted Clayton, although not entirely in jest. "I figured out the stocks at just the right time."

"And I quit smoking immediately and I wasn't even thinking about quitting."

"Hey! I haven't smoked either! Wait, I forgot. I never did smoke."

"Wow, what a memory. Have you had any strange dreams?"

"How dare you imply my dreams are strange," Clayton declared with mock indignity. "Besides, you haven't even seen them. Try proving they are strange in a court of law."

"Very funny but let's return to the topic at hand, which is your dreams."

"In one crystal skull dream I had, it was informing me to look at something near my feet. When I looked down I could see a tree growing out of the ground. It grew fast. I knew the tree was us."

"We were a tree?"

"It was a family tree with a radiance of energy bathed in prism light. I couldn't tell if the prism was from the crystal skull or the tree. The light touched me and surrounded me. The concept of death seemed transparent and I could see beyond it, like looking into another dimension."

"Maybe you were."

"I felt like an ancestor. I wanted to ask the crystal skull about it but I couldn't speak. Then you came into the dream light. You smiled and wanted to say something to the skull. You said, 'That is a wonderful tree', and touched me. I tried to come out of the dream by realizing I was dreaming. When I awoke, I felt a lack of direction in my life, an uncontrolled destiny. It still bothers me."

"Destiny has many mysteries for only one solution. Your destiny is greater than anything that happens to you."

"Emily, you are the adventure of my destiny."

"The great adventure of 'We'. I like it."

The sound of Dr. Hiller arriving home was nothing new to Emily, but this time she heard a female voice. "You have a very nice home."

Clayton and Emily moved to the living room where they discovered Dr. Hiller helping a rather tall blonde woman remove her coat. "Hilda Klaus, this is my daughter Emily and her...I'm not sure exactly...boyfriend but more Clayton. Hilda and I have been seeing each for a few weeks actually. She works in the administrative department at the university. When I returned from Toronto I suddenly had the urge to get to know her."

"I'm glad you did," smiled Hilda. "Anyway, I've heard good things about you both."

"Good things about us?" queried Clayton. "Dr. Hiller, I never figured you for a fiction writer."

"But it's all true!" dramatized Dr. Hiller, enamored by the energy of his acting. "Hildy promises to fly me to the moon so we can adjust its controls. Lindbergh should probably get the mission instead just in case there really is some unidenified man in the moon trying to control things. Isn't she fun?"

"What unidentified man?" queried Emily.

"You're right, it's probably a woman," volleyed Dr. Hiller. Luna the Tidemaker must be recruiting me to her cause."

Hilda remained at the Hiller household through dinner. When Dr. Hiller returned from driving her home, he was pleased to discover Buckminster Fuller visiting Clayton and Emily. Once Dr. Hiller settled into the conversation, Bucky began introducing scientific topics.

"I like your characterization of synergy," commented Dr. Hiller. "Since we know energy cannot be destroyed, a circular reusage of the energy source makes sense. Good luck getting the oil industry to buy your idea though. They see a millenia of profits ahead and they will control government if they can to make sure they get richer."

"Which of course is the paradox," began Bucky. "Some kind of alternative better uses of energy could be developed for the benefit of all but the economic elite will want to milk oil profits as long as they can."

"More instead of better for them, probably until the end of this century."

"And that is the 'glass half full' kind of thinking," commented Bucky. "The 'glass half empty' is wonderous but horrifying."

"What does that mean?" inquired Clayton.

"You are referring to Einstein's theories," remarked Dr. Hiller. "If Einstein is correct, a potentially very destructive force could be unleashed upon the world."

"What kind of force?" inquired Emily. Her mind produced an internal image of her most confusing, unexplainable memory, the crystal looking thing she saw in the sky at Fenway Park. "And who would have such a force?"

"So far no one," replied Dr. Hiller. "The scientific community should keep it that way."

"Science should try to keep the glass half full," suggested Buckminster.

"It sounds like science is afraid of a spill," contributed Clayton.

"Now you get it," Dr. Hiller and Bucky said in unison.

"Science is supposed to have all the answers," stated Emily.

"Science will always be an incomplete paradigm," declared Bucky. "The cycles of time needed to reinvent science are getting shorter. We can't imagine what the perceptions of science will be at the end of this century."

"The gap between scientific fact and fiction may become less pronounced," remarked Dr. Hiller.

"There is more to the third dimension than meets the eye," responded Bucky. "It's like finding a warm spot when you're swimming at the lake. It makes no sense. Neither do those spots that allow a peek into other dimensions from our own reality."

"One huge development in genetics could change the direction of mankind. It could change evolution," suggested Clayton.

"But everyone has faith in science and technology," said Emily. "Maybe someday we'll learn how to fly to other planets."

"That's easy," claimed Clayton. "All we have to do is build a machine that can travel through time and go way into the future and see how they get to other planets."

"See, faith in technology," beamed Emily.

After a momentary lull Clayton quipped, "Technology in faith would be an interesting angle."

"Yes," sighed Bucky, "it already is."

PART TWO

1939-1975

PRISM SHADOWS

CHAPTER ONE

UNEXPLAINED SKIES

Longview, Washington
June 1939

"I'm glad Jason gets to go on this little fishing journey. Where are you guys going?" Amanda watched as Floyd packed Jason's gear into his truck.

"Spirit Lake on Mount Saint Helens," answered Floyd. "Two of my buddies, Dan and Steve, are already up there. You met them at the big picnic last time you were here. They played in the bluegrass band."

"They were real good," recalled Jason. "Lots of people were stomping to their music."

"I hope you guys come home with more fish than empty bottles," quipped Amanda.

"Either way sounds pretty good," returned Floyd.

At the campsite, the first cork was popped as soon as the cooking fire was lit for an evening meal. The four men relaxed at the shoreline, watching Dan's two dogs run and sniff before the evening light disappeared behind the hills.

"When I was a kid, scary stories were part of the initiation into the neighborhood," remarked Floyd. "They always had a surprise hoax to go with the stories."

Jason stirred the fire with a stick. "I never did appreciate people trying to scare me."

"I would be afraid of overreacting and killing someone," added Dan.

"You always say that," proclaimed Steve.

"And it would be self defense," Dan returned.

"Nobody is telling any scary stories here anyway," Floyd arbitrated, "except for one real story that is." He glanced briefly at Steve.

"Okay, I'll tell the story. I hate telling this story because people think I'm lying or crazy."

"Both of which are true," kidded Floyd, "but tell the story anyway."

"My story doesn't have a big buildup or punchline. It's just something we saw."

"Which was?" inquired Jason.

"I don't know. We were staying at a friend's cabin on the Toutle River. Suddenly the dogs went crazy and we walked out onto the porch to see what was happening. There was a 'mountain devil' or something. It was about eight feet tall and was more hairy than furry. Two wolves were trying to get at him. He booted one out of the way to get a stick and then fought them off. When the creature noticed us it disappeared in the woods. The wolves took off but didn't chase him."

"Was it dark outside? Are you sure what you saw?" asked Jason.

"It was almost complete daylight."

"Why would people think you are lying if you have another witness?" Jason inquired.

"Ole Joe was a logger. He was killed cutting a snag when the tree went the wrong way. He didn't like to talk about the creature either."

There was a momentary silence of reflection by the men, broken up by the echoing sound of a huge belch by Dan. "Just thought I would change the subject."

Later that night Jason was disturbed from his sleep by the sound of the dogs whimpering outside the tent. After they ran off, Jason heard footsteps. "Why would the dogs be afraid of one of us?"

A faint moonlit shadow moved across the tent wall. "What the heck is going on?" Jason knelt and untied the tent flap, poking his head out into the moonlight. Movement to his right caused him to jerk his head in that direction. "All is well," his mind heard while his eyes glimpsed something faintly glow red and then fade near the trees. "What kind of animal was that? Maybe it was my imagination or I dreamed it or something. Everything seems to be okay." Hearing no other sounds, he drifted back into slumber.

Just before dawn all the men awoke at the same instant when Mount Saint Helens convulsed with a small earthquake. When all four men emerged from their tents, Floyd growled, "It's too damn early for me to get up yet."

"It's getting really cloudy," observed Jason. "Maybe it won't rain later when I get up."

"You mean when we get up," grumbled Floyd, reentering his tent.

The four men slept for about another hour. Again they all awoke together, this time to thunder and the sound of light rain.

"Dan, did you belch again?" yelled Floyd from inside his tent.

Before there was an answer, a number of objects began falling on the tents. "Knock it off you stupid bastards!" The strange bombardment lasted several more seconds. After a flash of lightning, more debris fell on the tents.

Each of the agitated men emerged from their tents but each was speechless. With another rumble of thunder the last of the debris hit the campsite.

"What the hell is this, a hoax?" complained Dan.

"How can it be?" asked Jason. "We saw some hit the campsite."

"Raining fish?" Floyd's bewilderment was fueled by intently watching several of the fish flop on the ground. "They're rainbow trout!"

"How can a thunderstorm rain fish?" inquired Steve.

The blustery wind and rain increased in intensity. "I vote for a postponement of fishing," proposed Steve.

"What about the fish?" asked Floyd.

"They seem very unclean to me," reasoned Jason. "Let's leave them for the mountain devil."

"Very funny," retorted Steve. "They seem to weird for me to think about digesting them anyway. They seem like they are part of some curse or something."

Despite breaking down the campsite, the stunned men had a number of questions to entertain. "What could possiby be the explanation for flying fish? Did someone with a catapult launch them from somewhere out of sight? Did some kind of volcanic activity launch them?"

Jason and Floyd decided not to make a big production of the flying fish story when they returned to the house. "Our wives didn't see what happened. They won't have any better explanation. Besides," continued Floyd, "I want to talk to Ruth before the kids hear my story."

When they arrived at Floyd's house early and without fish, the explanation was simple. "We were rained out."

Jason revealed the flying fish episode to Amanda during the drive back to Spokane. "It must have been hard to keep that story quiet," Amanda remarked.

"Do you remember any native legends about flying fish?"

"Not that I can recall."

"Maybe they were angel fish," suggested Lenny, bringing smiles to the faces of his parents.

"The whole thing seems like a bad dream," commented Amanda. "Have you thought about telling your story to the Spokesman-Review?"

"I don't want that kind of attention and I don't want to defend my story to them."

Amanda reached into the backseat to move her twelve year old daughter's reddish brown hair out of her face. "I wonder how many strange tales never get told."

"I wonder if scientists would believe your story. Is it part of our destiny when these kind of things happen?"

"Does destiny actually allow choices?" asked Jason. "We certainly didn't choose flying fish."

Several days later Jason telephoned Floyd. "Dan's wife works for the Chehalis newspaper and she saw this thing as a moment of fame, so she told them her version of the story. People have hounded me ever since then, like we are some kind of freaks."

"Just think if we had eaten the fish and we started flying ourselves?" joked Jason.

A brief silence followed and as if rehearsed, simultaneously the two men exclaimed, "We should have eaten the fish!"

* * *

"Sometimes I really don't know how you do it," Jason confided. "You devote so much time to volunteer work. Your 'Co-op Night' at the theater was a great idea.; admission for one can of food donated to the soup kitchens. And that's not to mention your farming plans."

"Getting the kids involved is the key," reflected Amanda. "Changing ten of the twenty acres of pasture and woods to crops is a family project."

"Because of that we can still keep the theater."

"It makes a modest profit. American families still spend an average of $25 a year on movies."

"Lucky for me the telephone company is somewhat depression proof. I think we'll be expanding for a long while."

"My job at the lumber mill wasn't depression proof but I still manage to fill my time with things to do."

"And I forgot to mention that you are the centerpost of our family. Thank you for bartering the piano lessons for Margaret. I've never seen her so happy."

"She's a happy kid. She loves everything, especially her membership to the Mickey Mouse Club. Speak of the devil!" Amanda exclaimed as Margaret entered through the front door.

"Lenny is still out feeding the horses. It's really a strange night. The sky is weird."

After turning off the barn light and stepping outside, Lenny's consciousness was seized by the grandeur of the northern skies on the first day of summer. "The Northern Lights. I don't ever remember seeing them before yesterday. They make the dark look crystal."

The 16 year old found a seat atop a wooden fence to observe the spectacle. "I feel it somehow. It reminds me of some other kind of light I've seen somewhere before."

Ten to fifteen minutes of discomfort on the fence gave cause to find a different spot on the backyard lawn. "What would a shaman think about the Northern Lights? It proves I'm not a shaman because I don't know. Mother thinks I have some kind of destiny. Maybe it will be one of my kids someday, or Margaret's kids who will have the destiny. I'm just not a very normal spiritual guy even though I have seen them both, the good spirits and the bad spirits. Not even busting my head open could change those memories. But there is more than that. Mom talks of the spirit of the land. What about the moon? The sun seems too far away but the moon belongs with the earth."

His attention again became focused upon the sky. "There are prism lights in heaven." Suddenly Lenny sat up straight. "This feeling, what is it?" Involuntarily his body poised for resistance. "I feel like a cat with its back up."

The sudden sound of two large thuds in the neighbor's pasture across the dirt road brought Lenny to his feet. "That scared the hell out of me! What was that? I'm going inside."

Within a few steps toward the house, movement of two lights in the sky captured Lenny's attention. "What is that? It looks like stars playing hide and seek."

One light moved steadily but slowly from west to east over the Spokane valley. In stark contrast the other light moved quickly near the slower object but then sped rapidly toward the foothills.

"An airplane, the slow light is an airplane."

The quicker light appeared again, this time slower with a multicolored glow. It zoomed to a position just below the airplane before circling above and below it in a matter of seconds. Six more little stars appeared and drifted together, exchanging little stars. As they began drifting away from each other, a huge spotlight appeared from above. "Where is that coming from?" Lenny cranked his head around but could only see the spotlight, not its source.

Hearing another loud sound in the pasture land across the road, Lenny observed the spotlight move to that area. Two large men seemed to materialize in the beam of light. Both immediately gave their full attention to something on the ground. Momentarily the spotlight disappeared and one lone hovering star shaped light remained.

"It's coming this way." Lenny did not move. He felt no fear. "I feel like a spotlight is on me but there is no light. I've felt like this before."

The sound of the croaking frogs in the irrigation ditch brought Lenny out of his stupor. "Where did it go? Some witnesses you frogs will make."

Before going in for the evening, Lenny pondered telling his 'science fiction' story to anyone. "Just because I love movies, people will think I'm making it all up. Maybe I'll wait to see if anybody else tells the same story."

In bed Lenny could not shake the residue of feelings from his sightings. "Maybe I should think of science fiction solutions to figure it out. Or maybe it was like when I was a kid, battling the devil."

"Did the strange light come from some other planet or dimension or something? Did they want me for something? The demon or whatever it was when I was a kid wanted me for something. The angel didn't seem to want anything."

Lenny could no longer distinguish destiny from loneliness. "I may be the only human being ever to go through this stuff. Or maybe I'm just the first. I want to learn to fly."

* * *

"Jerry found two mutilated cows on his property." Jason poured a cup of coffee for himself. "They were in the pasture just across the road.

"Jerry doesn't have cattle," noted Amanda. "Why would someone dump a couple of dead cows there? Were they butchered for the meat?"

"I saw them, the cows. There were incisions, like surgical incisions, but none of the meat was removed."

"It sounds like some sort of animal sacrifice. I don't think we should mention it to the kids. It will just scare them."

"You're probably right. I wouldn't know how to explain animal sacrifice to them anyway," agreed Jason.

"I feel like we should start locking our house doors at night but it was probably just a prank of revenge by someone."

"I can't imagine what pranksters would want with certain parts of the cow's guts. Not only were they removed but they weren't anywhere around the dead cows."

"It must be a bloody mess."

"Actually, no, they took the blood with them."

"I have only heard one story like yours," reflected Amanda. "A farmer out by the Idaho border blamed it on a devil worship group but there never was any proof."

"Be sure to give them candy at Halloween if they show up. We certainly don't need any of those kind of tricks."

CHAPTER TWO

CRYSTAL SKULL SPIES

Los Angeles, California
June 1939

"I can't believe Loretta is nine years old today," declared Al as he brought a stack of birthday party plates to the kitchen sink. "She's pooped out and in bed but she had fun."

"She has been a daughter of the depression but somehow we've managed," responded Al's wife, Zelda Merlin. "Hooray for Hollywood."

"I work long hours but I'm glad I have a job."

"Mr. Merlin, at least you enjoy working at the Disney Studios. I wish I could draw. I just get to be secretary for an IRS slob, but at least it's a job."

"We both deserve a vacation. I never have been on holiday since I moved to America."

"We could go to San Francisco, or maybe Seattle."

"Those places would be more reasonably priced than where I want to go, New York. This time it can be affordable."

"New York is on sale?" Zelda's lavender eyes widened to emphasize her sarcasm.

"Walt and Roy were supposed to go to New York with their wives but Roy can't go. Mr. Disney offered me Roy's place. He wants one of his sketch artists to see the New York World's Fair."

"I won't have any trouble getting time off," Zelda postulated. "This is a great birthday present for Loretta."

"It will be a month after her birthday before she gets to go to the World's Fair but I don't want to wait that long to tell her."

"It's exciting for me. I haven't been to New York since the parade for Lindbergh," revealed Zelda. "And I haven't been on a train since I left the FBI to move to Los Angeles to be with you."

Al held his tongue about his chance encounter with Lindbergh after the historic flight across the Atlantic Ocean. Only a fictional account of his immigration was revealed to Zelda or anyone else since the government changed his identity. "It is really nice to have Walt's help in making travel arrangements," he proclaimed, deflecting the direction of the conversation.

"I'm glad to stay out of it," confided Zelda. "Any additional suggestions will only weaken the budget and I'm just happy to be traveling."

"The trip should be wonderfully educational for Loretta."

"Something big is in her destiny so it makes sense she should experience something big, like New York City," reasoned Zelda.

"Speaking of New York, the Milton Berle Show is about to be broadcast. It's my favorite program, ever since it started on radio this year."

Zelda enjoyed Al's laughing as much as she did the comedian's jokes but tonight was different. Her employment responsibilities were bothering her. "I just want a simple life."

A burst of laughter from Al made Zelda smile but she missed the joke. "I want to quit," thought Zelda, "but I fear for my own privacy. After all, I doubt the feds will ever abandon general surveillance of my own husband. They'll never let me leave undercover intelligence."

Retiring to the kitchen for a glass of water, Zelda fought the urge to disclose her secrets to her husband. "We are a family. He should know about me. We are in love. We have been since we met in Washington, D.C. when the government took him out of Canada. I want to be in love and be loved. Keeping secrets is not right." But she did anyway.

A loud laugh from Al made her smile again. "Yes, I'm as sure as I can be. I'm in love."

After the radio program Al announced, "I'm going to stay up for awhile to make a budget estimate of our New York trip. I won't sleep until I do it anyway."

The task had been accomplished several times before. Al actually needed to make a late night private telephone call. "It's time to confront one of my secrets."

"Duty beckons," the voice on the line began. "This will be general eavesdropping and snooping. There are two separate assignments. First are the American Nazis in Los Angeles. Since Hitler conquered Czechslovakia in April there has been much anxiety by our leaders. Second is the communists in southern California. It is difficult to predict their direction in the event of war," stated the nameless voice.

"You must have the wrong number," answered Al in the appropriate manner to acknowledge his assignment.

"Is this the bus station? I was hoping to take a tour tomorrow," came the response indicating the when and where directives.

"Sorry, wrong number," remarked Al, confirming the assignment.

The phone call made him sad. Spy work for the government always did. "I want to get this finished as quickly as I can. The less contact with those intelligence boys the better." Less contact also meant less chance of Zelda suspecting anything. "I simply cannot imagine what Zelda would think if she knew I was an American spy. I certainly will never tell her about my activities with the other side, the Russians. I am not supposed to reveal anything of my background before I met her in Washington except, well except nothing I guess. She thinks I left Russia as an orphan kid. I'll go to the office, do some drawing and then do the undercover work. I'll end the day at the office, calling home before I leave."

"I hate it but I will honor my assignments as I always do. I fear governments but I also still fear Stalin. I wasn't able to keep my family away from the Soviets. I'm so tired of being a paranoid pawn. True freedom just isn't part of my life equation."

At the designated locker at the bus station, Al obtained his specific directions. "I doubt anyone in this depressed world hates their job more than I hate this one." He closed the bus locker door and departed for the home of a fellow animator. "After two or three or five drinks he'll innocently blab about his communist membership."

As planned, Al ended his day at Disney Studios, organizing sketches for 'Pinocchio'. He telephoned home at 5:45 before leaving the office.

Twenty minutes later Zelda glimpsed Al's 1936 Chrysler two blocks from home. "Look, I have to get off the phone. I'll let you know if there are any glitches in your surveillance plan, but there probably won't be any. Confirmed?"

"Goodbye Z," Zelda heard before the dial tone.

"I hate being called that," she thought as she hung up the receiver. "Only the FBI people call me that."

* * *

"I like riding on the train," announced Loretta, "but now it's dark and I don't get to see anything."

"Are you tired?" Zelda inquired, brushing back her daughter's dirty blonde hair.

Loretta nodded, her hazel eyes briefly closing. She offered no resistance as Zelda left with her to their sleeping quarters. Al smiled and waved to them as they departed but remained seated in his coach seat.

"My world as a child was so boring and dull compared to Loretta's. I have chosen to forget as much of Russian life as I can. How would I describe it, even to Zelda? Should I keep anything from her?"

Al consciously remembered his vow to forget. "It simply is not possible to reveal my secrets. They are dangerous. I'll never have true happiness but I can't let my problems affect Loretta's happiness. My secrets are solitary ones."

Walt Disney passed through the coach car and Al acknowledged his boss. "It feels odd not discussing animation with him. He always has something in mind." The hypnotic sound of the train on the tracks brought thoughts of his early days as an animator. "The hours were long when I began but it sure beat the job the government first provided as a stunt driver in movies. Now here I am on the way to the World's Fair."

In New York, Al did not spend time with his boss, who was there negotiating financing for a film. The Merlin family began with a casual day in the city, not worrying about seeing all the famous landmarks.

"Everything is so tall," remarked Loretta.

"With so many restaurants," began Zelda, "it is somehow more difficult to choose one. There seems to be so many good ones but just my luck I would pick the wrong one."

"I can't wait to have World's Fair food," declared Al. "I hope it isn't ridiculously expensive."

When the time came to visit the World's Fair, Al had to be reminded to eat. Built in Queens at a cost of $150 million, the 1216 acre site included fair attendance on a giant cash register, a 700 foot tall needle-like "trylon", a 250 foot parachute jump and such marvels as television, nylon stockings and "Elektro" the talking robot at the "World of Tomorrow".

"The World's Fair is crowded, expensive and fabulous!" Al crowed after one of many parachute rides. "I've never been in an airplane so the parachute ride is as close as I can get. I sure would like to be on the first ever transcontinental passenger flight from New York to Lisbon tomorrow."

The Merlin family attended the fair again on July 3rd. The 4th was their last day in New York. "Turn on the radio," requested Zelda. "The Yankee broadcast is about to begin."

Both Loretta and her father turned to look at her in surprise. "Today is Lou Gehrig Day at Yankee Stadium." Enough said. The family huddled around the Philco in the hotel room, joining millions of other Americans listening to the tribute to the iconic slugger stricken with an incurable disease.

"As much as I like New York," acknowledged Al, "somehow I think I am going to enjoy Chicago too. It will be different but I have a good feeling about spending a couple of days there."

"I want to go to the lake and go swimming," revealed Loretta.

Two days later, Loretta had her wish come true. Al rented a beach umbrella for the hot, humid weather and the family spent the entire afternoon at Lake Michigan. Each enjoyed a barbecued bratwurst for lunch.

"A boat ride on the lake would be so wonderful," stated Zelda.

"I'm not sure we can afford it," offered Al while changing the pages of his newspaper. Zelda withdrew her request.

"I like all the stuff we do," reported Loretta. "I would be happy just to walk on the dock."

A museum advertisement in the newspaper leaped into Al's consciousness. "The 'Skull of Doom'! That's the same crystal skull I saw in Toronto with Deborah." He thought about her briefly in a faded but warm memory. "She has probably changed. I doubt I would recognize her if I saw her but my mind can clearly picture the skull."

Al knew the museum ad would be meaningless to Zelda and Loretta but his mind became obsessed with the chance to see the skull. "I've been thinking about what to do in Chicago," he began. "I think we can afford a reasonably priced boat ride. I also want to go to a museum. This ad made me think of it so I want to go there."

Before retiring to the hotel room to get cleaned up after the day at the beach, Zelda had a referral for the boat ride. The particular sunset lake cruise also included a pasta dinner. "It has been a wonderful day," proclaimed Al, "but tomorrow morning we are going to the museum pretty early in the morning."

"We can eat breakfast at the hotel before we leave," suggested Zelda.

"What stuff is going to be at the museum?" Loretta inquired.

Al mentioned nothing about the crystal skull. "It is part of my past, before Zelda, and I should never cross that bridge."

"Museums are never the same," observed Zelda, "but there will be some amazing old things there."

"What is a 'Skull of Doom'?" asked Loretta, looking at the advertisement. "It sounds bad."

"It is a skull made from crystal," replied her father. "If it was bad they wouldn't let people like us see it. Other children will be there too."

After breakfast the three family members took a cab to the museum. There were two large families at the crystal skull exhibit when they arrived so Al escorted his family to other exhibits. More than half of the museum was perused before Al and his family arrived at the crystal skull.

"Maybe others won't have such an intense experience as I remember," thought Al. "Maybe it will be different for me too. After all, it is not isolated in a small room as it was in Ontario." His enchantment grew as he approached the artifact.

Privately Zelda became curious about others who came to see the exhibit. "What are they thinking? Who are they? Do they think it is evil?" She consciously tried to hold back some of her 'good' energy.

"What if there is a curse?" Her feelings changed with the minutes of the clock and she became less fearful. "My time with the skull is somehow precious or important. There seems to be some spiritual feeling. Can anybody else feel this?"

Zelda glanced at her family. "No, I'm sure the energy from the skull is being absorbed only by me. The color and hue of the skull changes with every visual angle. What is the skull trying to tell me?"

Looking at his wife, Al thought. "She seems just like any others who look at it. She is interested, even fascinated, but not obsessed or weird. Maybe my mind makes more of the crystal skull than it really is." Al allowed the energy of the skull to engulf him, "like standing in a rainbow." The energy of the skull reflected back to him the love of his family in a mild vibration, almost as if the skull were allowing only a minor share of its abilities.

"This is much better than my first time with the skull," deduced Al. "Maybe it doesn't recognize me. Those images of the Soviet Union in the skull were so long ago. It is like remembering a movie. The only thing that is the same is that feeling of lengthening hair or whatever. Oh, and the prism is the same."

Periodically Loretta moved to view the skull from a different vantage point. She remained patient throughout their time at the exhibit. "If I act grown up I'll get to do big kid stuff. Everyone tells me how smart I am so I should get to do big kid things."

Her heart began racing. "Is it scary? Don't show any feelings! Look bored and nobody will notice me." The longer Loretta stood with here parents, the more relaxed she became. "I like this but I feel weird. I feel numb or something, like I can't do everything. And my hair and skin feel weird." There was no panic in the youngster with the braided hair. "I want it to stop!" It did, but then Loretta began to have a perception of being turned inside out. She became small instead in her consciousness. "Everything is more than big."

No sooner was the perception realized of being tiny by Loretta when everything around her seemed to change. "Or maybe I'm changing and everything else is not. I feel really big, like a blimp. I can't move."

Just when Loretta thought about changing into another perceptional shape, her mother tugged on her arm. "It's time to leave. Loretta, it's time to go."

Loretta turned and watched the crystal prism fade from her mother's face. "Mother looks normal. Did they change like I did?"

As they exited after a cursory tour of the remainder of the museum, Loretta announced, "I'm different."

"Me too," agreed Zelda.

In a Mickey Mouse voice, Al chimed in, "Me two and a half."

Later, in the darkness of the hotel room, Loretta marveled, "How can mom and dad go to sleep so easy?" She listened to the rain on the fire escape outside the window. "I wish the rain wasn't covering up the full moon."

Her restlessness did not disturb her parents. She went to the window to watch the rain falling in the shine of the city lights. "The crystal skull is hard to learn. School is easy. My teachers think I'm lazy but I don't want to move up a grade."

Loretta stopped to view her partially illumined reflection in the hotel room mirror. "I look like a normal kid. I just want to be normal."

Climbing back into bed, Loretta thought about the other kids at school. "None of them learned to speak French. Dad taught me. Mom wants me to be a governor or senator or something. Being a movie star would be more fun. I could be like Dorothy in 'Wizard of Oz'."

"What am I supposed to do? I'm sure I can do what mom wants and still be a normal kid. But the crystal skull made me different. I don't get to be normal. They took me to the crystal skull because I'm special."

As the rain outside increased in intensity, Loretta grew more weary. "They didn't know what I meant when I told them I changed. Adults are like that sometimes." She bunched her pillow, welcoming ongoing slumber.

"Maybe the skull let me know being different is okay. Who was the most famous 'different' person ever?" Loretta contemplated her question momentarily. "Was it hard for Jesus to be different? I want to think about the crystal skull but I am ashamed. I know too many bad things and the crystal skull will know it. But how can I have dark secrets when I don't know what they are?"

CHAPTER THREE

LEFT FROM BOSTON, RIGHT TO TELEPATHY

Seattle, Washington
December 1939

Pulling up to his house in his 1933 Ford truck, Clayton could see the silhouettes of his ten year old son Mark and a neighbor boy throwing rocks into the early evening sky hues reflected off Lake Washington. Mark took off running when he noticed Clayton's vehicle.

It is time to eat!" The ten year old yelled as he vacated the waterfront and ran up the moderate slope to the house. "Dad, did you get the scones?"

"What is the magic word?"

"Two please."

Relishing the simple routine of the moment, Clayton reached into the bag and gave his son a scone. "Only one for now."

Emily was setting the table for dinner when Clayton arrived. "Did the kid scone you?"

"But of course."

"A sucker is born every minute."

"Please, we suckers are much more precious in these days of depression. Now a sucker is only born every three minutes."

She kissed him on the lips and returned to her task of setting the table. "Did you remember that the Fergusons are coming over for dinner tonight?"

"Really? I thought you were setting two places for each of us."

Emily barely chuckled. BAM! Clayton's fist pounded down upon the kitchen counter. BAM! "I don't want them here!"

"You have been working on that tantrum act for years and you still haven't got it right!"

"I think it's getting a little better!" Clayton exclaimed cheerfully.

"Is that dad's tantrum act again?" asked Mark while entering the kitchen.

"My reputation precedes me," chirped Clayton.

"Maybe it proceeds you," suggested Emily.

Emily loved her home, which had once been owned by her father. Dr. Hiller had taken a professorial job at the University of Washington in 1934 after a two year tenure at the California Institute of Technology. He married and divorced before passing away in the Lake Washington home in 1936. Emily inherited the house and the guest house, where her family was staying when her father passed.

Mark reacted to the knock at the front door. "I'll let them in!" His stocking feet nearly slid out from under him as he tried to run towards the door on the hardwood floors.

A smile graced Emily's face as she watched her husband trail Mark to the door. "It is great to be happy when so many people in the world are downtrodden."

"How ya doing hepcat?" Lonnie Ferguson was a dedicated follower of big band music and he loved to show it in front of Clayton.

"Hey, my 'alligator' friend."

Before settling in at the dinner table, Emily addressed the gathering. "We need a demonstration of the 'Big Apple' you two learned."

"We'd be happy to do that," Gertie responded, "but we'll go second."

Mark and eleven year old Tanya took the floor as Clayton assumed his position at the piano. Their routine was short, their steps were simple, but their act was well choreographed.

"That was cute as hell," announced Lonnie.

For Lonnie and Gertie's turn on the dance floor, Clayton put on the record "And the Angels Sing" by Martha Tilton and Benny Goodman. "I purchased it at the store."

At the conclusion of the dance routine, Lonnie gloated at Clayton's proclamation, "Crazy, man!"

The dinner was festive with salmon as the main course. In between bites, Gertie asked, "Did you hear that Al Capone is getting out of jail?"

"He's a crazy bastard," said Clayton, quickly covering his mouth in reaction to the dirty looks of the women at the table. "Sorry, I meant to say 'senile bastard'."

Lonnie laughed and added, "He is probably the one who invented the latest craze, goldfish gulping."

"Yuck," said Mark.

"Yeh, yuck," echoed Tanya.

"Goldfish are just like peaches!" Clayton exclaimed before slurping a peach slice from his plate. He received a loud round of 'yucks' from the table. Clayton changed the subject. "Wouldn't you like to have one of those televisions? They have some baseball games on television now in New York."

"Only in baseball season dear," corrected Emily.

"At the end of August, the Reds and Dodgers game was shown in New York," Lonnie contributed. "The announcer, Red Barber, said he had to practice at a Columbia college game just to figure out how to produce the broadcast."

"The Reds, those losers," lamented Clayton. "I hate the Yankees so I rooted for Cincinnati and got tortured four games to one."

"They won without Gehrig," said Lonnie. "That DiMaggio is great."

"So far," Clayton said, "there are only 400 televisions in the United States. But for me, it is a reason to stay on at the appliance store. Someday people will be buying lots of televisions."

"Your three year anniversary at the store is coming up soon," noted Emily. "I sure like your job better than the one you had building Grand Coulee Dam."

"What is television, dad?" Mark inquired.

Clayton looked around the table for help. "I'm not sure how it works exactly, just like I don't know how a radio works. There are invisible waves that go through the air which the television receives. Instead of only sound, it also has pictures, and scenes."

"Is it like a movie?" Tanya asked.

"No...I mean yes, there is movement just like a movie, but it is happening live," answered Clayton.

"We could watch the president giving speeches, like the one he is going to give at the World's Fair," remarked Gertie.

"We could watch everything," declared Emily. "My father was at a demonstration for the first television back in 1927. He was in New York."

"They could show movies on television," speculated Lonnie.

"Speaking of movies, we finally get to see 'The Wizard of Oz'," announced Gertie.

"It is supposed to be wonderful," acknowledged Emily.

In his best W.C. Fields impression, Clayton said, "I want to see 'You Can't Cheat an Honest Man' again."

"Not until we see 'Stagecoach' first," proclaimed Emily.

"We haven't even seen 'Gone With the Wind' yet," said Gertie.

Clayton changed his artistic impression to that of Clark Gable. "Frankly Gertie, I don't give a damn!"

* * *

"It snowed in the foothills," announced Clayton. "There may be more snow on the way." He kicked off his work shoes by the rear door. "It's time to cut Christmas trees."

"I get to go this year!" Mark moved closer to his parents. "Remember, you told me I can go."

"That's the plan," Clayton agreed. "Anyway, I like a little snow. Too much snow is difficult, and dragging a tree through the mud is not pleasant either."

"Where will you go?"

"We are going to Mount Si this year. We went there once before, three years ago."

Two days later the tree hunters headed toward the Cascade Mountain Range. "The journey is a strong all day hike if the trail is not covered with snow. If the weather is good, we'll mark the spots for the trees and return later. That way we can complete our climb. If the weather turns sour, we can get a tree at the most convenient elevation and head for home." At the foot of Mount Si was North Bend, a mountain town on the east-west highway across Washington. Snoqualmie Pass was another 25 miles east at the divide of the Cascade Mountain Range. "The trip around the north end of the lake and then southeast to Issaquah and North Bend is approximately 39 miles."

Mark was content to view the scenery of Lake Washington, the farms and rivers in the rolling foothills, and Lake Sammamish. When suddenly the mountain highway emptied out into a small valley, Mount Si loomed before them. "I see the mountain!" exclaimed Mark, anxious to begin the trek. Within twenty minutes the group was ready to hike.

"The trail is clear except for debris from the windstorm the other day," Lonnie observed. "The Douglas firs are sure easy to see since all of the leaves have fallen from the maples and alders." All of the chosen trees were marked within the first half mile of the trek but the hikers continued upward on the trail.

"I need to remove a layer of clothing," Clayton announced. Soon the other hikers were joining him. Occasionally the hikers gave Mark a moderate boost but mostly he traveled at the same pace as the adults.
The hikers nearly made it to the top when they encountered snow that was determined too difficult to negotiate.

"The view is glorious. Except for a few low clouds blowing by, Seattle looks like I could hold it in my hand," Lonnie exclaimed.

"Since this looks like the end of the hike, I am going to eat. I'm hungry," Clayton announced while opening his sack lunch. Mark was pleased that his mother included a scone with his food. Several bold little birds called "camp robbers" visited them and ate scone crumbs out of Mark's hand.

"Oh my, I'm getting stiff and sore already," Lonnie announced when he stood up to leave.

Roger, who accompanied Lonnie with the group to the mountain, said, "I'll be a walking cramp tomorrow."

"It's all downhill from here, in a hurry," Clayton remarked. "It won't take long to get back to the trees." Along the way, Clayton stopped to address the others. "Mark spotted a tree that we like better than our first choice. It is worth the extra distance of dragging it down the trail." Everyone agreed to wait for Clayton but he instructed them to go on ahead to their own trees. "We'll probably catch up with you before your trees are cut."

The cutting went smoothly and Clayton dragged the tree to the trail. Switchbacks on the trail meandered to an open area where a gully and another hill were in view. The meadow area between the trail and the gully was partially covered in snow. Clayton was adjusting his gloves and his subsequent grip on the tree when he felt a nudge from his son.

Looking down, Clayton saw Mark pointing straight ahead at a moving shape nearly 200 feet west and probably 150 feet lower in elevation. "It looks like a black bear," Mark whispered as they continued to watch the rapidly ambling creature heading to an unknown destination. It suddenly stopped, listening and perhaps sniffing.

"Shouldn't a black bear be in hibernation?" Clayton asked, not expecting a response from his son. "But you're right, it looks like a bear."

"He's moving!" The animal then began walking on two legs down the hill at an aggressive pace, the snowy areas having little effect on its progress.

"Oh my goodness," Clayton whispered. "That is a great ape of the northwest."

"Wow," said Mark, not understanding what his father had said but impressed with his sincerity
nonetheless.

The mountain ape acknowledged the presence of the two humans by looking their way. It did not break stride.

"Did you hear that?" Mark asked his father.

"There was no sound from it," remarked Clayton.

"But it told us to stay here until it was gone."

"Yes it did son."

The task of transporting the tree down the trail was hardly noticeable to Clayton. The aura of adrenaline flowed from he and his son and both kept their heads on a swivel to detect another sighting. Clayton's mind raced to comprehend what they saw. "What will I say to my friends? For years, I have wondered about the possible existence of a mountain ape." Clayon recalled discussing a possible mountain creature with people from a number of tribes when he worked on the dam. "I never could be sure if they were pulling my leg. After all, I was a naive east coast white man." None of the things he thought to say came to mind when Clayton and Mark reached the others.

"Did you see the ape?" Mark barked his inquiry from about 30 feet.

"What ape?"

"The ape that looked like a bear," answered Mark.

"You saw a bear?"

"I am not sure what we saw," said Clayton in a tone to quell the energy of the conversation. He looked at his son, who recognized the look from his father to not continue the issue. The unspoken communication was like getting the look not to misbehave or to remember to keep a secret.

"Shouldn't a bear be in hibernation by now?" Lonnie inquired.

"That's what dad asked," reported Mark.

"I wish I could go back and preserve a footprint," Clayton thought, "although I wouldn't really know how. I bet a footprint would look much different than a bear paw print. I wish someone else could have seen it."

Both Clayton and Mark were sitting in the backseat, limbs from two Christmas trees obscuring their rear window view. "I would like to see a footprint too," Mark said to his dad.

Clayton glanced at his son, realizing that Mark's comment seemingly was a reaction to his thoughts, not his words.

Similar to when Mark approached the other hikers, he blurted out the news about the sighting to his mother when they returned home. "We saw an ape but it looked like a bear!"

Amanda laughed. "What do you mean?" She looked suspiciously at her son and husband, expecting a fictional tale.

As Mark told his story he realized it was being absorbed but necessarily believed by his mother. Aside from the occasional looks to her husband and his confirming facial expressions, the look on his mother's face transformed from being entertained to the look of concern and then to bewilderment.

"It was less than a football field away," added Clayton to the story, "but it also was out in the open."

"And it told us to stay where we were!" Mark exclaimed.

"It spoke to you?" Emily asked, again looking toward her husband.

"Not exactly, we didn't hear anything."

"Then how could it tell you something?"

"I do not have an answer to that one," Clayton returned. Deliberately changing the tempo of the dialogue, he eased into a kitchen chair. "I guess it is one of those things we will just have to figure out some other time."

Emily recognized the routine and her husband's facial expression. The topic would best be discussed without their son.

"It thought the words to us!" Mark interjected, also recognizing the look on his father's face.

"Oh, I see," said his mother.

Mark also recognized the facial expressions of his mother and he realized the topic had reached its conclusion for the present time.

"It is time for both of you to clean up for dinner," Emily commanded. Clayton initiated a race as he began an exaggerated quick walk and Mark responded. "No running in the house!" By then Mark had already caught his father and was trying to push him out of the way with a cunning laugh.

Later that night, in the quiet of their bedroom, Clayton and Emily discussed the mountain ape phenomenon in detail. "Do you suppose the ape wanted you to see it?"

"I like hearing as many questions as you can muster," Clayton said, "but I have very few answers."

"You should draw a picture of the creature while it is fresh in your memory."

"It's fresh alright. But you know I am lousy at drawing. A picture of mine would not convey my actual memory. Mark could draw a better picture than I could."

Before she drifted off to sleep, Emily planted another thought in Clayton's head. "I bet there are not very many people who have seen both a mountain ape and the crystal skull."

"And a flying, hovering something else I cannot explain," Clayton remarked, remembering the object that emerged from the Boston harbor in 1927. "I still don't know what to call it."

In the essence of his being, Clayton questioned, "Is there some sort of ultimate meaning to all of this?" I cannot escape the feeling I already know the answer.

"I sure would have liked to have been able to talk about the mountain ape with your father," Clayton told Emily. "This surely would have supported his contention that science is incomplete and does not have all the answers."

"That position is unpopular with scientists."

"Bucky Fuller used to say how science is heading in wrong directions instead of what will help everyone and the planet. I wonder what he would think of the mountain ape?"

"Even progressive scientific thinkers would only consider it a beast. They would have someone here to shoot it in no time," proposed Emily.

"Why do you suppose one hasn't been shot already? Why is it the Indians are the only people who seem to know anything about the creature?"

"You and Mark know more about it now."

"Somehow it seemed like he was protecting us, like some kind of guardian. I say 'he' but I really don't know. It seemed friendly but then again so can bad guys. Are they good guys?"

Emily contemplated her reply. "Worrying about what we don't know is blind fear. What we do know is that it is good to keep an open mind."

"No matter how open my mind is, the memory of today won't ever escape."

CHAPTER FOUR

A NEW LIFE IN A COLD WORLD

Los Angeles, California
February 1951

"A date which will live in irony," Al thought as he perused the gifts he purchased for Zelda on Valentine's Day. "I buy the presents when it actually is my birthday, the one nobody knows. All of my documents indicated I was born on July 31, 1897. I really don't mind very much. I am actually 56 years old on this day instead of age 54 as the rest of the world believes.

"Do I feel old?" It was a question he entertained by himself the entire day. In many ways his world drained his exuberance for life. On the other hand, his 21 year old daughter was expecting a child. "I have all of my life as a grandparent ahead of me."

Loretta and her husband Mark lived near Fort Dix in New Jersey, where he was stationed. "Despite the Korean War, Loretta's world is so incredibly different than I ever could have imagined. The nation has a strong economy and a massive boom of postwar babies is underway. The nation is connected by television. And my least favorite, the world now has atomic weapons."

The sound of the front door scattered his daydream. "I want this to be a romantic, fun day." He smiled when he saw the box under her arm. "I love chocolate birthdays."

The following morning Al left for the studio before sunshine poured into the bedroom to wake Zelda. "Valentine's Day turned into a wonderful night." The sex from the night before still resonated through her senses. "Back to the real world." She walked through the house while the coffee was brewing. "It has been several years since Loretta moved but I'm still not used to being alone in the house. It gives me too much time to think."

Zelda moved in for a closer view of her face in the mirror. "My eyes look 52 today." The increasing gray in her light brown hair did not bother her. She had maintained her figure, save for 12 to 15 pounds which appeared after her daughter reached womanhood.

"My sweet pregnant daughter." Somehow the spontaneity of the smile in the mirror and the brightened
look of her eyes surprised her. "I feel good. I had so much anxiety about the world when I first heard Loretta was pregnant. My worries solve nothing and help nothing. All I should really fret is what I can help to control. Being the best grandmother I can be is easy to control. I should be happy!" Many times in her life Zelda tried to reason her way out of depression. Her government job did not help because she still needed to hide her actual undercover clandestine activities for the Federal Bureau of Investigation.

The late mid-February morning temperature was slightly above sixty degrees and Zelda drank her coffee out on the porch. "I love watching the distant ocean view. It gives me the feeling of having no obstructions between me and the remainder of the planet." Between cups she returned inside. Listening to the television while the pouring her coffee, Zelda heard the news that Sugar Ray Robinson won the middleweight title the day before. "Al won his bet," she thought happily. When she was nearly finished
with her second cup of coffee and toast with honey, she heard the telephone ring.

Picking up the receiver just after the third ring, she paused in a moment of recognition. "Al always tries to answer the phone after the third ring, like it is some sort of superstition. Is it?"

"Comrade," the male voice on the line said before she spoke.

"Hello?"

"I am sorry." The line went dead.

"It is one thing to have a party line, but a communist party line?" She giggled at her own joke and felt an anticipatory joy of wanting to tell her husband the story. Her mood quickly changed. Any association with communism, like them calling the house, was bad news in this day and age.

"They were expecting a "comrade"? Zelda searched the house for electronic bugs.

* * *

"The year 1951 is a time of strange news, mostly bad," mused Al. "Julius and Ethel Rosenberg received the death sentence for selling atomics secrets and the next month the United States detonated the first hydrogen bomb. The end of the world seems imminent."

"Everything in the news bothers me," Zelda proclaimed. "It does not help that Loretta is 3000 miles away. Pregnant pictures are not enough for me."

"I try to cope with everything the best I can. Movies, television, and new gadgets keep me involved with something nearly all the time."

"I like the gadgets too. I still cannot imagine power steering. Vibrators for beds is the funny one."

"When 'Your Show of Shows' is on, you seem to forget about your anxieties," noted Al.

"Those are temporary remedies. 'Streetcar Named Desire' was another temporary fix, but I am glad we watched it twice."

In mid-June, a live human birth was televised for the first time. The event crushed Zelda emotionally. Al was not home to watch the telecast but he was not surprised at the sudden change in his wife. "I am going to be with Loretta when the baby is born."

Arrangements were made for Zelda to fly to Fort Dix. Loretta's due date was July 1 but fortunately Zelda arrived six days early. Katherine Tessa O'Donnell was born the next day.

Al learned by telephone that he was a grandfather. "I cannot believe how overwhelming my emotions are. I'll book a flight to New Jersey as soon as we hang up." He laughed at himself after making the reservation because he 'blabbed' about the baby with complete strangers.

Al opened a bottle of vodka. "This toast is to my granddaughter, Katherine Tessa." His second toast was for his daughter, and then one for his wife, and for his son-in-law, and then for himself. His sixth toast was again for the new baby. "One more toast to Loretta." There were still more tears before he passed out on the couch.

* * *

After one week in New Jersey, Al needed to return to California for work. He resented having to leave but he also knew he had timely spy responsibilities. "I hate this double agent crap. This has been going on since the last year of the war. The only time I didn't do it was during the war. Either side would have me killed if they knew about me."

Zelda was scheduled to return four days later but she moved up her reservation one day. "I want to surprise Al and figure out something nice to do for him. I'll figure out something."

When Zelda arrived at home, she was disappointed Al was not there. " He didn't know I was arriving early, so forget about it." She put down her luggage and plopped into an oversized chair in the living room.

The telephone rang, causing Zelda to flinch. The phone was within easy reaching distance but she hesitated, wondering what to say if it were her husband. Then she laughed at herself. "Why would Al call home if nobody is supposed to be here?" The phone rang again and she answered with a held back laugh.

"Comrade!"

"Hello?" Zelda said cautiously. "What number are you calling?"

"I'm so sorry." The line went dead.

"One time is perhaps an accident but two of these phone calls rushes way beyond coincidence." Adrenaline overcame her fatigue and she went through her habitual routine of checking the house for electronic bugs, something to do while collecting her thoughts.

"Wait, what's this on the dresser? It's a key to something, specific to the number engraved on it." She examined both sides of the key and returned it to the dresser. Zelda then noticed a note extending out of a magazine written in Russian. "The only part of the note I can decipher is the number 264, the same number engraved on the key."

Zelda poured herself a glass of scotch, gulped it down, and called her FBI contacts to set up a meeting. "I need to know what the government knows about my husband."

Al arrived home about 7:30. "The pickup truck is gone. Was it stolen?" He was greatly relieved and pleased when he opened the door to find the answer to his question. "Zelda's luggage is here!"

The sound of an automobile on their long dirt driveway caused Al to peer out the window. At first he did not recognize the vehicle because it was out of context. "That car belongs to my Soviet contacts. Why are they here?" He felt an immediate surge of anger and resentment. When the car door swung open Al was already in the front yard.

"Comrade, I am sorry to come here but we knew your wife left in the truck," said the well-dressed spy.

"What is this all about?" Al asked in Russian.

"Unfortunately, your wife has accidentally intercepted two of our calls to you. My FBI contacts inform me that she was at the bureau office asking details about you."

Zelda had nearly returned home when she saw the black 1948 Buick turn from the road onto the driveway to her house. "I've never seen that car before." Her instincts indicated caution was needed. She parked the truck in the walnut grove and slowly advanced towards the house. The long shadows of the oncoming dusk made her more confident in her stealth.

Two men were on the porch, speaking in Russian at first. She recognized her husband's voice, in English.

"Did the FBI give her any information on me?"

"They really know nothing about our operations," said the second man, this time speaking in English.

A sudden fear of being discovered came upon Zelda. Her training and instincts told her to be the aggressor, to use the element of surprise. She emerged from around the corner of the house with her handgun drawn. "Good work Al. What do you use for bait to catch a commie?"

She expected them to be startled. She expected to disarm the Russian. She expected to shoot first if trouble started. Zelda did not expect her adversary to be ready to shoot. She was hit just above the belt. "Son of a bitch." Falling and rolling to her side in agony, her eyes settled on the ocean view. "No obstacles." She then looked toward her husband.

Al got up to move to her side when the Soviet contact shot his wife for the second and fatal time. His head drooped and he let out a sigh. His approach to her was slow.

"I can take care of the body. Let's move her to the trunk," the Soviet commanded in Russian.

As Al dropped to one knee to look at his murdered spouse, a lifetime of resentment and anger welled up inside of him. He continued looking at her, scarcely wondering about his own fate, until the Soviet put away his gun. Wasting no time, Al scooped up the gun Zelda clutched and turned toward the Soviet. Without pause he shot the "comrade", who tried to say something while at the same time clutching the gushing hole in his neck where much of his tonsils formerly were. The Soviet spy looked surprised as he fell backwards.

Al turned again to Zelda and tears irrigated the aged lines of his face. He felt a momentary feeling that he was glad she was able to spend time with their grandchild. "What a world of shit. Why can't we just be people?" he pleaded to the universe in Russian.

Not since his escape from the Soviet Union 24 years earlier had Al felt such fear. "What should I do? I feel very old and tired and spent." He briefly considered his options, including burying the bodies. "But then what will I do, join the Soviets?"

A mood came over him and his mind created a vibrant physical sensation. "Think about Loretta and Tessa." Al could feel himself holding his granddaughter. It made his decision very simple. "I need to be on the side of the good guys."

He called the FBI. "I have a big problem and it cannot be discussed on the telephone." They arrived fourteen minutes later. He told them the truth about his secret life as a spy.

The official story was concocted by the FBI. "Zelda was killed by an intruder. She shot and killed him before dying. You discovered the bodies when you came home."

The police accepted the story without difficulty. "Did the FBI mandate their acceptance? I appreciate their alibi but at the same time I know the government will have expectations of me."

* * *

Being a witness to the murder of Zelda was the worst experience of Al's life. Calling Loretta with the news her mother was dead continued his brutal torture.

As for Loretta, bitter sadness accentuated the chaos of implementing quick travel plans to California. "Flying will be difficult for the baby so we're going to travel by train. She should be at ease with the rhythm of the rails. I miss Mark terribly. I'm so thankful he was able to have time with Tessa before he left for Korea. Mom too. I am equally as thankful she was able to spend time with us."

Loretta had never attended a funeral before her mother's ceremony. "I am surprised there are so many people here I do not recognize," she told a neighbor. "And for some odd reason, the thought occurrs to me that I never want to wear black again. I am proud of my father. I know how difficult it is for him to conceal his emotions. I'll never forget his tears. Last night was the first time I ever saw him get drunk. He drank vodka until he passed out in the chair."

The casket was open for the funeral. Loretta was fearful of seeing mortal wounds and was relieved when such was not the case. "Still, nothing about my mother looks peaceful." Loretta placed a photograph of her mother holding Tessa in the casket. Al also put a photograph in with the body, a picture of the family at the 1939 World's Fair.

Loretta and Tessa moved out two weeks before her apartment lease in New Jersey expired and returned to California. She nonetheless informed her father, "I have no desire to stay in the home where mother was killed."

"I don't either. I put the house up for sale." Al rented a home for his daughter. He decided to scale down to a smaller house for himself. In so doing, he gave his daughter furniture and other household goods as well as $3000 for her renewed life in California.

The federal government found suitable employment for Al being a sketch artist for the police and court system and he subsequently purchased a home in Los Angeles. His confession to the FBI about being a double agent changed his responsibilities with the government. "Oddly, the FBI was somewhat impressed that I was able to successfully hide my role with the Soviets from central intelligence as well as from my wife. How perverted is that?"

Al was also able to sever his ties with the Soviets. In a carefully orchestrated and wiretapped phone call, he exposed the Soviet spy group to the FBI. "It is time to leave the espionage game for awhile," he informed them. Surveillance will be very heavy. Continued spy duty is impossible."

The Soviets agreed with him. "It is hard to believe the bad guys never found out about my betrayal of them."

"Is destiny still outside of my control? What about the destiny of Loretta and her family? Is the whole truth part of that destiny?"

CHAPTER FIVE

MARK OF FAMILY, MARK OF WAR

Seattle, Washington
October 1951

I'm tired of reading." She put down her book, a text describing how the Celts believed in shaman transformation into animal form. "The quest to make sense of the crystal skull and the sasquatch is never ending but sometimes it drains me. And there is virtually nothing to make sense of the unidentified flying object my husband watched in 1927, or what I might have seen. Only the reports of flying saucers in the past few years by the American public validate us. Anyway, it is nearly time for my favorite television show."

"I hope Mark is doing alright today," Emily said, as she did dozens of times each day. Her brain was able to register twin images of him. One image was of her son stationed in Korea and the fear and uncertainty associated with that reality. Like side-by-side television sets, the second image received was seeing Mark with his baby girl and his wife before leaving. "I am so thankful Clayton and I were able to travel to see the newborn baby before Mark was sent overseas."

The introductory music and the big heart on the black-and-white screen snatched the attention of Emily. "'I Love Lucy' is on!"

Clayton missed the first ten minutes of the show but he quickly shifted into laugh mode. "It is especially nice to hear Emily laugh so hard. She gets so tied up in her many conflicting emotions and fears."

When Emily dashed off to the bathroom after the program, Clayton picked up the book on the end table. "Celts", he said, "not my type of reading, like most of the stuff she reads. But then again, she grew up with a physics professor. Research is a way of life for her."

"Research to me is more of a face to face exercise." Many times Clayton thought about giving up the search for answers during the 18 years since relocating to Washington. "Other people are not obsessed after a sasquatch sighting. Maybe obsession is normal for me. The crystal skull was viewed by many people. Did it have an impact on anyone else like it did me? I'll never know, but I can still feel it inside me."

"I am so glad you were able to watch the program," Emily announced when she returned to the living room.

"It kind of makes me miss show business," Clayton said. "We could have made a show like that if they had television available when we were younger. You are just as scatterbrained as Lucy is!" He did not wait. He pounced on her for a short tickle.

Emily smirked, trying hard not to give in to the tickling. "Mind over matter," she said. There was a brief gasp of laughter from her and then a second attempt at a solemn face. "Mind over matter," she repeated, barely getting the words out before squirming and squealing with laughter.

"You know one thing that I really like about tickling you?" Clayton asked. "I get a full hand reminder of that classy chassis of yours."

"You like a cheap feel?" Emily asked, placing his hand on her breast. "You like a cheap feel on a 50-year-old woman?"

"You won't be 50 for a little while yet," Clayton responded. "What do you say about letting me passionately attack you while you are still young?"

"I won't be young for very much longer. You better get started."

Sometimes Clayton wondered if Emily grew tired of the forever search to explain the unexplained. "It takes a world war to distract her," he thought. "She did have a period of indifference until 1947 and the Roswell mystery in New Mexio. That was just one too many unexplained phenomena for her, especially after the Ken Arnold sighting earlier that year. She has devoured anything she could read on anything remotely weird or conspiratorial since then."

Neither Emily or Clayton objected to any beliefs or ideals of their partner. "It is difficult to shape a viewpoint about the larger philosophical picture," Clayton admitted. He regularly included the Bible in is reading materials although he was not particularly religious. "Somehow scriptural readings bring illumination to ideas. It is as if there are hidden messages."

"A strictly scientific viewpoint is not possible," Emily agreed. "Most people know nothing about the sasquatch, or they think it is a myth. Scientific evidence once seemed impossible for the great apes in Africa and now they are considered our ancestors. Where does the sasquatch fit into the lineup? One thing is for sure, the sasquatch is at the top of the food chain. No one has found a partially eaten carcass of the as yet unidentified species."

"As for the crystal skull, not everyone has the same experience so opinions are expected to vary," Emily continued. "The scientific outlook of the crystal skull is that it is simply a work of art, no more and no less. Since modern technology cannot reproduce it, the crystal skull seems to be a miniature a work of genius similar to the grandiose pyramids of Central America where the skull was found."

"It is a good thing we all appreciate open minds," Clayton observed. "Intellectual dialogue is always more interesting with sympathetic listeners. Having an open mind also makes it easier to poke fun at oneself."

"We are not as open minded about alien theories. It is ironic to be waiting for some definitive proof of unidentified flying objects despite your sighting."

"There is nothing I can prove about my sighting or about yours," returned Clayton. "Nonetheless, an open mind is the best course of action for everything. A quiet mouth is also a good idea. Not very many people can discuss the crystal skull, the sasquatch, or alien sightings without also entertaining the idea that the believer is nuts. Unfortunately, the sasquatch sighting story followed Mark throughout his school years. It was a valuable lesson in discretion for our entire family."

"It is no wonder Mark didn't grow up to be a science fiction writer or something with what we've seen."

"He grew up with a general appreciation of what was valued by his parents, namely music, baseball and intellectual pursuit. We are just not real good at any of them."

"Except you with music. Everyone forges their own path," Emily reminded her husband. "You never pushed Mark into music beyond some basic concepts before he began school."

"He wanted to be a drummer."

"There is nothing like pounding headaches synchronized with loud and bad percussion," stated Emily.

"Which is why I'm not a drummer."

"He did well singing in choirs."

Clayton momentarily left and then reentered the room bringing snacks from the kitchen. "Mark mastered the guitar much better than I was able to. Remember when I brought home a guitar when he was 15? He took right to it."

"I think he just wanted to do something better than you," grinned Emily.

"Females liked it. Mark once admitted making up mushy songs and that he hoped his teammates didn't find out."

"His baseball teammates may have been more kind," his mother advised. "Mark's friends in high school had great respect for his never say die attitude when it came to baseball. He grew up with us very frustrated Boston Red Sox fans for parents who were thousands of miles away from their team."

"There is no question that baseball is revered more highly by me than any other skill a person can develop," Clayton reasoned. "There are many doctors and lawyers in the world but there are only 400 or so major league baseball players at any given time."

"Sometimes I wonder how good of a player Mark might have been if he didn't rip apart his throwing arm in that sledding accident. Was he 13?"

"Yes. I was amazed he tried so hard to throw left handed," acknowledged his mother.

"It was an uphill struggle. He just wanted to be able to play first base. He was a good pinch-hitter. To his team, Mark was the heart and soul."

"I loved those games."

"Those heart memories will stay with me until the day I die, maybe even the next day."

"We didn't feel the same way about his grades," Emily teased. "Academic pursuit was not a high priority for him."

"He wasn't terrible, he just didn't care very much."

"'Life has too many opportunities to get slowed down with studying', he used to say. But eventually he developed some memory techniques. His test scores improved and everyone thought he was working harder."

"I was as amazed at his B average at Central Washington as his staying there for a full year," remarked Clayton.

"Central's cowboy culture was a shock for him. Even the girls seemed foreign."

"I think it was the never ending winds in Ellensburg that drove him out."

"So he went from smelling cow shit to a different culture shock at Fort Dix. Once he was reassigned from tank mechanic to the medical corps, he was sent to Letterman Army Hospital in San Francisco for extended training. That's when Loretta captured his fascination, his love and his future."

"We've been doing this for days."

"Doing what?" asked Emily.

"Anything sentimental," responded Clayton. "Since we heard the news about Zelda we have been obsessed with recalling fond memories."

"We hardly knew her. The day we met her was when she was leaving New Jersey."

"It was fun meeting someone who loved our grandchild as much as us."

"We had such a wonderful image of her. The intrusion and murder is all so gruesome. The whole story seems incomplete with no way to conjure a closure. It was sure nice to talk to Mark yesterday."

"I thought his call might go through the new transcontinental dial telephone service but it was through military services," noted Clayton. "I loved his story about losing a bet on the Giants. There are no Yankee fans in this family!"

"He sure didn't want to talk much about Zelda."

"Mark deflected the topic. He just wanted some happy talk. He has had plenty of sad conversations with Loretta already."

"The death of Zelda makes me wonder about reincarnation. Do you suppose, if reincarnation actually happened, that it could happen on a nonlinear basis?"

"Meaning what?" Clayton asked.

"I just had an idea that maybe all time periods could be used to learn lessons of the soul. Maybe Zelda was reincarnated into a period hundreds or even thousands of years ago. It would not be the same for everybody."

"Do you mean that you don't think she went to heaven?"

"I am not saying that," answered Emily. "But maybe some people have to complete all of their soul lessons before they go. Maybe they experience other religions, spiritual experiences, or even races. Maybe Zelda will experience old age in another lifetime."

"I can envision time and eternity as the same thing. Maybe some people are sent back in time with
insight from the future."

"Please clarify," his wife requested.

"Maybe they become the Einstein's or the Edison's or prophets."

"Do you suppose that our exposure to the crystal skull and the sasquatch could have originated in other lifetimes?"

"As you know, I can answer any question," stated Clayton.

"Yes of course, as long as you do not have to answer correctly. I get your point though. My questions cannot be answered definitively."

"It is enough for me to have experienced stuff that normal human beings cannot imagine. If I try to forget about it all, the crystal skull somehow gets in my mind and starts it all over again. I only hope some of these mysteries in life can be explained."

"Which mystery would you like to solve first?"

"That's easy." Clayton paused for effect and for the look of earnest curiosity on the face of his wife. "I want someone to cure the curse of Babe Ruth on the Red Sox."

* * *

"It sure was nice of Al to invite us to stay at his place in L.A.," remarked Clayton as he grabbed his sack lunch before leaving for work. "He just moved into the new house a couple of weeks ago."

"It will be grand to be at Tessa's first Christmas," beamed Emily.

"More like grand as in grandma and two grandpas."

"We talk to Loretta each week and she seems ready to deal with the holiday season. Still, Zelda's absence could make things tougher for Loretta and Al. Did Loretta seem okay to you when you talked to her?"

"We didn't talk for very long because Tessa was wailing. What a singer my little grandchild is."

Emily giggled as Clayton kissed her goodbye. "I wish Mark was home for Christmas."

"He will be with all of us loved ones in spirit."

Loretta made dinner for her in-laws and her father the day after Christmas. To her mild delight, the elders drank a considerable amount of alcohol. With any inhibitions liquored away, the conversation turned to odd or unexplainable experiences in their past. "Mere coincidence is not sufficient to explain the four of us all seeing the crystal skull," Al stated, but otherwise thought, "not to mention that three of us saw it in Ontario in 1927 not more than a few weeks apart with the Mitchell-Hedges family. That was in another life for me."

"It is a strange play of destiny but thousands of people have actually seen it, " Loretta surmised.

"Strange things do occasionally come our way," stated Emily.

"Another thing we have in common," Al added. The room was silent as the listeners were not sure if Al was including the murder of his late wife in his sentiments.

"At the risk of being considered mental, I have a story about a sasquatch that Mark and I saw. You have heard the story, right?" Clayton asked Loretta. After her acknowledgment, Clayton proceeded to describe the sighting of the sasquatch in 1939 to Al.

Steadfastly remaining quiet about his life before Zelda, Al could not help but think, "I cannot believe the coincidence that someone else in the world has experienced both a sasquatch and the crystal skull. I wish I didn't have to keep quiet about my 'Yellow Top' sighting in 1927. Beyond strange is the fact that Loretta has seen the skull and not a sasquatch whereas Mark has seen a sasquatch but not the skull."

"What is next, aliens?" joked Emily. Noticing the nervous expression on Clayton's face, Emily decided to omit the space alien topic from all conversation.

CHAPTER SIX

CRYSTAL CLEAR OVERSEAS CONNECTIONS

Spokane, Washington
November 1951

"There is much I don't understand and sometimes cannot accept in this modern age," Jason remarked while tossing the newspaper on the coffee table. "America is now 'Babyville' and television cut movie industry earnings in half. Of course one of those million or so television sets purchased this year was ours."

"But you are leading up to something specific you don't understand," predicted Amanda.

"Or accept."

"Nor do I," Amanda said, recognizing the direction of the conversation. "I cannot understand or accept why Lenny was recalled to active duty in Korea after serving our country in World War II. By the way, Margaret called today. She was just checking to see if we had heard from Lenny."

"Is everything okay with her?"

"She is doing great."

"Good, good, now I have something to show you."

"What are you, some kind of pervert?"

"Of course I am, but not just now." He took Amanda's hand and led her out the kitchen door. "I got my first company car."

"Wow, it's government green."

"It is a 1952 Chevrolet and at least it doesn't say 'Pacific Northwest Bell' on it."

"Maybe we could take a joy ride to McCord Air Force Base."

"Not with this car but we can take a trip over there if you like." Jason carefully removed several leaves that had fallen on the windshield of the new vehicle.

"Margaret wants us to come for Thanksgiving. I sort of kind of told her that we probably, likely, might, possibly, definitely, positively maybe, for sure try to make it."

"It must have taken a long time to say all those words. Thanks for running up the long-distance bill."

Turning on the television set, he asked, "Did you hear about the color television broadcast, the first one?"

"I bet color television sets are expensive. Anyway, I hope they are for awhile. Movies won't have the market on color soon enough."

"There is some good stuff on TV. 'Superman' and Edward R. Murrow are on tonight. Milton Berle is on too."

"They are on the same show?" Amanda again teased.

"You should be on TV," Jason teased back.

"Do you mean like Dinah Shore, or Lucy?"

"I am thinking more along the lines of Gertrude and Heathcliffe, the two seagulls on the 'Red Skelton Show'."

"I am going to ask Sandra if she wants to go with us when we go to Tacoma to see Margaret."

"She probably has plans with her aunt and uncle. She sure is anxious for Lenny to get back home. Only a couple more months to go. I know they both are anxious to start a family."

"When we go to Tacoma, maybe we should take the television set with us," suggested Amanda.

"I have a better idea. Let's buy them one for an early Christmas present when we are there. I would rather buy one over there than drag one along with us."

"You know, I could get to like you," smiled Amanda. Then she changed the channel.

Jason slumped into his chair, his thoughts centered upon his daughter Margaret and her indirect journey from growing up in Spokane to living in Tacoma. She had been married for just over a year, a bride at age 23 to Lieutenant Walter Thomas Johnson of the Air Force. Both graduated from the University of Idaho in Moscow in the same year. Walter, drafted into military duty in June 1951, was shipped out to Korea four months later in charge of the fueling of cargo planes. "He is not expected to be stateside until after Easter. We still hardly know him," thought Jason. "Sometimes I feel guilty for only thinking about Lenny being overseas and in danger. Margaret faces it twice as much as I do each day. Someday I need to tell her what a hero she is to me."

* * *

Several weeks before Jason and Amanda were to leave for Tacoma, Jason dropped a thunderbolt on his wife. "This may come as a surprise but I think we should sell the theater."

"But that theater is a part of us, both blessing and vanity. Why do you have a change of outlook?"

"It is just all this communist crap. What if we unintentionally show the wrong movie and we get blacklisted or something? I don't trust anyone anymore."

"Our partners thought this communist crap was going to be a problem years ago."

"Which is one of the reasons they sold their interests to us," Jason continued. "They saw television as the biggest reason though."

"And now we get to watch the commie trials on television," Amanda noted ruefully.

"Anyway, let's think about it for a couple of days." However, by that time, the couple had already developed a plan to market the theater. "Newspaper ads are the first step. We should wait a little while before we put up a 'for sale' sign on the building. I don't want to alarm our regular movie patrons." Despite their intentions, many of the theater regulars began asking Jason and Amanda about the proposed sale. Those concerned movie patrons turned out to be a blessing in disguise as a purchaser was found by word of mouth.

Much to the relief of both parents, Margaret was not surprised and did not oppose the sale. "The theater will never slip from our memories of family history. The golden age of movies is gone for us anyway. All of this supposed Communist inuendo in the arts is dangerous and it takes some of the fun away from owning the theater. It's just some government mind control thing anyway."

Jason was a war veteran and Lenny was a soldier but none of the family trusted the United States government. "I have been suspicious of our government since the internment of Don Yamamoto in World War II," Amanda insisted. "That left a horrible scar for me. Lenny and Margaret both worked as pickers for Mr. Yamamoto on his farm."

"He is a nice man," Margaret remembered. "And Rodney was the sports editor for the high school paper when I was editor."

"A lot of people came to the 'welcome back' celebration you organized Amanda," Jason remembered. "It was ironic that the community mostly contributed vegetables and fruits to the Yamamoto family when they returned."

"That was an emotional time for them. Their spirits were hardened during their internment. I don't want to know what they went through."

"The Roswell stuff also really reduced my trust in our government," Jason acknowledged. "All of America was duped by that one."

"An alien spacecraft crashing is a world changing thing. We deserve to know the truth, even if it was just some secret new kind of airplane."

"The government fears a 'war of the worlds' type of panic, like there was during the Orson Welles broadcast. But that was 13 years ago and the world is more sophisticated now."

"Sophisticated and stupid at the same time."

"It was after the Roswell incident when Lenny first divulged to some of his friends the unidentified flying object he sighted in 1939. Although he previously kept quiet about it, the experience changed the direction in his life. I still think going into aviation mechanics is part of his quest to understand the sheer magnitude of what he witnessed that summer night."

"Being in aviation mechanics also keeps Lenny near pilots, some of whom occasionally let slip a tale of unidentified flying objects," Amanda added. "Generally, those stories are scarce. Pilots do not want to invite ridicule. The government doesn't like those incidents, even if the source is reliable."

"We never questioned his judgment or integrity. Other people would. We just asked questions about angles, viewpoints, colors and potential speed calculations. Never once was there a hint of 'are you sure'? Somehow, it all seems relevant. The mystery of alien visitors is likely tied up with other strange phenomena, all of which seem to be part of a purpose. The term 'flying saucer' was coined right here in Washington. It's not surprising it was the same year as the Roswell thing. The unidentified saucer objects were reported flying near the location where we experienced the flying fish in 1927."

"Everything these days makes me believe more in my grandfather's prophecies, but I still get surprised. It makes me believe there is a destiny involved even if it takes years or generations to happen. I feel it is naive to worry about my personal role but I hope the family destiny will manifest itself through intention. Each day the tumor of destruction in the world is a challenge of destiny."

"A challenge to everyone's destiny. The atomic bomb is a nightmare beyond even the most depraved minds. Each day we awake to a world of fear."

"Although racial discrimination and prejudice have been part of my native ancestry, hatred of another people I will never understand. And now our son and our son-in-law have been sent back into the theater of hate, the new 'us and them' of the Cold War. I remember talking about building a bomb shelter many times."

"I do too. Ultimately your idea that a bomb shelter is negative thinking is why we didn't build one."

"I hate everything about atomic warfare. It makes no sense to unleash anything so devastating upon the world. It is a literal opening of Pandora's Box. How can anything so toxic and deadly be limited to the area near the explosion? I am convinced that not enough is known about radiation to risk it upon the earth."

"I am convinced the government knows very much about radiation but risks it anyway," remarked Jason. "I am also convinced that the expanding activity of reported unidentified flying objects is an indication that alien life is concerned about potential of nuclear war on earth. The ramifications haunt me."

"My spiritual energy has been focused on everyone coming home safely from Korea. My heart pours out to them all the time."

"Hopefully our prayers will be answered." Privately Jason thought, "Although my past nullifies my chance to get to heaven, I believe my prayers will be heard for my son and for Walter."

"I pray everyday for Lenny and Walter but sometimes the outside world crowds in on me with its hatred, war, and degradation of the planet with its modern secrets. I go for walks when I feel ungrounded."

"In our own ironic fashion, our last movie as owners of The Emerald Theatre is "The Day the Earth Stood Still". Jason and Amanda sat in the audience and after the film they drove home as movie patrons instead of owners.

"What now brown cow?" Amanda asked her husband as their car passed the Idaho-Washington border.

"Moo!"

"Which reminds me, the price of horsemeat has tripled in Portland."

"Did I moo that badly?"

"No, I just know Portland is one of your favorite places." Amanda accepted the expected dirty look from her husband.

"Now, there is a place to test nuclear bombs!" He smiled through the purposely exaggerated frown on his wife's face. "Really, I'm just prejudiced because of the time I got in a fight with those thug bootleggers and I'm not real fond of the followers of the Oregon football team."

"Hey, I thought of a question for you to ask at work."

"Which is?"

"The price of a phone call has doubled in some of the big cities from five to ten cents. If it does here, do you get a raise?"

"There is no way. They will probably buy one of those big UNIVAC computers, since the Census Bureau bought the first one."

"That is a big machine to just do counting."

"Professional football could use one of those. Norm Van Rocklin had 554 yards passing in one game this year. That record won't be beat for 50 years, maybe more. Do you want to bet on the Browns against 49ers championship game?" Jason challenged.

"Who do you think will win?"

"Otto Graham hardly ever loses, so I like Cleveland."

"Okay then, I'll take San Francisco, and I want the stakes to be dishwashing for a week."

"And if I win, you will polish all of my shoes?"

They shook hands on it and promptly forgot all about the game to be played the following week. However, Amanda did make an informal mental count of Jason's shoe inventory.

* * *

"Being here in Tacoma is like living in prayer time on a full-time basis," noted Amanda.

"We all live in hope and fear but I am glad we do not discuss it continually," Margaret emphasized. "However, experiencing it together helps beyond words."

"I feel the same. I feel better being here, like something good is going to happen."

"Just the same, I don't want to just sit around when you are visiting," explained Margaret. "Since you like unsolved mysteries in the world, I planned a trip to a museum to see a particular exhibit. I highly doubt it is a 'skull of doom' as described in the ad, but the fact that it originated or was found in the land of the Maya makes it more fascinating."

"It is some kind of crystal skull, right?" inquired Jason. "I've heard something about that before."

"They must use the 'doom' term to sell tickets," scoffed Amanda. "I doubt anyone is dropping dead when they see it."

The following day Margaret and her parents went out to breakfast but arrived several minutes before the museum opened.

"We missed the rain!" Jason exhorted. "It rained buckets during the drive but somehow it mysteriously stopped when we parked at the diner."

"You came to see the skull, huh?" The security guard addressed them as he unlocked the museum
door.

"We wanted to get an early start," stated Margaret.

"Has it been a popular exhibit?" Amanda inquired.

"There never seems to be a big crowd but some people come back day after day."

"They must not be doomed," quipped Margaret.

The security guard let out a short but hardy laugh, his indigo eyes complementing his smile. "If anyone is doomed, it's me. I am here every day."

Being virtually the only people in the museum, the three family members went directly to the exhibit. The skull was enclosed in a small roped off area with a light shining on it from above and below. Wordlessly they established their positions in front of the skull. Based upon independent whim, each changed their position occasionally for the purpose of different vantage points.

"There is some sort of pulsating quality or energy or aura about the crystal skull," Amanda thought. Her mind began racing but somehow she realigned her thoughts around feelings of her grandfather. Her mind sped through fragments of images, the order and the intensity of each image varying and sometimes reoccurring.

Jason was at once transfixed by the skull. He took the time to read and absorb the display. "As an artifact, it is beyond compare. I wonder about the 'skull of doom' label but we have no fear for our safety." His eyes traveled from the skull to the display and back a number of times when he felt a jolt of energy like electricity, emanating from the skull. "What was that!" his thoughts screamed. "Is there movement within it?" With his eyes glued to the skull, Jason could feel a mounting energy, a tension, as though he was waiting for an answer.

Margaret was at first amused by her parents. "Their evident fascination is rewarding. I picked an interesting activity, one that my parents will remember." She read the display, taking several glances at her awestruck parents between sentences. After finishing the script, Margaret squatted to see if she could see any brush or scratch marks on the artifact. From the lower position, a reflecting light from the skull paralyzed her briefly. She stood up slowly, her eyes fixed upon the crystal skull. "I feel some sort of message. What is it?"

Many memories of her life came to mind as Amanda viewed the crystal skull. At first a feeling of ancestral energy from her grandfather accompanied each memory but soon the image of her grandfather faded from Amanda's mind. It was replaced by a feeling that something was amiss in her environment.

"It's Lenny," Jason said simply, reacting to the change in energy and expression from his wife.

Margaret tried to remain calm. "We know nothing, but I think father is correct. It is something about Lenny." Her inner mind saw first her smiling husband and then an anguished brother.

Helplessly, silently, the three family members stood with their eyes fixed upon the crystal skull.

Margaret flinched. "I felt the snake." She snapped to attention. "The snake is somehow a symbol that Lenny is alright. Somehow the snake helped him." The strange sensation passed. "Lenny is just fine," proclaimed Margaret. "And so is my husband."

The brilliance of the light in the skull seemed to increase and its hue seemed to change, as if there were an injected happiness. Everyone in the group breathed easier and then stepped out of the way for other spectators advancing to the exhibit. There was very little conversation among the three as they absentmindedly shuffled through the remainder of the museum.

"Something good did happen," remarked Margaret after everyone was in the car.

"Of course there is no way to know for sure but I agree," Amanda responded. "It felt like a turning point for something good."

"The world needs more 'glass half full' people like you," quipped Jason.

Amanda gently placed her hand on her husband's shoulder. "The way of a positive destiny should show us how to get the glass full again, with something good in it."

* * *

Lenny rolled over to his side again in the infirmary bed. "I don't want to be in Korea." He did not blame his illness on anyone. For 18 of the first 21 hours he was sick, he slept. After that he had minor vomiting and a minor bowel movement before falling asleep for several more hours. For the next 40 hours, Lenny just remained on his side, not able to eat, drink, pee or poop, consuming only a few glasses of water during that time.

"We are not sure about your virus," the doctor informed Lenny during his first day in the infirmary. "The medicine I prescribed initially may have induced the vomiting. Perhaps the best medicine is

simple rest for now. Hopefully you will be able to hold down some food soon, which I think will help us in
developing a remedy for you."

Some 38 hours into the 40 hours of viral torture, Lenny questioned his remaining mortality. There, lying in the dark, he felt an image of light in his mind. "I feel love and healing energy being received. It feels like family." A memory came to Lenny's frail mind, a story of an Egyptian shaman. He consciously enacted the symbolism of the story upon himself.

"First visualize the virus in my body." It was relatively easy to do because the adverse force had been within him for days. "Picture and feel the lines of gravity extending through me to the earth's core through jagged pathways."

In the stillness, Lenny commanded his thoughts, "Wait for my symbolic healer." In the dark, with his eyes closed, Lenny became aware of the presence of the healer. He knew its deadly python form. "I can feel it move about the room. Now it is over me and around me." Lenny could sense the fangs and the bite of the snake was no surprise but still it made him writhe. "I can feel the snake burrow inside of me. I can feel the huge reptile moving through various areas of my body." Hope sprang through him as the snake began its healing process. The snake was eating his disease and relief was immediate.

Within minutes the snake left his body. Lenny was aware of the snake in the room, purging the virus into the bowels of the earth. Knowing that he could bring the snake back again, Lenny said, "Thank you for your healing help." The physical feeling of release from his meditation was familiar. "It's like the night I saw the space craft or whatever it was."

Before fading into deep slumber, Lenny projected a prayerful thought to his loved ones halfway around the planet. "I am okay. I am better."

Two days later, Lenny watched the medical attendant on shift move toward his bed. "I understand you were the one who found me."

"You collapsed near the latrine. It was dark and in the pouring rain. I was lucky to find you when I did, although we are not sure how long you were on the ground."

"I feel much better today. Thanks for saving my life."

"I just got you out of the rain. You mostly healed yourself. You baffled the doctors. You had us worried for awhile," Mark admitted. "For some reason I knew you would be okay. I had some sort of feeling you are supposed to be alive for something better than this war."

"You have no idea," Lenny joked. "I appreciate you coming around to check up on me. You were in here the other day during your day off."

"I wanted you to pull through because you're a Washington guy; Spokane, right?"

"That's right. Where are you from?"

"I was born in Boston but I mostly grew up in Seattle," Mark replied as he rose from the bedside chair. "I was here on my day off to say goodbye to a guy from Massachusets. He had some great Ted Williams stories."

"You guys were talking about something else, another subject. I couldn't help overhearing."

"Many of the soldiers coming through here tell me stories. I think it is a combination of facing mortality and being hushed up that makes them want to tell me things."

"Hushed up about what?"

Mark looked around the room and peeked down the hallway. "It will happen to me soon enough. The big brass doesn't know what I've seen and heard."

"The skies are full of mystery."

"So you have seen things too? Be careful who you talk to. I have heard rumors about rumors and none of them are good."

"Pilots have been grounded who report strange activity."

"It's bad for anyone who has seen the unexplained. Some of them have died mysteriously. I fear for my own life."

"And it is very simple to make it look like they died at war. Who questions that?"

"Have you seen anything yourself?"

Lenny briefly considered his own unexplained sighting as a teenager but instead began, "When I was on my way to Haneda Air Force Base in Japan, this strange, very bright light started coming at us. The pilot moved out of the way but it came back at us, split in three places and then sped away faster than anything I've ever seen."

"Doesn't sound like one of ours," quipped Mark. "Were you told not to say anything about it?"

"I was advised by the pilot but I was never ordered to do so. Let's hear your story."

"I don't know what I saw. It moved very fast and had some kind of a wave in front of it. When the colors in front of it ran together, it disappeared."

"Doesn't sound like one of ours."

"That's what got me interested in talking to people about what goes on up there besides war. Have you heard of 'foo fighters'?"

"I've heard of them in Europe."

"Me too and a few stories kind of like that around here. Anyway, one strange ship enveloped a bomber plane in an amber light."

"What did the aircraft look like?"

"Apparently it was a perfectly round, luminous circle. It was around the airplane in different positions, causing most of the instruments to malfunction."

"Then what happened?"

"The whole thing lasted about 16 minutes and then the craft sped off to the northeast and disappeared."

Lenny slumped back in his bed. "Why hide stories like that from the public? My parents love that stuff. They don't tell those kind of stories to anyone else but to me and my sister."

"My parents get obsessed with that stuff too. They are real cautious in what they say."

"Because the powers that be want to prescribe electric shock treatment to anyone who reports a sighting."

"Now that's something to reverse engineer."

"Anyway, thanks again for everything. Mentally and spiritually, I feel much better. My release from military duty in 22 days seemed like an eternity away during my virus. It will be several more days before my strength is likely to return but my wartime will end soon."

With optimism and vigor increasing progressively, Lenny's dreams began to be like visions. In one particular dream he saw a flying disc disappear, but he also recognized a wrinkle in reality where it went. He followed that wrinkle without conclusion. "There is another level of existence or reality just beyond my reach. I get a feeling of serenity just imagining it."

In his last day at the infirmary, Lenny dreamed about a son. He pictured a totem pole with images he somehow recognized as his ancestors as well as himself and his son. "It is a totem of peace," a voice in the dream told him.

"My ancestors are not from a tribe who used those kind of totemic symbols." The dream informed him the "sasquatch" was named by totemic tribes. Then Lenny saw the totem pole enter a vortex or wrinkle as in the previous dream.

"It is best not to try to decipher my vision dream," Lenny thought after he awoke. However, his anticipation to return home to his wife was magnified.

"I'm going to have a son," he told a nurse.

"When is your wife expecting?"

"Probably in ten or eleven months." The curious look on her face was the most pleasing memory of Lenny's time in the infirmary.

CHAPTER SEVEN

DENIAL DENIED

*Los Angeles, California
December 1951*

"The worst is over," Loretta lied to herself. "Nothing could be worse than making those calls."

She leaned over the crib but moved her head suddenly so her tears would not fall on her daughter's face. "You are too young to know about being sad." Loretta grabbed a baby blanket to dry her cheeks.

"How can Emily and Clayton possibly accept this as part of destiny?"

Loretta's knee buckled and she grabbed the crib for balance. After a quick glance at her sleeping child, she moved to the bed. "I'm not the first woman this has happened to, what am I supposed to do? I should be tough."

Ignoring her own words, Loretta instead silently watched her fleeting inconsequential thoughts with her mind's eye. "None of it makes sense. Somehow the best thing is to not feel sorry for myself."

The telephone rang but Loretta ignored it. "Life is so unfair. Wasn't my mother getting murdered enough?"

The baby stirred in her crib, momentarily distracting Loretta's thought patterns. A cold shiver radiated from Loretta's heart throughout her body. "What a strange time to have this feeling." She rolled up her sleeve to look at her forearm. "I'd swear every hair on my body is growing. That's silly. You can't see a hair grow."

When Tessa awoke, Loretta quickly picked her up and held her. "I wish we could hug your father."

* * *

"There's no training manual for this. What are we supposed to do?" Emily reached for the last tissue in the box.

"Loretta's comment on the phone about being in denial made me think," Clayton responded in a soft voice. "We are in denial too I suppose. It doesn't make any difference anyway."

"I guess we should get our stuff together and get out of here. I am suddenly very anxious to go home."

"Am I ever grateful we decided to drive to Carlsbad after Christmas," remarked Clayton. "It would have been difficult being around anybody at Al's house right now."

"I would like to see the baby again but I wouldn't be able to handle it. We need to be alone together."

"Loretta and Tessa probably do too."

"I just want to get home," Emily reiterated. "We don't know when Mark is going to arrive but I want to be there plenty early."

"Our son, the Army medic," Clayton said quietly, softly. "We'll need to support Loretta and Tessa any possible way we can. Going through this twice in one year is too much."

"This is the blackest, most miserable day of my life," sobbed Emily. "Watching our son being buried won't be any easier. I wonder if we will ever know how he actually died."

CHAPTER EIGHT

SKULL MATES IN PRISM

Spokane, Washington
February 1963

"I've made good time." Amanda cautiously negotiated the 1962 Cadillac DeVille through the rough icy spots at the bottom of the hill on Pines Road where she turned east toward the entrance to South Pines Elementary School. "I guess I'm not late. Their appointment with the dentist isn't for another half hour." Amanda had volunteered to pick up her nine-year old twin granddaughters Marlene and Elaine so Margaret would not have to leave her job as a dental assistant.

To her amazement, one car was surrounded by a mob of children. The dark haired granddaughters were not among them and made their way to their grandmother. "What is all the excitement?" Amanda asked the girls.

"It is Bumpy Wills' dad," answered Elaine.

"He's a fifth grader," added Marlene.

"His dad is a fifth grader?" Amanda teased.

"No grandma!" The twins responded in unison, somewhat in competition with Amanda's laughter.

"I know who he is. Everyone in Spokane does. Maury Wills was the Most Valuable Player and the first to steal 100 bases," Amanda informed her granddaughters.

"Everybody in school knows that!" Marlene said.

"Yeh, everyone," followed Elaine.

"So you think you are smart," teased Amanda. "But just remember, you both are only fourth-graders… and you're only girls."

"I think boys are dumb," announced Marlene. Her sister nodded in agreement.

"I do too," said Amanda. "They're just as dumb as girls."

The twins were with Amanda when both Jason and Margaret arrived for dinner.

"Congratulations on the good checkups girls," Margaret announced.

"So I don't get to pull any teeth out of my grandkids?" Jason kidded.

"Guess what girls? I have some good news." Margaret paused for a moment of obvious suspense. "You two are going to be Star Lighters in September! As you know the present Star Lighters are thirteen and their time on the talent show is done."

"The Star Lighters have always been the same twin girls," remarked Amanda. "Now my two grandtwins are going to be the greeters and sing the jingles for the sponsor, Boyle Fuel Company. That means Marlene and Elaine will be on 'Starlit Stairway' for several years to come, right?"

"Let's hear it girls," Jason requested.

The twins jumped to their feet and got in position. In perfect harmony they voiced the provincially famous jingle. "Fairfax 8-1521, Fairfax 8-1521, when you need coal or oil, call Boyle." The girls then excused themselves to watch television before dinner was ready.

"It is times like this that I wish they had their father," said Margaret. "I can't believe the plane crash was four years ago. Their only memories of him are what they can remember before turning age five. They know he died in the crash of a fuel plane at the Fairchild base, but hardly anything pleasant."

"How is the romance between you and Mr. Jacob Manfred?" Amanda inquired.

"He is great, really."

"Are you great too?" Jason asked.

"I'm fine. I just don't want to rush anything." Margaret's answer was apparently accepted. A brief silence in the room ensued before Amanda changed the subject by dropping the silverware she was transporting to the table.

The noise startled the 65 year old Jason but he quickly yelled, "Fumble!" and pounced upon the fallen silverware.

"You are almost retired. You should be more careful about jumping on the floor," reminded Margaret.

"I have worked at the telephone company for 37 years," noted Jason, "and we just don't get to jump on the floor very often there."

"That's because you were in management," teased Amanda.

"Although I do not consider myself a workaholic," Jason confessed at the table, "I am unsettled at the prospect of having no real daily shedule."

"I'm surprised," Amanda said. "I thought you were looking forward to the benefits of a less stressful existence. Money is not an issue with the pensions and AT&T stocks and options you have."

"It has definitely been a benefit to work for a company whose parent is AT&T. The truth is, I am just sad to be leaving when technology is growing so quickly. The recent hotline established between the United States and Russia is a perfect illustration. Then there is the technology not of this earth, used when astronaut Gordon Cooper orbited the earth 22 times."

"Not to mention your belief that advancing technology and electronics will eventually allow contact with alien life," noted Amanda. "The downside of technology is a Christian soldier necessity of protecting 'in God we trust', the technology for and against nuclear holocaust. We have to trust John F. Kennedy, our president who is nearly the same age as our son. We surely cannot trust Khrushchev."

"You are going to do just fine in retirement," Margaret proclaimed. "You will have the finances to work on all sorts of electronic projects. You'll always be a gadget man."

"That's true girls," Jason told his granddaughters. "I love new stuff. Our family was the first around here to have two television sets and later to have a color television."

"There is one sure fact about retirement for you," Amanda said, "you are going to have ample time to enjoy your grandchildren."

"Amen to that," Jason responded. "I almost wish we still had the theater."

"You can do some of what I do, with me," suggested Amanda. "There are at least three of the six horses we have that wouldn't mind letting you ride them."

"I couldn't keep up with you. At 61 years old you are still at the front of the line when it comes to everything, including community volunteer work."

"More than anything, I enjoy being a grandmother, and a mother, and a wife. I am the matriarchal leader of our little tribe and my role is to spoil rotten my grandchildren, children, and husband. It is a most pleasurable pursuit. We are fortunate to have both of our children living in Spokane."

"I admire both the toughness and the tenderness of our daughter," Amanda said to her husband over breakfast one morning. "She is tough in the way that she deals with adversity yet she is a tender human being."

"She devoutly attends the United Methodist Church with her children. She is virtually the only family member to become consistently involved in organized religion."

"That started after seeing the crystal skull. Her faith bolstered her after the death of Walter."

"And then there is Lenny the school teacher and baseball coach and his life of perpetual progress," Amanda remembered. "He and Sandra are the happiest couple I have ever seen and they love being parents."

"October 30, 1952, the day Mickey was born, was the happiest day of Lenny's life."

"I love my grandchildren equally, but Mickey changed me."

"That's because you were happy he turned out to be a boy," commented Jason.

"I suppose you are right but its more than just that. It is as if my ancestral spirits are giving me prophetic visions of him. His path is to be different. It does not matter so much what it is that will be different in Mickey's life, I just know a different spiritual path will be his. And it has nothing to do with the Cold War or money or politics, but it will be significant. I'm sure of it."

* * *

When he saw the ad in the newspaper, Lenny called his parents. "You have talked about the crystal skull so often and now finally I get to see it. All I know about it is from you both and Margaret. I really want to see it."

Although it would be some six days until the crystal skull exhibit, Lenny immediately became anxious. "How should I prepare? Should I prepare Sandra for the experience? Should we take Mickey with us? Should I view the crystal skull with my family or alone, or both ways? Am I making too much out of all this?"

In general, Lenny tried to work at activities to keep his mind occupied. "Teaching school and organizing the practice schedule for the upcoming high school baseball season is good for that." Not wishing to increase any anxiety about the skull, Lenny rarely discussed the upcoming exhibit with Sandra until the day before the exhibit.

"Say Sandra, what do you think about taking Mickey to the crystal skull exhibit?"

"Your family takes the crystal skull very seriously. If Mickey doesn't like it, he might be a nuisance. And it also might cut our time at the exhibit. I think we should go again with Mickey after we know more of what to expect."

"Mickey may not have an adult appreciation of the artifact but he is not too young for the experience," surmised Lenny.

"When Margaret heard about the plan to see the crystal skull exhibit, she also made a secondary plan to take the twins on a separate occasion."

"I asked my sister if she thought the crystal skull would be the same? How could a piece of crystal change very much? Margaret surprised me with her answer. She said, 'Well, I've changed'."

"So you think it will affect you differently?" I asked.

"I don't really understand what that means," admitted Sandra. "I'm sure I will understand more about all the fuss when I actually get to see it myself. What did she say?"

"Basically, she was aware that her shift to a more spiritual life occurred after she observed the crystal skull. She also said there is more to her spiritual side than what people might think. Margaret believes what other Christians believe but also more simple things."

"What kind of simple things?"

"Like everyday miracles, and I don't mean Jesus sized miracles. She considers the mind, body, healing, childbirth, and spiritual energy to be miracles. She says she marvels at the heartbeat of each new day."

"It's no wonder she turned out to be a singer with that disposition," Sandra remarked. "She probably was some kind of a bird in a former life."

"I wonder what my mom and dad are thinking about seeing the crystal skull. I have a hunch my mom is more excited about it than my dad is. He probably doesn't want to make a big deal out of it."

In fact, the topic of the crystal skull was scarcely discussed by Jason and Amanda until the day before they would see the exhibit. "Amanda, I am surprised, but for some reason I have confrontational feelings about the crystal skull. I have a notion that concentration is the key to obtaining answers about various mysteries from it. My theory is that no one knows how to use the energy of the skull."

"Maybe it is as simple as concentrating on what you want to be resolved. Most people probably view the skull with anticipation, or anxiety, or simply not knowing what to expect. That means the energy route is not necessarily an intended one. Maybe it is even the path of least resistance."

"Perhaps there is more than one way to enlightenment? I want answers to my mysteries from the crystal skull. Concentration hardly seems dangerous."

"Anyway, think how little you have been thinking about retirement," Amanda teased.

"I spend too much time thinking about the sasquatch and alien life except when I watch television. I love the comedy shows, especially 'Candid Camera', 'The Beverly Hillbillies', Danny Thomas, Dick Van Dyke, and Andy Griffith. And I love 'My Favorite Martian'."

"And a few more."

Later that evening, Amanda giggled at her husband's laughter in the living room. "I am so glad you were able to put your crystal skull anxiety away for awhile."

"Ray Walston as the alien! I have to laugh at myself because I doubt I would be able to focus on alien life in the presence of the crystal skull with a mental image of 'Uncle Martin'. Maybe I'll just think about 'The Twilight Zone' on the way to the exhibit.

* * *

"We need to prepare ourselves for the fact that other people likely will be viewing the exhibit with us," Jason said at breakfast. "When we saw the crystal skull in Tacoma, no one else was there for much of the time."

When they arrived at the museum, the other three people in line walked toward the crystal skull exhibit with them but quickly departed for the restroom. Afterwards, those particular patrons left for other areas of the museum.

As the family approached the crystal skull with seemingly choreographed slow, cautious steps, Lenny began laughing. "We look like something out of a 'Three Stooges' movie!"

"I am glad you left me out of that analogy," volleyed Jason.

Reaching the exhibit, Lenny stopped suddenly. "Wait!" Everyone halted immediately, which
prompted a teasing smile. "Is anybody scared?"

After a momentary giggle the remainder of the family pushed past him.

"What brought that on?" Lenny questioned himself as he joined in assuming positions around the crystal skull. The practical joke type of gag is unlike me, especially now. My family members take this exhibit very seriously. Maybe it was an unconscious way of trying to control the energy flow." As he moved closer, his wonder and growing appreciation of the artifact caused a big and involuntary smile on his face. "It feels like it knows me."

Lenny's antics were quickly forgotten. The focus of Margaret became increasingly intense and selfish. "I have no interest in how the others are reacting. They can tell me later. The energy flow of the crystal skull is very familiar. It is like being inside a sound I cannot hear. There is a vibration, a frequency. I wonder if there is a melody waiting to be discovered." She soon became somewhat stunned by the overall sensation. "Think of a specific topic, something to ask the crystal skull. What about the future? No I do not want to know that," she deluded herself. "How about the past?" Briefly, an image subliminally registered in her head. It was a totem pole... and an ancestor? "Do I need to know my past to know my future? No, it is the future by itself. No, I do not want to know the future." And so her thoughts volleyed until she realized she feared the future. "I fear my own mortality and that of my children. I have lost a husband. Will I lose another one?" She feared losing a parent. "No I do not want to know about the future. I want happy songs."

The first reaction by Jason to the crystal skull was to admire it, which he continued doing throughout his experience. He posed a question in his mind, expecting the skull to reciprocate telepathically. "Do you have a connection with alien life?"

No answer was forthcoming so Jason tried to think of nothing. "I wish that I had not asked a 'yes or no' question. But it is what I wanted to know. I also wanted to know, 'Do great American apes, or sasquatches, exist at the present time?' Jason chuckled to himself. "I asked a 'yes or no' question again." He continued gazing at the crystal skull. Unlike his experience 12 years before, the crystal skull did not change. He could see no changes in color, or light, or pulsation.

Nearly ready to discontinue his pursuit of questions and just enjoy the exhibit, Jason formulated an afterthought mental question. "Are the sasquatch and aliens related in any way?" Still the skull did not change in the eyes of Jason. But his personal energy and mood shifted dramatically. For some reason, he was overcome with a sense of guilt. Jason was always free to acknowledge his appreciation and thankfulness for his life and his family but the feeling of guilt sometimes visited him nonetheless. "The murder of a murderer by me so many years ago precludes any chance of redemption for my soul. I know that. It separates me from the rest of my family, a dirty secret."

"But why do I have these feelings of guilt now? Is it some sort of message? Am I trying too hard to figure out some sort of message?" Jason looked at his family members and the feelings of guilt subsided. "Is that a message?"

Almost immediately when Amanda looked into the crystal skull she had a feeling of empowerment. "I feel larger than life, as if my family could fit inside me, or on my shoulders. I have a feeling of enormous size and strength but my body has not changed."

Someone Amanda did not know walked up to the exhibit. The feeling of being large and powerful changed to a feeling of smallness, like one molecule as compared to the universe. The feeling of empowerment continued however. "I have a mind's eye image of time and I am the medium, no, the middle. I can sense my grandfather at the bookend of past time."

"Who is at the future bookend?" Like some dreams, details streamed together and were unclear. "It is my grandson Mickey. He is an adult in my image of him but I cannot see the details of his face." The image of her grandson in the future depicted movement, but no specific activity. She was following him. Amanda could feel herself move internally, shifting to follow Mickey's path. "Where is he going?" After she asked her mind that question, Mickey began changing with each step. "He is growing in size. Is it evolution?"

"Oh, excuse me! I am sorry!" the new person at the exhibit said after he bumped into Lenny. Everyone shifted a step to allow the new person space to view the exhibit. Amanda's thoughts and feelings quickly shifted into neutral. "It is like a campfire nearly going out but managing to rekindle itself in a different pattern than it had previously burned."

At first Amanda felt an overwhelming sense of forgiveness. It made her smile as she recognized the crystal skull somehow reflecting her own energy. Then she had a near breathtaking moment of consciousness. "Forgiveness is emanating from my entire family simultaneously, like teamwork," she admired silently. "Does one of us seek forgiveness?"

Her entire being filled with true inner joy. Amanda felt her tears mingle with her joy. She did not wipe them away.

* * *

During most of the drive home from the museum, Sandra was quiet, content to gaze at the beginnings of spring green on a sunny day while Lenny was lost in his own thoughts. "I just figure she will want to discuss the crystal skull experience on her own time."

When they arrived home, Sandra sat alone in the living room. After several minutes, she picked up a Bible and began reading about Moses. She read three chapters. Her eyes then wandered onto a footnote regarding the name of God told to Moses by God. "I remember translations of God's name being 'I Am That I Am', or 'I Am Who I Am', or 'I Am What I Am', but the footnote provided yet another version. The original Greek translation for Yahweh also included 'I WILL BE WHAT I WILL BE'. She sat there thinking about possible different interpretations of God's self-administered moniker.

"Hey Sandi, are you hungry?" Lenny walked into the living room. "I'm going to have some of that leftover fried chicken."

"Can we talk about the crystal skull a little bit first? I'm not really hungry."

"Sure we can. I'm not really hungry either. I was just looking for something not important to do."

"The crystal skull was much different than my expectations," stated Sandra. "It was interesting to watch your family during breakfast. They were getting mentally prepared for something weird but at the same time they had a great deal of respect for the skull."

"Mostly, I tried not to discuss the crystal skull with you very much before we went to the exhibit. I had never seen it myself but I had preconceived expectations based upon what I heard from my family. I wanted you to have an open mind about the skull."

"Thank you, I guess. I'm not sure how to explain my experience, so tell me what it was like for you," Sandra requested.

"Well, at first when I was kidding around, it seemed like I was trying to manipulate the focus of energy, to be in control of it."

"But how could you do that with so many other personalities involved?"

"It did not occur to me. I didn't plan what I was doing, it just happened."

"Okay, go on," instructed his wife.

"Then I just felt good, like I was supposed to be there. I started grinning and I couldn't stop. The crystal skull seemed to get kind of foggy, except for a couple areas of prism light. It was bizarre, like a climate change."

"Really, I did not see that at all. I saw sort of a purplish blue color, like a light bruise."

Her husband gave her a quick, puzzled look before he continued. "The foggy look of the skull lasted until that guy bumped into me. You could not see that, huh?"

"I did not see the foggy part. I definitely did not see it and we were both looking at the skull when the new guy fouled you."

"After that," Lenny continued, "I had this weird feeling about all of us, but mostly about Mickey."

"Wow, the colors are different but I felt the same way, especially about Mickey. There seemed to be something ancestral about it."

"Which is weird. We have very different ancestral backgrounds."

"You know yours better than I know mine. I know who they were but not much about them. The only thing in common with your ancestors is that our mothers are both half native," she said. Lenny did not correct her statement. Sandra's late mother was half Pauite. She and her father were both killed in an automobile accident before Sandra was a teenager .

"None of my feelings about Mickey, or anything for that matter, seemed negative while I was looking at the skull," Sandra reflected.

"That is the same with me. I just had these real strange sensations of changes, like changes of dimension or size, or something."

Sandra was momentarily quiet, pondering what her husband had said. "Do you mean shape shifting like a shaman?"

"I didn't think about it that way, but maybe."

"Did I ever tell you about my great great grandfather?" Lenny shook his head no so she continued. "I probably should have but I really do not know very much about him. He was a chief."

"Really, he was a chief?"

"In the southern Idaho area, he was known as Chief Bigfoot. Did you know that 'Nampa' means Bigfoot?"

"But he was not a sasquatch."

"Well, no, but he was a very large being. He was well over six feet tall and had feet that were nearly fifteen inches long."

"Was he a shape shifter?"

"I always thought only shamans could be shape shifters."

"My great grandfather was a medicine man and shaman," Lenny stated, "but I never heard any stories about shape shifting."

"You don't think the skull is trying to tell us that Mickey has shaman abilities, do you?" Lenny did not answer because he simply did not know. He thought about his mother's viewpoint on these matters until Sandra changed the direction of the conversation. "Do you think the expectations and perceptions of others have an effect on what we perceive from the crystal skull?"

"You ask a lot of tough questions," said Lenny with a chuckle. "But it does not seem so. My sister became much more religious after she saw the skull the first time but nobody else had a similar experience."

"Weird," Sandra mused. "For some reason, one of the first things that I did when I got home was open up the Bible."

"Did you turn to any particular section? Were you led to a message?"

"I Will Be What I Will Be."

"Yes you will and what does that mean?"

"In Exodus, God identifies himself as 'I Am That I Am', but a footnote said the original Greek text also indicated an identification of 'I Will Be What I Will Be'."

"What does that mean?"

"I don't know. You ask tough questions," answered Sandra. "Maybe it means God will be this to the Christians and will be this to Native Americans and will be this to Hindus and so forth. That would mean we are all on the same team."

The telephone began to ring but both of them knew that budding insights from their crystal skull experience would fuel the fire of many future conversations. "Let's not give Mickey any preconceived ideas about the skull before tomorrow."

One notion became immediately clear to Mickey the next day at the museum, his parents wasted no time going through the facility. "They sure are in a hurry. This has been pretty good."

"The best part is at the end of our little tour," his mother informed him.

"And we are looking forward to spending more time at that exhibit, the crystal skull," added his dad.

When they reached the skull there were two other people there, apparently deciding to leave. Each parent became became immediately consumed with the skull, a situation Mickey found fascinating.

It took a couple of minutes for the crystal skull to capture his interest. "It is just strange." An odd feeling passed through him. "Maybe the skull thinks I'm strange. It think it wants me to know it's a good thing."

For most of the remainder of their time at the crystal skull exhibit, Mickey tried to figure out what the artifact actually was. "I don't care how it was made or anythings else about it. Is the skull alive?" When the crystal skull seemed to change color, Mickey was not surprised. "It wants me to feel the colors." When the skull emitted a sort of electrical, spiritual vibration, Mickey simply accepted it.

"I think the crystal skull is one of the good guys. Superman could use it."

* * *

For the remainder of the day, Mickey felt like something new was going to happen. It did not. "I'm trying too hard to think about the skull. I need to get my chores done."

Splitting firewood required focus. Each swing of the axe eased Mickey's mind. He gathered up an armful of wood and one peice escaped, hitting him on the top of the foot. "Ouch! Gravity hurts!" The pain passed and an unseen frequency or energy field passed from the wood he was holding. His heart energy reached back.

"I feel it! What is it? I feel the wood inside me!" The crystal skull came into Mickey's mind. He walked up the stairs at the back of the house, pausing a moment to look at the star filled sky.

"I think the crystal skull is special for me. It has some old secrets."

Later that night before falling asleep, Mickey thought about how little his friends were interested in hearing about the crystal skull. "Mom and dad sure were interested in what I thought. They didn't tell me much about what they thought about the crystal skull. They just wanted to listen to me. I didn't tell them everything. I couldn't."

Mickey expected vivid dreams. "I wonder if I'll tell anybody if I have a skull dream?" The most intense dreams began just before dawn. Mickey saw an image of his Grandmother Amanda growing younger and going back in time to greet her ancestors. They were his ancestors too. Somehow Mickey recognized his great great grandfather Strong Eagle. He was reaching across the generations to point out Mickey specifically to a white shaman. The two of them were smiling at a bear but the bear changed into a man with fur! Mickey realized the fur man was himself but he continued changing. He could feel himself getting smaller until he was back to his own form. It was then the crystal skull appeared in his dream. The skull was telling him it was going to be important to be happy with people and help them.

When he awoke in the morning, Mickey had an overwhelming desire to divulge his dream to his Grandmother Amanda. "I'll tell mom and dad but I want to talk to grandmother first. A medicine man turned into a bear? She'll know what it means."

CHAPTER NINE

A PATH OF PROGRESS, A STREET OF TRAGEDY

*Seattle, Washington
June 1963*

"Would you ever want to move back to Boston?" Emily asked her husband as he walked through the back door, her speech slightly slurred from the late morning vodka.

"I have thought about it at times. It's just not the same as it was. We remember Boston but Boston would not remember us," stated Clayton.

"Because our friends are here?" She reached for the vodka bottle but reconsidered, deciding to fix some lunch instead.

"That's right. Besides, how would we live? We have the music store to rely on here. I think it would be difficult starting over somewhere else, even Boston."

"We should change the name of the store. We make more money selling music records than we do musical equipment. Maybe we should call it something like 'O'Donnell Play Music Store'."

"That sounds like a store for little kids but your suggestion is well taken."

"Do you want some lunch?"

"I have to finish changing the oil in the truck and then I will be in," answered Clayton as he exited out the back door.

As much as he tried to be lighthearted, there were times when life with his wife could be grim. "I have never stopped loving her and I never will. She is just in such a dreadful rut, almost as bad as it was after our son was killed in Korea. The years after Mark's death brought a dreadful cycle of prescription drugs and alcohol for her. I am her only reprieve from depression. There is no reprieve for me. I'll just try to stay busy running my music store. It is going to pay off. I figure rock 'n roll music is going to continue to grow in the upcoming decade."

Clayton listened to the end of the song playing on the truck radio after he finished changing the oil. "'Rhythm of the Rain' is an appropriate song for a band from western Washington." He headed back to the house, trying to think of an afternoon activity for his 61-year-old wife and himself which would discourage her from drinking away the day.

Frequently Emily wondered about her grandchild. "Would I have less depression if we still had Tessa in our life? I am sure of it. But Loretta seemed to disappear from the planet about the time Tessa turned four years old."

The birthday card Emily sent to Tessa for her fifth birthday was returned to her with a brief note from Loretta. "I have remarried and will be relocating, although it has not yet been determined where." What was worse, her new husband did not want any further connection with anyone in Loretta's life prior to their marriage.

Despite the daily alcohol intake, Emily maintained a constant admiration for her husband. "His love for me has never wavered and I appreciate it. My love for him and my empathy for his patience during the darkest times is my motivation to someday get better."

The twelfth birthday of Tessa was approaching. "I wish I could see her, talk to her, watch her play, or whatever else she does. Would she resemble Mark? All I know is that I always spend more money on booze around Tessa's birthday than at any other time of the year."

The late June weather was warm and clear and the nighttime temperature was in the low 60s, a wonderful Seattle night. "It's a great night to go to a drive-in movie to see 'It's a Mad, Mad, Mad, Mad World'." Emily usually was agreeable to a drive-in movie, more so than a movie theater because she could take booze with her and drink in the car. Her husband was aware of her reasoning but very good or very funny movies had the knack of grabbing her attention. "She will drink less than she would at home if her focus is on the screen."

"Cleopatra" was the only movie in the recent past that Emily enjoyed in the theater. She also enjoyed the Alfred Hitchcock movie "The Birds" but it frightened her so much that she stayed up late and drank after they arrived home.

Clayton's plan worked. There were so many stars and so many crazy antics going on in the "Mad,Mad..." movie that she largely forgot about alcohol. During the drive home a story about a new procedure for retinal operations in the eye was on the radio. "Not for this cowboy," said Clayton. "What if they screw up? Does your brain get laser beamed?"

"In this day and age I am sure that such a medical procedure is safe. They had the first lung transplant this year."

"And there was the first liver transplant."

"I could use one of those."

Clayton cringed and redirected the flow of the conversation. "There are many firsts this year. The nuclear reactor in New Jersey and the Polaris missile on a submarine are firsts."

"Not to mention the first woman in space."

"I didn't realize there was a race for space for women but I guess you have to give that one to the commie bastards."

"We sold $250 million worth of wheat to those enemies," remarked Emily.

"I wouldn't have but nobody asked me. How could the United States possibly trust Khrushchev after he nearly caused the destruction of the earth with last year's Cuban missile crisis? Now he says that 'de-Stalinization' allows no individual liberties for the Soviet citizens. What a nice guy he is."

After a momentary pause Clayton switched on the radio again, changing the station to hear music. "The Times They Are a Changin'" by Bob Dylan was playing and both Emily and Clayton remained quiet during the song. "Here we are in our 60s in age making our living from record sales."

"Will the changing times be good or bad?" Emily asked.

"The answer could be both."

"You know more about that government stuff than I do. I don't trust any government agencies. I don't trust anyone watching over me except you."

"Not everything is a conspiracy."

"It could be. After all, life is an illusion."

"I'm sure the government doesn't tell us everything but that doesn't mean life is an illusion," argued Clayton as he opened the front door of their home.

"What if aliens are trying to make information available to us humans but the government won't share it." After switching on the lights, Emily opened a bottle of gin.

"Or at least control the information. The whole Orson Welles 'War of the Worlds' thing gives them an excuse because they think the public can't handle the truth."

"I'll bet the crystal skull and aliens are connected."

"I wish we could find out somehow," acknowledged Clayton with a yawn. "Space ships don't seem to be anything worldly. President Kennedy's plan to put a man on the moon by the end of the decade may be somewhat far-fetched but I like that kind of commitment to space technology."

"I love having an Irish, Harvard educated president."

"You are still fond of anything to do with New England. I got a kick out of his 'Ich bin ein Berliner' comments in his speech in West Berlin the other day. He is just another Irishman like me who likes German beer."

The following morning Emily shuffled through the unopened mail while waiting for the televised Martin Luther King speech to begin. "How in the hell is anyone supposed to figure out zip codes? What is so zippy about them?"

"'Zip' is an abbreviation for Zone Improvement Plan."

"It's a good thing you handle paying the bills. Oh look, there's Dr. King."

"There are supposed to be a couple hundred thousand people there."

"I have a dream," thought Emily during the televised oration. "What a beautiful speech." She looked at her husband, always supportive. "He's happy despite me."

"Free at last, free at last, thank God almighty free at last," echoed Dr. King's words.

"I want freedom," thought Emily. "I want freedom from alcohol. I want Clayton to have freedom from my alcoholism as well."

When the speech was finished, Emily announced, "I want a new life."

Clayton's eyes went wide in surprise but his response was silent.

"I want more peace of mind. I know my drinking has been the worse part of 'for better or worse' for you. Now it's time for me to get medical help and quit drinking."

"I have confidence in you. What prompted all this?"

"I read a book called 'The Feminine Mystique' by Betty Frieden. She claims bored housewives are unfulfilled women. I don't want a new career but I do want a new personal identity."

September was a tough but good month for Emily, spending more than half of her time in a clinic for alcohol recovery. Both she and Clayton expected a physical hell but only Emily had to experience the sickly purgatory. She expected to deal with demons. "I just need to let them fuck me and get it over with. Maybe thinking about something else will help."

Serendipity in the form of a letter did help. "It's from Anna Mitchell-Hedges! I haven't heard from her in years." Perusing the letter Emily learned of the death of Mike Mitchell-Hedges four years earlier and of Anna taking the crystal skull to exhibitions across the continent. "I can't believe she was in Spokane earlier this year. I would have gone if I would have known."

Each day Emily began meditating with a picture of the crystal skull Anna had enclosed in her letter. She tried to mentally create a crystal skull experience based upon her memories. The process was a metamorphosis. "The color of my hope and healing changes everyday like a different color of the crystal prism."

While she grew stronger in rehabilitation, Emily nonetheless kept her crystal skull exercises to herself. "I might get committed for idol worship, matter over mind." Something about the minor guilt of her secret skull "affair" made Emily feel alive. "Making up silly myths at my age," she skoffed to herself without revealing her methods. "Besides, I get strong thoughts about Tessa when I meditate about the skull. Is that intuition? Is my granddaughter okay? The stronger I get the more hope I have of seeing her again."

Emily began to enjoy what previously did not matter to her. "Nothing has made me feel better since I began rehabilitation than the Dodgers beating the Yankees in the World Series. Sandy Koufax kicked their butts!"

"The World Series was a good diversion for us forever Red Sox fans because the Yankees lost," agreed her husband.

In October, Clayton had an announcement for Emily. "Record sales at the store have been really good. It looks like we can afford to go to Dallas for Thanksgiving after all."

"That makes me happy. I haven't seen Victor since his wife passed three years ago. I haven't flown anywhere in years. By the way, I heard the east coast radio stations are playing songs by some English band, 'The Beatles'. Has anyone asked about them?"

"Never heard of them. Sales are still steady for 'Surfin' USA', 'Wipeout', 'Sugar Shack', and 'He's so Fine'. I hope everyone's records sell."

"I just thought of something important about the trip. I need to go shopping!" exclaimed Emily.

"Things really are getting back to normal around here."

* * *

"Victor, I'm the last person in the world who should say this," began Emily, "but you look like you could use a drink. You have been restless and detached since we got here yesterday. What is it?"

"I'm sorry I haven't been a better host," her 69 year old brother responded. "It will be over soon. Where's Clayton?"

"He's still in the shower. Vic, I know you are not a President Kennedy guy, but can we go to see the motorcade? We certainly didn't know he was coming to Dallas when we planned our trip here but we sure would like to see the old Irish boy."

"Don't say that about me not being a Kennedy guy. I didn't vote for him but it's important that people don't think I'm against him. Sure, we can go. I know a safe spot."

"I'll make some breakfast before we go."

At the table, Victor announced, "Look here," pointing to an ad in the Dallas-Fort Worth newspaper. "It is sponsored by the 'American Fact-Finding Committee'. Never heard of them. They claim to be neutral but they attack all of Kennedy's policies." The 'committee' calls themselves an 'unaffiliated and nonpartisan group of citizens who wish truth'.

"That sounds like the right wing extremists in this country," noted Clayton.

"Don't say that," warned Victor. "I don't trust them anymore. Too many things are going on."

"That ad makes it look like somebody is getting ready to blame somebody for something," remarked Emily.

"They'll probably blame the wrong people for the wrong reason," speculated Victor with an absent minded expression.

Victor knew the city well and found a place to wait for the motorcade where they could sit on a brick flower bed planter. They all stood up to get a better view when the Lincoln Continental convertible passed in front of them and Clayton snapped a photograph. Emily took a quick peek at her brother who was himself straining to get a good look at the president, the first lady and Governor Connelly. Their view was a good one but it lasted perhaps fifteen seconds. Some of the crowd began dispersing as the president's car turned the corner and went out of view.

"I know a good place for a Texas barbecue lunch," said Victor. He winced at what sounded like three separate firecrackers in the distance.

"I wouldn't be shooting off firecrackers around the Secret Service," said Clayton.

Just before entering the restaurant, Emily pointed to people on the opposite side of the street. "What's going on? It's like you can see a rumor spreading." When the slow moving wave reached their side of the street, Emily stopped a woman whose face resembled the horror of knowing she was about to vomit.

"The president has been shot," the woman said hollowly.

Lunch was quickly forgotten by the group. Instead they proceeded directly to Victor's 1961 Chrysler so they could listen to the radio. Just after arriving home they heard the news that the president was dead. The ensuing confusion prompted various possible theories from the three. "Is it a coup attempt by Lyndon Johnson? Did he organize the assassination through connections in his home state? Is it a Soviet plot for retribution of their failed attempt to place missiles in Cuba? Is it the Cubans? Is it a worldwide left-wing conspiracy?"

"I fear a right wing extremist conspiracy," expressed Clayton. "The Dallas locals on the street were suggesting that possibility. The newspaper ad today points that way too."

"It's more than that," postulated Victor. "This whole thing is not a surprise to some people, some who have nothing to do with politics."

"That makes it a conspiracy," declared Emily. "How do you know anything about any of this?"

"I don't know, I don't. I have just heard rumors."

Partisan politics were put aside as Victor, Emily and Clayton remained glued to the television. The many times Emily wept was noticed by Clayton. "I am proud of her for still rejecting alcohol during this crisis. Maybe being around big brother helps."

Later in the day the three learned of the arrest of Lee Harvey Oswald. "I know the guy who found Oswald a job and an apartment after he moved back to the United States from Russia," noted Victor. "He asked me about apartments in the area. He was working for some bigshot Texas oil man with CIA connections."

To a certain extent, there was some channel flipping among the three major networks but for the vast majority of the time they watched Walter Cronkite on CBS. On the third day Emily joined her brother and husband after washing the dishes. "They are about to move Lee Harvey Oswald to another location," Victor informed her. "I guess this means no government overthrow is likely." Suddenly a man jumped in front of Oswald and shot him point blank in the torso.

"I cannot believe what we just saw," Emily stated as tears scattered down her cheeks. "It happened so fast."

"That has to be the first time in the history of global television that a homicide was witnessed live," surmised Clayton.

"They are already identifying the shooter as Jack Ruby! I met him once," remarked Victor. "I purchased scalped tickets from him for a Texas versus Southern Methodist football game several years ago. Somebody sure must have something on him to make him do that."

"Maybe the whole thing is a mafia conspiracy," suggested Emily. "The Kennedy brothers were after the mafia."

"The CIA knows how to use the Mafia," Victor noted quietly. "The CIA is everywhere and is much different than people think."

"They aren't in outer space," quipped Clayton.

"Don't be so sure," answered Victor.

The exhausted trio refrained from further speculation. The only thing to do was simply watch. All network programming was suspended after the president was killed but people were not watching less television. Indeed, the entire nation was being held together by the live telecasts. "Television has become like a friend to a bereaved family," Clayton observed.

"This whole funeral business for President Kennedy is so sad," groaned Emily. "Still everyone wants closure to these days of fear and tragedy."

"Prominent people in the world die every year, including Robert Frost, Aldus Huxley, and baseball great Rogers Hornsby this year," noted Victor, "but this is the biggest."

"But I think no other single death in this century will have such an impact on America," added Clayton.

Emily could not recall previously seeing her older brother cry except when they were children. "I am sure he had his private emotional moments when father passed, but I didn't see them."

After the horse with no rider with a boot turned backwards in the stirrup was broadcast, Victor declared, "I'm with you two. I've never witnessed an exhibition like that one before. That image that will never leave me."

"Everyone's eyes are on Washington D.C. but I'm still afraid of Texas," revealed Clayton. "What are investigations going to find? Where will it lead?"

Just as Emily could never remember Victor previously weeping, she similarly did not remember hearing her brother previously praying. He did so when they sat down to Thanksgiving dinner six days after the assassination of the president. Everyone helped in the preparation of the meal. "I am so glad for the fellowship of our time together," Victor informed his guests. "I know it's not the best way to spend a vacation."

Clayton and Emily were to leave the next day. "Our one and only trip to the state of Texas has been more unpredictable than anyone could have imagined," commented Emily. "All of us are still in a state of shock over what happened. At least now we know there was not an attempted takeover of the government or an invasion by another country. Television programming and sporting events starting up again seems like medicine for our festered mental and spiritual wounds."

"Television coverage will be different from now on," predicted Clayton. "America's 'need to know' about politics, war and scandal will never be the same."

"The Cold War has already crapped on us," added Emily, "and it isn't getting any better."

"Still," cautioned Victor, "it may be dangerous to know even some of the truth. The Cold War isn't what people think. I think it is part of a bigger, secret war."

* * *

"The world certainly changed in our absence," reflected Clayton after returning from Dallas. "Our home feels like a haven of security."

Having arrived home on a Friday night, Clayton spent the following day at the music store. The weather cleared after an early morning rain. Emily bundled up for the 45 degree weather, which seemed very cool after their stay in Texas. "I want to spend much of the afternoon outside." She built a fire by the lake and began reading a book.

It was not long before one of her neighbors briefly joined her. Emily read another two or three pages and then was joined by an elderly neighbor couple. Afterward, she had to laugh at herself for considering them elderly. "I am 61 years old and the neighbor couple is perhaps two years older than Victor. It helps to think young."

Before the afternoon was finished another five people came and went, some of them actually bringing some driftwood to throw on the pile for future fires. The one common theme in all of their conversations was the assassination of the president. Emily grew tired of recalling her tale of the Dallas trip after the third time, "but it is just as well to get most of the story telling done in one day. At least this way the story told will be nearly the same for each neighbor."

The early darkness surprised Emily. "The days are much shorter than in Dallas. I shouldn't be surprised after a few decades in the northwest."

Clayton left for work before daylight and returned home in the dark, although the time span was just over nine hours. "That's a nice beach fire," he said as he approached.

"I have been out here most of the afternoon, except for an occasional trip to the bathroom. Some of the neighbors have stopped by to visit with me."

Clayton threw a couple of pieces of wood on the fire. "Let's roast hot dogs."

"That makes me think of Fenway franks."

"Speaking of Boston," Clayton said, "I forgot to tell Victor that I still have the Red Sox hat. He always wanted to buy it from me."

"What is left of it. It is too worn out to wear anymore."

"I will get a new one when the Red Sox win the World Series. Someday the curse of Babe Ruth has got to end."

"Curses; do you still think they are real?"

"You have asked me that many times. They certainly are to people who think they are cursed. Maybe that is what breaks them, convincing people they can break them."

That night Emily dreamed of her late son Mark riding with Jackie Kennedy in the presidential motorcade. When Emily awoke the next morning the crystal skull came to mind. "Anna mentioned in her letter that the skull was going to be exhibited at the 1964 World's Fair in New York. After that it is going to be tested extensively for several years. Why didn't they exhibit it at the Seattle Worlds Fair? I wonder if Clayton is up for a trip to New York?"

In her private meditations while still in bed, Emily tried to bring the crystal skull to mind in a similar manner to when she began rehabilitation but she had trouble concentrating. Her energy became restless as though the life force in her itched. "Something's wrong. Is this intuition? I should call Victor. Maybe something is wrong with my granddaughter instead."

CHAPTER TEN

RUN FROM THE PAST, TRIP INTO FEAR

Colville, Washington
November 1963

"Why isn't everyone scared like me?"

Tessa glanced through the doorway between the living room and dining room where her little brother Randy was working on a jigsaw puzzle. "He's only seven. He doesn't really know about being scared. I'm only twelve years old but I know enough to be scared of the world."

Now in the sixth grade, many times she had practiced the drills at school in case of nuclear attack. She learned to hide under a desk. She learned how to sit with her back against the hallway wall, hands clasped to brace the back of her neck. She watched a movie about the devastation of the atomic bomb. "And I know the drills won't help."

Tessa thought about the Cuban missile crisis the year before, when the world was waiting for the end. "I will never forget how scared I was when I rode my bicycle anywhere, knowing I might be alone when the bomb was dropped. Would it matter? Would it be better to see my mother and brother die before me? Would we die together at the same time?" Tessa never worried much about her stepdad. "I don't like him very much."

Tessa turned her attention back to the television set. "I wonder why mom and my stepdad Teddy stopped watching. They weren't watching when Oswald got shot. I had to tell them. They only watched television for a while after that. Maybe they are just afraid of what might happen next."

"Randy is lucky. He doesn't have to be afraid."

* * *

Before putting on her sweater, Loretta briefly examined the bruise on her arm. "How should I explain this one if the kids ask?" She saw herself in the mirror shaking her head sadly as she was pulling the sweater into place. "Tessa will know how it happened anyway. She isn't fooled by excuses. Sometimes I wonder how I fool myself."

The funeral for the slain president was about to begin on television. "I hate the world sometimes. Most of the time I blame my hatred on my parents. But in my heart I know many of my problems are my own doing."

In 1956 Loretta and Tessa moved to the Colville Indian Reservation in eastern Washington. She married Teddy that year and one year later their son Randy was born. "He is such a beautiful child. He looks like Teddy in some ways but I can also see so much of my father and mother in my son's features. Somehow I want to block them out mentally as much as I can."

But she thought about them now. "I cannot help it. This whole assassination thing and ideas of conspiracy makes me think about my parents. It was nearly eight years ago that my father told me the truth about what happened to my mother and about their lives as government operatives." She remembered it somberly now. "I simply accepted his story and moved away with Tessa to Colville." She left her widowed father a note: "We are going away somewhere that I hope you will not try to find."

"Why live in Colville? It just is so much the opposite of Los Angeles." She actually did not plan to go there specifically, she just started driving towards Canada. There was a "help wanted" sign in the store where she stopped for groceries. "That is a good enough reason to start a new life here."

Loretta always thought it was extremely unfair that she took her young daughter out of the lives of her
late husband's parents. "But it had to be done. It is all or nothing. Besides, my father would contact Mark's parents to find out my location." Many times, Loretta wanted to change her mind about Clayton and Emily; almost every time a new bruise appeared on her body or face.

"They are only a couple hundred miles away as the crow flies but I cannot contact them. It is all or nothing. Besides, my husband would treat me with extreme vengeance."

As Loretta watched the funeral procession for John F. Kennedy on television, her tears were nearly constant. Those tears however were actually for the memories of the funerals of Mark and of her mother.

Tessa knew very little about her real father and even less about her grandparents. "I know my dad died in war while helping others to heal from wounds. Mom says my grandparents have been dead for a long time. She hardly knew them or remembers them herself."

As for the parents of her real father, she had no memories of them. "I remember getting birthday cards and Christmas presents when I was younger. They are probably dead now too. I remember drawing a picture with color crayons for them when I was little." Tessa put it in the mailbox, addressed simply to "Grandma and Grandpa O'Donnell". She was surprised and disappointed when the mailman gave it back to her at the mailbox the next day, explaining it needed an address and a stamp. "When I asked mother about it she told me nobody knew where they moved. There were no more cards or gifts from them either. They probably died and went to heaven with my real dad."

"Not everyone gets to go to heaven. I am sure mother will go to heaven. I am also sure my stepdad Teddy will go to the other place."

* * *

Some of Tessa's friends at school had developed an interest in boys but Tessa did not see why boys were any different than any other friends until kissing was explained to her. "Yuck! I remember Teddy and mom kissing but they don't do it much anymore. Maybe kissing makes things worse and that is why they quit. It would sure make things worse if I started kissing the boys at school."

Tessa knew she was different from her classmates. "Having a dead real father is very different." But it was more than that. "Mother always tells me that I am 'a very special being'. It has to be true, I just don't know why. It is probably one of those, 'you'll know when you get older' things. Maybe I have to figure it out for myself. I'm sure it is going to be different than being a princess or president of the United States. My father probably would have known if he was still alive. One thing is for sure; very special people get to go to heaven. I will just have to figure out the way there myself."

On the last day of November, Tessa was surprised to wake up to four inches of new snow. There was no school that day anyway so she convinced Teddy to get the sleds out right after breakfast. She found a nearly fully used candle and tried to get the sled runners as slick as she could.

"I want to go sledding too," insisted Randy.

"That's fine with me just so long as I can go to the bigger hills with my friends later this afternoon," Tessa announced. Privately she thought, "If Randy gets left behind, he'll put up a fuss and get in trouble. Teddy can be real mean to him when he gets in trouble. He is meaner to Randy than to me, probably becuse he is a boy and is supposed to be tough. I hate it when Randy gets punished, especially when Teddy has been drinking."

Sledding was a great deal of fun. Tessa and Randy worked up a sweat hauling their sleds up the hill time after time. There were several other kids there too and they traded sleds, toboggans, and innertubes. Some of their energy was spent just laughing really hard because some of their crashes were so funny.

Before Tessa and Randy came in for lunch they made snow angels in the yard. "Let's make believe real angels will be able to see the snow angels. That way the angels will know there are children in the house who need their help," Tessa explained.

Randy was tired after lunch and wanted to watch television. He patiently watched the end of the football game his dad was watching. He missed the morning cartoon shows but he did not mind. "Sledding is more fun. There are some good shows on television in the afternoon anyway," he told his sister. Teddy went into town and Loretta did not care which shows Randy watched, but she joined him for "My Friend Flicka" and "Rin Tin Tin."

Tessa was not real interested in the shows. She waxed the sled runners again and waited for her friends to call on the telephone. The exhilaration was worth the wait. "It sure is harder to climb the bigger hill though." As Tessa grew increasingly tired she paced herself by accepting rides on the four person toboggan. "That way I don't have to drag a sled by myself when I walk back up the hill."

There were a couple of near disasters. One time Tessa was lying on her sled while going down the hill when several kids failed to get off the trail as she approached. She swerved to miss them and crashed into a fallen tree, snapping off a couple of dozen small branches from the long dead Ponderosa pine. She was not harmed. The second disaster did not involve Tessa but she saw it. A boy visiting during the long Thanksgiving weekend accidentally put his lower lip on the metal part of the steering handles. He pulled away instinctively, leaving the contacted part of his lip on the sled. His scream was bloodcurdling as he rolled off the sled partway down the hill. His friend steered the sled to the bottom of the hill with his feet while the new kid kept his sleeve against his wound before they rushed him home.

As darkness approached Tessa sat on a tree stump waiting for her turn on the toboggan. Waiting with her was Bart, a 15-year-old ninth grader. Both of them were tired and little was said. "He is a high school boy. He won't want to talk to a sixth-grader."

"Look at that!" Tessa was startled because Bart gave her a nudge with his elbow. "Look at that!" He pointed to a rocky but treeless hill about 200 feet from them.

Quickly, yet with little effort, someone had emerged from among the huge basalt areas and was walking up the hill towards another set of rocks.

"Wow, look how fast he is walking!" Bart said, climbing to his feet. "What is that?"

"Look how big it is," stammered Tessa, mildly afraid of saying something dumb.

For just a moment the object of their attention moved completely away from the rocks and had a completely snowy, white background.

"Is that a bear? It must be," remarked Bart.

"It is as big as that tree," observed Tessa, "but it walks like a man. Shouldn't bears be hibernating?" She suddenly felt bigger herself, bigger than Bart. She felt like every hair on her body was growing. Tessa tried to ignore the sensation as she continued watching.

Just then the creature turned his head as if it was looking back at them. The two of them could not see any distinct features in the twilight and neither of them spoke. They just continued watching for the next several seconds until the creature could no longer be seen.

"I can't believe we saw a bear," exclaimed Bart.

Tessa did not comment. She did not want to say anything stupid. "Bears do not look like that or walk like that," she thought. "I have seen a bear before, at Twin Lakes." She briefly recalled surprising a bear while riding bicycles with other kids on a camping trip.

Nervously Tessa ventured a comment. "I don't think it was a bear." Bart did not disagree.

Later that evening, Tessa told her family about what she and Bart had seen. "I think your imagination has created an image different than reality. Did Bart think it was a bear?" Loretta asked.

"I think he did, yes."

"Then he was right," Loretta returned. "He is older and was probably less frightened. His imagination wasn't playing tricks on him."

"We've seen a bear, Tessa and me," volunteered Randy. "It was real scary."

"It was closer than the bear you saw today," Loretta continued. "And it was light outside then. You just could not see the bear very well tonight."

During the conversation, Teddy remained quiet. Typically he was known to venture an opinion about virtually anything regardless of whether or not he had a factual or rational viewpoint. "It could have been something different," he finally said.

Tessa was mildly surprised at his limited support. She did not ask for his opinion. "He probably said what he did because he wants me to do something."

In her bed that night, Tessa resolved, "I'll get one of my friends to go with me tomorrow to look for footprints." It did not take very long for her to begin drifting off to sleep after exerting so much energy during her activity in the snow that day. She heard Teddy ask her mom to get him another beer before she succumbed to slumber.

That night, Tessa's dreams were strange. She got up to go to the bathroom at one point and when she went back to bed her dream continued where it had been interrupted. She later told her mother, "I was lost. Everyone I thought I might know turned out to be someone else. They looked like people I know until I got closer but there was something different about everyone. They had braces, or a mustache, or something different. It was like there was a someone else for everyone. Even you seemed different. And nobody recognized me. And my dream last night was the end of the story from dreams the three nights before."

Her family members never were particularly interested in her dreams. "I am not surprised by my dream. I dreamed the same four part dream story once two years before this one and once the year before that. Maybe it is just part of being 'very special' as mother always says."

After breakfast she tried to quit thinking about her dream but she could not. "There has to be some kind of meaning I am missing. Why couldn't anybody recognize me? In my dream I can know the others even if they don't look like they usually do. There must be one simple answer. I must have changed. Somehow I must look different to them."

If this dream were to happen again sometime, Tessa wanted it to end differently. "It is possible. I just need to find the one person in my dream who recognizes the changed me. Who will that be? And how can I recognize him if I don't know who he is?"

A wave of relaxation came upon Tessa and she welcomed it. Her resolve to figure out the dream was at least partially successful. "Now I know it is a 'he' who will change the ending of my dream. I am sure everything will have a happy ending."

It was early when Tessa started her day. Only Randy was awake, quietly playing with his Lincoln Log set, designing and building a house with the wooden toys. Both children grew up learning how to be quiet when everyone else was asleep. "Getting Teddy mad in the morning makes everyone have a bad day." Tessa thought. She made them both a bowl of cereal. As she ate, she did her usual practice of reading almost everything on the cereal box.

While pouring another bowl of cereal, Tessa suddenly remembered, "I am going to find the footprints of what we saw yesterday." She jumped out of her chair to peer out the window, looking at the sky to see if more snow might be likely. She watched steady drips directly in her sight line.

"It is melting," she said, somewhat surprised at her spoken words rather than a silent thought. Randy paid no attention to her, the sound of crunching cereal occupying his ears. She looked at the clock. "It is 7:15, not even light out yet." Her heart sank. "It will be melting much more quickly when the sunlight is full. It is windy too." She knew what that meant, a "Chinook wind". "The snow will melt fast. The playground at school tomorrow will be a huge, sloppy field. I remember the teacher making a boy wear a plastic bag dress last year because he had got too wet during recess to wear his pants."

She went back to her cereal. It would be impossible to find any footprints on the rocky hill today.

Waking at about 7:20, Loretta knew her children were awake. She could hear the cereal being poured into bowls in the kitchen. She was also confident Tessa would be fine taking care of the early breakfast so she thankfully rolled over to go back to sleep. "I can get 45 minutes to an hour more sleep," she thought to herself. Before long she was dreaming again. The real early morning dreams were the ones she remembered best and somehow she thought about that in her dream. It was like it was a signal of premonition narrated by her dream voice instructing her how to remember it:

> "Riding in a car, relaxed, I suddenly discovered I was alone in the back seat. The dream driver was no longer there and the automobile was moving by itself. I felt the car leave the road and plunge downwards into water. My mind skipped the details of my escape from the vehicle and I found myself swimming upward toward the surface. The water was not uncomfortable or cold, but I began to feel alarmed that I could not reach the surface very quickly. I was running out of air but still I did not panic. Somehow I understood I was still in the midst of the dream. Maybe I could save myself but I was not worried. At the same time I realized I could scarcely hold my breath any longer. Glimpsing the surface, I tried to convince myself to try harder. My increased effort was using up my oxygen! I had to try to breathe! I took a short involuntary breath but I found that the water did not bother me. I made my body function somehow but I knew I would not make it to the surface. My mouth opened and water entered my body, yet I was conscious. Am I drowning? No, I was just changing. My mind found a way to deal with the water. But I no longer wanted to be in the water

so I willed myself awake, or at least to another dream segment. It was the crystal skull! It has been a long, long time since I dreamed about the crystal skull. I moved closer to pay attention to it. Suddenly the skull became alive. Or maybe not alive, it was just becoming human looking. Was this the person the skull was patterned after? It was a woman with dark hair and dark eyes. Someone called to her. The skull went back to crystal. Someone is saying something."

Loretta woke up. Teddy's finger was in her vagina. "Roll over. I want a quickie before I have to get up."

Loretta did not typically dwell upon her dreams. "They just are another world I visit but seldom understand. I know psychologists or psychiatrists or hypnotists or whatever think they can decipher meaning from dreams but I doubt it. That kind of analyzing is like trying to interpret a painting that someone only described to you."

Nevertheless, both the crystal skull and surviving drowning during her dream stuck with Loretta. As in the past, she wondered about any hidden meaning. "It just seems like the dream is alerting me of potential change. The skull changed. My body changed to breathe underwater. Is something else going to change? Who was the face on the skull? She seemed like some sort of new friend." Somehow this unknown friend was giving Loretta the feeling that she would be safe despite changes, whatever and whenever they were.

Loretta took this to mean her family would be safe as well. "We just need to stay on the positive side of the world." The term "accentuate the positive" rattled through her brain many times in the next two days. It seemed to be an old lesson revisited and nothing creative. "I am probably just reacting to the whole assassination thing." Still, she found herself smiling and hugging her children more often than she usually did. "The correct path should be a happy one, even if I don't know where the path is headed."

* * *

Late Tuesday afternoon it began to rain. The upper 30 degree weather was chilling and Tessa and Randy stayed inside watching the

"Captain Cy" and "Wallaby and Jack" cartoon shows with live studio audiences comprised of children. "Mom, that acrobat kid is on again!" Loretta took time from heating up leftovers to watch but otherwise she was content to read a book.

Teddy was later getting home than usual. "He must be at the tavern," reasoned Tessa. It was not an unusual occurrence but it sometimes spelled an obnoxious time when he arrived home.

"Leftovers again for dinner? Are you just too lazy to buy something else or are you just too lazy to cook?"

"Dinner will be ready soon," Loretta quietly informed her husband. "Could you please move your archery stuff from the kitchen table?"

"For leftovers? I ain't finished making arrows yet."

Tessa walked into the kitchen. "What do you want?" Teddy angrily asked.

"Should I set up the TV trays?" Tessa asked calmly, trying to defuse the situation as she had at other times in the past.

"Shut up and get out of here!" Teddy yelled, shoving her back out of the room.

"Please calm down, you might hurt her."

"You shut up too you dumb cunt!" Teddy screamed, squeezing his wife's arm hard enough to make her wince.

Entering the kitchen, Randy ran toward his parents. "Leave mommy alone!"

The drunken parent let go of his wife and delivered a backhand to the jaw of his seven-year-old son who fell backwards, banging his head on a kitchen cabinet. Randy was stunned but not unconscious.

Loretta reacted by pounding her fists anywhere she could upon her husband, including one blow to the back of his head. Although not knowing specifically what might happen next, Loretta always followed her own advise, "I would rather be the object of abuse than my children."

Teddy punched her just below the collarbone and Loretta staggered backwards against the kitchen counter. He again grabbed her roughly by the arm and picked up a large kitchen knife, holding it to her throat. "I'm tired of you getting tough with me!"

"Put down the knife!" Tessa screamed at her stepfather. Loretta had her back turned to her daughter but Teddy could see her distinctly. He let his wife's arm drop and lowered the knife from her neck. Tessa held tight a partially completed arrow to Teddy's bow. The string was drawn as far as her adrenaline would allow.

"You're a tough little cunt, just like your mom."

"Put it down honey," Loretta recommended.

"Shut up!" Teddy yelled, backhanding his wife with the hand still clutching the knife. He followed that hit to her arm with consecutive punches to her torso, confident Tessa would never let the arrow fly.

He guessed incorrectly. "Holy fuck!" The arrow entered his body at the rib cage. Stunned and furious, he turned toward Tessa. She was fearful for her life but remained standing in the same place, horrified at her own actions. Teddy was hurt but nonetheless charged at her with a kitchen knife. Loretta tried to reach for him but missed.

Randy did the only thing he could, sticking his foot up while still lying on the floor. Teddy tripped, twisting to miss the kitchen table. He put his arm up to protect himself during his fall but subsequently the knife in his hand bounced off the table into his neck. The arrow broke off after his body hit the chair before hitting the floor.

The bleeding was heavy and profuse. Loretta stumbled to the phone to call for an ambulance.

Tessa let the bow drop to the floor, taking a couple of small steps backward. She wanted to help Teddy but she was still afraid of him.

Randy walked toward his father. "He's real bloody."

"I think he's going to die," stated Tessa.

It took at least fifteen minutes for the ambulance to arrive. Tessa and Randy were sent to their rooms while the medical people removed the dead body. Both were silent except for the mild sounds of sobbing.

"Some 'very special person'," Tessa sobbed. "This is not what should happen. How can I ever find the way to heaven now?"

CHAPTER ELEVEN

ALONE PATH OF FREEDOM

Los Angeles, California
December 1963

"I wonder how long I've slept?" Lying in a hospital bed, Al squinted at the clock on the nightstand. "I'll be glad to get these digestive tests finished. One more day in here." He gulped down a glass of water with his medicine.

"At age 68, I feel lucky there has not been a lifetime of ailments. I'll be retiring soon. Maybe my physical problems are a signal to retire very soon." The timing of the problems was not lost upon him. His most severe problems began when President Kennedy was killed.

Although the television in the hospital room was on almost continually, Al spent most of the time wrestling with his own memories. "There are a lifetime of thoughts that I have never been able to discuss with anyone. I wonder about my daughter. I know she lives in Washington. I could have her found but it is better to respect her wishes to be left alone. My grandchild is now twelve years old. It probably won't happen but somehow I hope to be able to see them again before my days on earth end. And if I have any other grandchildren, they will get the same respect and love I have for Tessa. I sure do not want to meet Loretta's husband. He mandated that not only me but also Clayton and Emily would not have any contact with my daughter."

In anticipation of his hospital visit, Al compiled a personal history for Tessa to be given along with the proceeds from his will. "Who would believe such a story? During the previous night at the hospital his mind became obsessed with how he should have better described the Black Virgin of Kazan Icon, one of the greatest of all Christian relics from Russia. "It was the miracle icon, representing the Holy Mother of Russia. I saw it only briefly but I helped smuggle it out of Russia during the Revolution."

"It was all so long ago, back when I believed a Christian relic could make a difference. The murder of my wife, of both wives, hardened my heart against God."

"Still, the icon representing the Holy Mother of Russia many times comes to my mind when I think about the crystal skull. From the sixteenth century I think, it had all those rubies, emeralds, pearls and hundreds of diamonds. The White Russians maintained it had powers to sometimes heal the blind."

"Certainly, I never told anyone of my role in the smuggling of the icon, not even members of my family. I sometimes cannot help but wonder if Stalin somehow knew about it. As one of Trotsky's personal drivers, I overheard too many things. I saw the writing on the wall for Trotsky's demise. That is why I agreed to the hideous plan when I was 'volunteered'. I thought my life might be spared. But I could foresee my own demise as well. I had no remaining living family at that time and I knew that I would be used like a test rat. Or test ape as it were. Only in those distant memories do I think of myself as Alexiev Bubkov."

The attention of Al was turned to the television set when something about Lyndon Johnson was announced. "The whole Kennedy assassination ordeal has been so unnerving. At first I thought that son of a bitch Khrushchev finally got him. As much as any person in America, I fear a Soviet attack."

His convictions were not changed when later he learned Lee Harvey Oswald was arrested. "I remember Oswald. The American government asked my opinion about the former Marine when he moved to the Soviet Union in 1959. Was he the only gunman? Maybe but Oswald probably also was ordered to take the action he did."

After the arrest, when the cameras caught Oswald saying he was a patsy, Al was not so sure about his conjecture of orders for the alleged assassin. When Oswald was shot, confusion reigned. "There are a number of potential suspect organizations. Anything could have been plotted and anything can still happen. The Cold War isn't what people think.

The Secret War is becoming much more important. The silent weapons of data processing and international banking and manipulating natural and social energy at every level, even the Vatican, will outlast the Cold War. They believe in their power against nature, against love. Just thinking about it all again makes me feel like crap. I need to get some sleep."

Later that evening, Al's thoughts returned to his final days in the Soviet Union before his escape. He read again what he wrote about his personal story to leave to his daughter. "Will she believe it?" Weakly, Al felt his hair tingle in a remotely familiar way. "There's a full moon tonight."

"The experiment was such a devious plan by Stalin. It was from the mind of a madman. Not even Hitler would have devised a program so far-fetched and ridiculous. Nonetheless, it happened. I recognized the innuendo of my knowing too much about too many things and the message between the lines was perfectly clear. I should 'volunteer' for the program to prove my loyalty. What a joke."

"Volunteer I did but I escaped after the first injection. The science of the experiment I do not understand, including what was actually injected into me. It was some kind of extract from an ape. Was it some kind of sperm or blood? Through all of the years I never could guess what it was and there certainly has been no one to ask. But I fully knew what the purpose was. Stalin wanted his scientists to find a way to produce a hybrid of ape and man, a subhuman being. Such a being could be bred in large numbers to establish a new kind of army. Stalin hoped the new kind of soldier would have at least the basic mental capacities of a human with the strength and dexterity of an ape. My sperm was planted in both a woman and in a female ape. I escaped from the Soviet Union before any results were known."

Al winced at the recollection of how difficult it had been to describe those details in his personal history. "Failure in the tests would have meant certain death. Success would have meant briefly prolonging life."

Feeling his medicine having an effect on his staying awake, Al clicked off the light on the nightstand and gave in to sleep. The debate in his mind about rewriting his complete personal story would have to wait until morning.

A few hours later, Al awoke thinking about the day his daughter was born. "It makes me smile even now. I was so glad Loretta turned out normal. Every parent is glad about that but it was extremely true for me. I could not help but harbor doubts because of the beginnings of the ape experimentations on me. It was one of the few times I ever attempted a prayer of thanks and appreciation to God."

After getting up to go to the bathroom, Al returned to bed. He decided perhaps some kind of prayer was in order at that very moment. "I don't know what words to say but I guess that does not matter. God, I apologize for not being good at praying. Please grant your blessings upon my daughter and her family." When finished, he was not satisfied with his prayer. "Oh well, I know I cannot be content with it because I don't deserve to be asking God for anything. For that reason, I am not sure my prayer will be heard anyway. It is not time to dwell on such a matter. I lost control of my whole life after I saw the crystal skull the first time yet I want to see it again. Was it a coincidence? But everything turned out fine with Tessa and Loretta. Everything is fine except my spy suff. Neither side is a good guy or bad guy completely and I don't even want the edge side of that coin. I want to go back to sleep. Amen."

At approximately 3 o'clock in the morning, the door to Al's hospital room opened and a man peered
into the room. Very quietly he approached the sleeping patient. Still there were no signs he had disturbed Al enough to wake him.

Carefully, the man looped a belt around the left arm of Al and subsequently secured it to the bed frame. Cautiously moving to the other side of the bed, he grabbed a pillow from the unoccupied bed in the room and suddenly forced it upon Al's face. Anticipating the reaction of Al, he used a knee to hold down the patient's right arm during the expected confrontation. In terror Al awoke and began to struggle.

In a hushed voice, the aggressor proclaimed, "It is time to die Alexiev!"

Al fought as well as he could. During his struggle, in his mind, he was indeed Alexiev again. A fleeting image of the crystal skull raced past his thoughts. "My secrets are being extinguished. I can't get past the negative."

As his life began departing from him, he was flooded with a new feeling, a strange feeling. "It is a sense of a new kind of freedom. All I ever wanted was real freedom." His thoughts raced much faster than his fight to live. Alexiev felt throughout his being that his freedom from everything before meant freedom toward something new. "At last, zero."

His acquiescence to the new freedom was accompanied by two words from his killer. "Goodbye comrade."

CHAPTER TWELVE

GRACE BALLS OF FIRE!

Spokane, Washington
May 1975

"Hello, I'm here!" A couple of minutes later Margaret joined her mother and her father in her childhood bedroom for her Saturday morning weekly visit.

"Hello dad!" Margaret said cheerfully, trying to perfect her casual act against the shock of seeing her thin, jaundiced father. Cancer had stripped him of perhaps 60 pounds from his days of a slightly plump 195 pounds. "You look chipper today."

Everyone in the family knew, as did Jason himself, that the disease would claim him soon. How soon was not known. It was a topic no one wanted to discuss.

"Your father and I have been talking a few things over," Amanda said, "and we think it is a good idea if you could ask the girls to make arrangements to come visit your father pretty soon."

Jason smiled at Margaret. "Don't be alarmed. I'm not going to kick the bucket yet. I just want to have some time to pay my respects to my loved ones."

Tears began to accumulate in Margaret's eyes and she tried hard to not let them streak down her cheeks. "They can't come home this weekend but they probably can make it next weekend. They both are writing reports due soon in several classes."

"My little twin Cougars. That should work out just fine," Jason said. He chuckled briefly. "Notice I didn't say I was in a hurry, or to take your time?"

Margaret could not help but smile. Her father's request seemed sad. "I sure am grateful he did not request a last heartfelt conversation with me today. Still, I will have to prepare the girls for what they will face. It has been several weeks since they visited their grandfather and his appearance has changed."

Amanda had finished making lunch for her daughter so they excused themselves to go to the kitchen. Jason seldom had much of an appetite. "Lenny and Sandra are going to visit us tomorrow," stated Amanda. "Your brother seems to be pretty good at hiding his grief, but I know he worries. Sandra tries her best to help him deal with it all, bless her heart."

Margaret nodded her affirmation of what her mother just said as she continued eating her sandwich. After a gulp of apple juice she asked, "What kind of talk do you think dad has in mind for the girls, or for me?"

"I don't know dear. He will probably let them know how proud he is of them and how much he loves them despite having such a rotten mother," Amanda stated with sarcasm and a twinkle in her eye that was quite familiar to her daughter.

"It is a miracle indeed. Of course, I could have been much more rotten if I tried to be just like my parents."

"And I'm sure your father will agree when it is his time to give you his respects."

* * *

In the following weeks, Jason regretted not being able to appreciate the transformation of nature from spring to summer. "I can see only bits and pieces of spring."

Margaret and Amanda found at least a partial cure for his anxiety. "A hospital bed with wheels!" Jason could thus be moved into the living room with hillside views in the large picture window and into the dining room with views of the creek and pasture.

"This is nice," acknowledged Jason. "Before I could sit in a wheelchair to see outside but it was hard to stay comfortable."

With the summer solstice approaching Lenny announced, "It bothers me that dad has to spend all of his time indoors. I'm going to build a ramp to move either the wheelchair or the rolling bed out to the yard. The bed is light enough to be pushed by most people, except you mom. It isn't going to help anything if you hurt yourself."

Enjoying the temperatures in the low 80s on a mid June evening with Lenny, his father recalled a similar time of year in the distant past. "It was 48 years ago when you took the header onto the cement floor and busted up your skull. I thought for sure you were a goner."

"I must not have thought I was a goner, but I do think about it once in a while. I think I maybe knocked some wires loose and that is why I have no sense of smell."

"Maybe. Some people say that everything happens for a reason but I sure have not figured out a reason for that one."

"There has already been enough weird stuff in our lives for creating our own kind of reality, our own different way of looking at things. I agree, cracking my head open didn't seem like any kind of silver lining for that."

"Much of my time lately has been spent trying to reconcile many of those bizarre things in this world. Where do the UFO phenomenon, and sasquatches, and the crystal skull fit into the scheme of things?" Jason sincerely inquired. "How are they reconciled with the Christian view of the world?"

"And why does our family get so genuinely caught up in these things?" Lenny added. "Why is it that only some people have these kinds of experiences? Everyone else thinks weird kind of stuff is crazy."

"Not everyone, but the vast majority do indeed. I actually really have enjoyed the increasing popularity of the bigfoot in recent years."

"Like the two bigfeet made from plaster you gave me for Christmas?" Lenny inquired with a smile in jest.

"They were supposedly made from real footprints. But it doesn't matter if they really were. It seemed like lighthearted symbolism of our family experiences."

"When Mickey visits, I sometimes see him standing on those two big feet in his bare feet or in his socks. I have seen him talking on the telephone and take off his shoes without thinking about it, standing there until his conversation has ended."

There was a pause in the conversation after a brief chuckle, both still enjoying the moment.

"Dad, as far along as your cancer is, I cannot begin to tell you how grateful I am that you can still laugh about things. You are still very mentally alert."

"Did you think I was just going to be a bitter old vegetable?" Jason inquired and then did not allow a response. "I guess that could have been a legitimate fear by all of you but I just have too much to think about."

"Are you trying to be a philosopher in your old age?" Lenny asked with a sarcastic smile inherited from his mother.

"Not really, but a few clues to the mysteries would be nice. The crystal skull is still a real strange one for me. Lately I have been trying to think of it as a technological work instead of for the purpose of art or religion. Maybe it has ancient knowledge like a computer. Or maybe it is a key to space travel by aliens."

"We'll never know, I guess," sighed Lenny. "But it makes you wonder about how many other ancient mysteries have been lost and will never be found."

The screen door to the ramped porch opened and Sandra walked outside. "Hey boys, it is just about time to eat. Do you want to eat out here Lenny?"

"No, we were just about ready to come in anyway. 'All In the Family' will be coming on soon, dad's favorite show."

"Sandra, you just get better looking everyday," Jason stated.

Lenny was busy transporting his father up the ramp. "It's a good thing she is crazy," he said loud enough for his wife to hear, "otherwise she never would have fallen for me with a family like ours."

* * *

After finishing finals at Western Washington University in Bellingham, Mickey came home to Spokane for a week. "To finish my degree I need to attend summer quarter in a couple of weeks but I am going to see about a part-time job next week," he informed his grandmother on the telephone.

Mickey was told about his grandfather's wish to see family members several weeks earlier when the Western baseball team traveled to nearby Cheney to play Eastern Washington University in a season ending three-game series. His college baseball career was thus ended but the switch hitting centerfielder had lettered all four years, three of those at Whitworth College in Spokane before transferring to Western. He announced his future plans before baseball season ended. "I am going to remain in Bellingham for graduate school in the fall."

The 22 year old had no particular place to go until later that evening and he was more than content to spend time with his grandfather. After discussing the baseball season and the grind of finals week, Jason turned the conversation towards more intimate subjects.

"I know you enjoy college life and the academic world, but what do you suppose is in store for you in the grander scheme of things?" Jason asked.

"The plan now is to eventually get a doctorate degree and become a college professor and baseball coach," answered Mickey.

"I already knew that."

"Mickey Galvin probably doesn't sound like a professor's name, but that's okay. I always seem to be different anyway."

"That actually is more like what I'm talking about. You are more intellectually and spiritually different than any kid, maybe anybody that I have ever known. It seems like someday you are headed for some great contribution to our planet."

Mickey laughed in an easy manner. "I don't know about all that but sometimes I do feel I have some out of the box destiny. Of course grandma and dad have always insisted upon some kind of destiny like it is an ancestral duty."

"The idea of such a destiny was provided by your great great grandfather," Jason stated. "I wish I could have known him. It would have been very nice to pick the brain of a shaman about mysteries like the crystal skull and the sasquatch and even space aliens."

"Many times I have wrestled with ideas of destiny. Does everyone have a destiny? If they do, then it seems free will would not matter." Mickey paused to see if his grandfather was going to provide any dialogue on the subject. He then continued, "On the inside cover of a class notebook I recently wrote: Destiny Is for Those Who Believe in It."

"And do you believe in yours then?"

"I don't know what it is yet but yes I do. If I believe in it, then I will create it as best I can," answered Mickey.

"There seems to be the beginnings of a new respect for American Indians. Do you suppose that is part of it?"

"I'm only part native," Mickey said, "and all sides of my family are a part of me. So it has to be more than just that."

"My side of the family never seemed interested in the notion of destiny and they were not particularly interested in our ancestors."

"I have a different way of looking at things sometimes," Mickey admitted, "but I can't help but wonder if there isn't something in your line of ancestors that has a spiritual link to me. I honestly do not have the same feeling about my mom's father and his ancestry."

"What do you mean?" Jason asked, reaching for a glass of water.

"I don't know. Maybe it is crazy but it seems like maybe somewhere in your Scottish-Irish lifeline there was some kind of wizard or shaman or something."

"That would be a new one on me," Jason said with a tired grin.

"Maybe it is because of mom and grandma, but you have always seemed so racially tolerant and fair. That's not just it but it seems like part of it."

"I do not really mean to pry, especially since I've never been particularly a religious man, but are your spiritual beliefs more Christian or more native?"

"That is a tough one. I don't think about spiritual matters as an either-or. I do seem to have more unusual episodes than any of my friends."

"What do you mean?"

"I cannot begin to explain it all, but I guess I can give you a couple of examples. This might seem crazy, but many times when I'm traveling I project something like a force field around the car. I obviously cannot see anything, but I can feel it. I can feel the energy as it surrounds the car. I think it has saved my life a couple of times too."

"I must say I've never heard of that one before. That does not seem like an Indian or white thing necessarily either. Tell me your other example."

"This one was actually in a class I took. At Whitworth, they had a required class called 'Interpretations of Jesus'. It was a remarkably liberal class given the school is Presbyterian based. Anyway, the final in the class was a creative project to indicate an interpretation. One gal danced, people wrote songs and poems, there was artwork too. One guy even made a replica of the Dead Sea Scrolls."

"So what did you do?"

"Writing is the only thing I can do. I wrote a story and included some wild and esoteric pictures from magazines for effect."

"What was the story?"

"I had no idea what it was going to be when I first sat down to begin writing, but it ultimately became 'The Story of Life as Told by a Raspberry Bush'."

"Hello!" Jason said with a mild laugh. "How is that an interpretation of Jesus?"

"It really is the Genesis story at the beginning of the Bible. When plant life was first created, it was a perfect world for them until the sun went down. Then all of plant life was in fear until the sun rose the next day. The plants then recognized the sun as their savior and in respect all plants from that day forward leaned toward the sun during daylight. When animals and man showed up, the plants had purpose. Of course, the intellect of plants is limited, so they are not supposed to understand everything. But they understand their place in nature and the appreciation of creation and of their savior, the sun. They do not understand why mankind, with a superior intellect, cannot figure out the same for themselves."

"Wow, how did that fly with the instructor?"

"It was 60 percent of our grade so the highest possible score was 60. I received a 59, the highest grade in the class. Someone told me it was the highest grade ever in that class."

There was some noisy activity in the other room and Mickey heard his grandmother call to him. "There is no hurry, but when you get a chance could you get something for me from the top of the hall closet?"

"I'll be right there," he called out and then turned back to his grandfather. "You know grandpa, I really never talk much about these kinds of things with anybody else but you and grandma. I have personal talks with mom and dad but they are not the same."

Jason smiled, feeling an eternal embrace. "So let me ask you, in a more casual mode, what is it that you would really like to be?"

Mickey stood up, ready to help his grandmother. "I guess I would like to be a bra designer."

"What?"

"What can I say grandpa? I really like tits."

* * *

"I still think I could handle most of everything that needs to be done with you," noted Amanda, "but the part-time nursing care at home really does help."

"You are 74 years old and still strong," conceeded Jason, "but my retirement benefits pay for it. The best thing for me is to have some of the burden eased for you. The thought of you as a soon to be widow is still foreign to me."

Occasionally Amanda did leave the house with her husband unattended. "I am out of coffee filters and butter and I need to go to the post office," she announced while gathering her purse and keys. Once outside, Amanda could see a black curtain across the distant horizon with intermittent flashes of lightning.

"I thought I could smell rain," she said aloud. "We could use it." It was the summer solstice, the longest day of the year in terms of daylight.

Glancing at the storm clouds heading eastward, she noticed the velocity of the winds increasing considerably. "It is starting to look like 'the Wizard of Oz' out there," she thought, feeling a sense of urgency to get home. The last mile of the four mile trip to the grocery store and back produced more anxiety as the storm front grew closer.

When she arrived at home, Amanda felt a sense of relief. "Was I worried about getting wet? She scoffed at the thought. "We need rain but I still want to run from it."

"It looks like a gully washer is headed our way!" Amanda announced as she closed the back door behind her. "It is windy too! It almost looks like Dorothy is headed over the rainbow."

Hearing no response, Amanda went into the room where Jason was in bed. "I'm not feeling very well," he said quietly.

Somehow in her heart, Amanda recognized the moment. "You old fart, you aren't leaving just yet are you?"

Jason opened his eyes and saw the tears streaming across the face of his wife of nearly 55 years. "No, I am not leaving just yet." He smiled weakly.

"Do you want me to call a doctor?" Amanda asked as bravely as she could.

"No, no, somebody else. Call our neighbor, Reverend Welker."

"You mean Reverend Walker," Amanda corrected him.

"Whatever," Jason mocked in his Archie Bunker impression.

Amanda laughed briefly, interrupted by her own cough from the sniffling which accompanied her tears. She made the call from the bedside telephone to the surprised neighbor. Neither Amanda nor Jason had ever attended his church but he agreed to come immediately.

"What is this all about?" Amanda questioned her husband, stroking his hand.

"I'm not any good at this stuff but I think I need to try to make a certain kind of peace. I'll need you both."

"Let Divinity purify your pain."

The storm outside grew louder with the rushing gusts and the sound of the advancing thunder. The fiberglass roofing over the back porch rattled helplessly. Lightning flashed brilliantly nearby, lighting up the room during the instant radiance. "He is completely ignoring the violence of the storm," Amanda silently noticed.

"I'm going to call the kids," Amanda said to her husband, who did not object. She hid her feeling that
there was likely little time left.

Amanda called Lenny first because he had farther to drive. Sandra and Mickey responded immediately and they were virtually on their way before Lenny hung up the phone. After the call to Margaret was made, Jason said, "I wish that idiot she divorced would have been faithful to her. She is going to need some comforting."

Amanda remained calm during the phone calls but the tears burst forth again. "You are still thinking about the welfare of our children, a good dad all the way."

The doorbell startled Amanda to her feet. "The reverend must be here."

Within a minute, Amanda escorted him to the room where her husband was waiting. After their initial greetings, Reverend Walker directed the conversation toward the purpose of his visit. "Not having attended our church, I was surprised by your request for me to visit. What can I do for you?"

Jason looked to his wife and then back to the reverend. "I do not have much time left it seems. I've never been a religious man for a very personal reason. I need to confess something and I wanted Amanda to hear it."

"You do know I am not a Catholic priest," the reverend offered.

"It doesn't matter what denomination you are," said Jason. "You are a neighbor."

"Go ahead then," Reverend Walker said, pulling up a chair to the bedside.

"It was a long time ago, after the war." Jason grimaced somewhat, forcing him to pause. "In the war, World War I, my whole platoon was wiped out except me. I survived with a black soldier from another platoon who became my friend. We had a long wait until help came and we had some rough action, just the two of us. Neither of us would have made it without the other."

While Jason paused to gather his thoughts, Amanda became concerned about his comfort. "Can I get you anything dear?"

"No, no, please stay here." Jason continued his confession. "After the war, we made plans to visit each other. I went to Alabama, but when I got there I found out my friend had just been lynched. I could not bear to go to the funeral and quite by accident I found out who killed him. So I found where he lived, waited in his house, killed him and left town. No one really knew I had been there and nobody suspected me."

There was a moment of stunned silence before the reverend responded. "So you have carried this burden with you since then?"

Jason nodded affirmatively while holding back his emotions.

"The war had not ended for you, Jason," Amanda said softly. "You were still fighting for freedom."

"It was still murder," Jason stated, looking into the eyes of his wife. He turned to the reverend, "I chose to neglect religion because I knew I didn't have a chance."

"I cannot say you did the right thing," the reverend said. "All I can advise is to make penance with God, to repent."

"I have not kept count but I have probably tried at least 10,000 times, just in case God might listen. Despite my hopelessness I always had the desire to be as good of a husband, and parent, and neighbor as I could."

Amanda, although remaining quiet, found her emotions unrestrained. She ran her fingers through her husband's gray and white hair. "You saved lives too. The man you killed probably would have killed others."

The reverend began scanning the faces of his neighbors incredulously as a flash of lightning eerily lit up Jason's face. The booming thunder followed quickly.

Jason continued speaking with more sorrow than before. "I'm not expecting to be forgiven. I just wanted Amanda to know about it, with at least some peace from God for her, so she can tell our children. That's all reverend. Thank you."

"The children will be here soon," Amanda said. "You can tell them then if you want."

Jason managed a weak smile. "Goodbye reverend."

The reverend stood up and placed his hand on Jason's shoulder. "God will hear your repentance.
Peace be with you neighbor."

The reverend was escorted outside by Amanda. She shook his hand before he slid onto the driver's seat of his car. Almost simultaneously with the car door closing was a frightfully brilliant flash of lightning, striking the pine tree near them. Both the reverend and Amanda cowered as a limb of the tree crashed down upon the front end of the reverend's car. Neither of them was hurt but both flinched with the subsequent booming thunder.

"Somehow the tree is not on fire," noted Amanda. The first traces of rain were beginning to appear and it would not be long until the rainfall would be heavy. The air was electric and another nearby flash of lightning and subsequent thunder followed.

"Look!" Reverend Welker exclaimed, pointing to the ground behind Amanda.

There on the grass were several balls of fire, seemingly with no flames. The balls of electric energy moved slowly between Amanda and the house. "Will they catch the house on fire? What are they?" Amanda shouted.

Several more fireballs appeared, encircling Amanda and moving near the reverend's car door. "Can you get away?"

Amanda stood still, not sure which way to turn. "Will they hurt me?" She remained speechless but a brief thought passed through her mind. "I should be afraid but I'm not really. How will I describe this to Jason?"

"What are they?" Reverend Welker asked with great anxiety, fearful to step out of the car with a fireball of energy in his path. A fallen branch from the pine tree burst into flame on the other side of the car.

There was no time for analysis and rational reaction was not forthcoming. Instinctively Amanda raised her hands and held them at shoulder level. Her palms faced the fireballs and each seemingly held their position. Wordlessly she moved her hands slowly back and forth before raising her hands higher. Finally she stopped and commanded, "The spirit of the land forgives you Jason!"

"They are lifting off the ground!" The astonished reverend watched Amanda beckon them towards her hands and they responded! Another flash of lightning was farther away and the thunder followed less quickly. The electric energy balls remained suspended, moving away from the house and the car. "They are getting closer to your hands!"

The reverend watched in terrified disbelief as yet another lightning flash occurred. This time with the thunder a torrential rain began to fall. The fireballs began to flicker and gravity reclaimed them. When they hit the ground, perhaps grounded, they were extinguished. Amanda felt her hands drop to her side.

The reverend quickly exited his car and ran several paces to her. "Great Mysteries of God! Are you all right?"

She looked around quickly. "Yes, yes, I am fine," she announced while walking quickly to the house. Her adrenaline surprised her. "I need to check on Jason!" Half turning her head, she shouted, "Thank you for being here!"

The reverend quickly surveyed the dented fender and broken headlight on the front of his Buick. The rain had extinguished the flaming branch on the passenger side of his car. In a state of complete awe and wonder and without haste he walked through the rain and again entered on the driver's side. The rain flying into the open window brought him back to reality. He quickly reached for his electric window switch after turning on the ignition. With the windshield wipers on at the fastest tempo, he finally departed.

"You would not believe what happened out there." Amanda kicked off her shoes and left them on the covered porch. As she passed the refrigerator, she grabbed a dishtowel hanging on the door and began wiping off her arms and wet hair while she kept walking down the hallway.

"Lightning struck…" Amanda stopped in midsentence after seeing her husband. "Oh no."

She did not have to check. Amanda knew he was gone. She sat down in the chair the reverend had used. A duality of feelings passed through her. "I feel so sad and suddenly so lonely. And at the same time I feel a sense of relief that his long suffering has ended."

"Goodbye my darling," she said softly. Tears joined the rainwater on her still wet face. "I am sure you will experience forgiveness on the journey."

Amanda sat gazing at Jason, her swirling emotions laced with wonder at the timing of his passing with the strike of lightning and the ordeal with the fireballs of energy. Just as she began to ponder how to explain to her children the events of the evening, she heard the back screen door.

"Hey! What happened to the pine tree?" Margaret had arrived.

The time of transition had begun.

CHAPTER THIRTEEN

REKINDLED KINDRED

Seattle, Washington
October 1975

"This is one of those times when I sure miss Emily," Clayton noted in his journal. "I know her passing three years ago is part of life. I am thankful she died in her sleep without suffering. I am very thankful for that but I wish she was still alive for this glorious month. The Red Sox are in the World Series."

"The Red Sox team has the look of a champion despite being the underdog to the 'Big Red Machine'. We have the Rookie of the Year and the American League Most Valuable Player in one player, Fred Lynn. Maybe this year, some 57 years after their last World Series title and 55 years since the trade of Babe Ruth, just maybe the curse of the Babe can be broken."

All of Clayton's friends heard him speel his opinion. "Sure, all of us Red Sox fans all suffered broken hearts after the 1967 World Series when Bob Gibson and the St. Louis Cardinals defeated the Sox in seven games. But this year is different. Besides Fred Lynn, the Red Sox have another great rookie, Jim Rice. Each rookie drove in more than 100 runs. The Red Sox won the pennant without Carl Yastrzemski having a good season."

"It is a time to believe in miracles." During the playoffs with Oakland, Clayton received a telephone call that sweetened his life in yet another miraculous way, eclipsing the Red Sox making the World Series.

"Hello, is this Mr. Clayton O'Donnell?"

"Yes, this is he."

"You probably don't remember me." Tessa paused, her nervous anxiety overcoming her. "This is your granddaughter Tessa."

As her words registered, Clayton's first reaction was to regard the call as a hoax. His own tears told him otherwise. "Really?"

Within a week, Tessa visited Clayton at his home. He had sold the home on Lake Washington after Emily passed and he now owned a smaller dwelling overlooking Puget Sound at Redondo Beach, 20 miles south of Seattle. It had been 22 years since Clayton had seen Tessa and he was not sure how to act when she arrived. When first he saw his long estranged granddaughter after he opened the front door, he felt the expression and smile of his late son on her face. Clayton simply cried.

Tessa made it easy for him. "Oh grandpa." She walked through the door and hugged him. "I wish our reunion would have happened sooner."

She stayed with her "Grandpa Clayton" for three days. They fished off the pier and had dinner at nearby Salty's Restaurant on the first day. By then Tessa had become acclimated to the Red Sox cause. "I have lived in southern California for about twelve years so I am a Los Angeles Dodgers fan. Since Oakland beat the Dodgers last year, it is easy for me to root for the Sox against them."

Clayton and Tessa watched games two and three of the playoff series together. Boston won all three games to sweep the series and Tessa was quite surprised to see tears of sorrow amidst tears of joy of her grandfather. "You don't know how much Emily would have loved to have shared this exact moment with us."

"Not only is her spirit here with us, her spirit helps make this moment as sweet as it is."

* * *

After returning to Los Angeles, Tessa watched the broadcast games alone. "Don't worry grandpa," Tessa said on the phone after the Red Sox lost game five of the World Series. "The Reds lead the series three games to two but something good may be just around the corner."

"I appreciate your support," Clayton responded, "but a Red Sox fan learns to live with disappointment."

"Its just that curse of the Babe thing ripping at you. Think positive. No matter what, it has been a great season."

"Well, I am so glad you called. I don't mean to be pessimistic, but all Red Sox fans know it takes a World Series championship and not just an American League pennant to end the curse."

As game six progressed, so did the melancholy feeling of Clayton. By the bottom of the eighth inning, he was silent and listless although the Red Sox managed to get the tying run to the plate. "Don't get your hopes too high," he cautioned himself. "But I really can't help it. What a big letdown it will be if the Reds hold their lead and win the series."

A couple of pitches later Clayton surprised himself with how high he jumped into the air. "Bernie Carbo! A three-run home run to tie the game!" Still on his feet, Clayton loved hearing the sound of his own voice doing an impersonation of the cowardly lion in the "Wizard of Oz" movie: "I do believe in miracles, I do, I do, I do!"

Then he settled back into his chair and watched as the tension mounted in extra innings. Reds manager Sparky Anderson had used eight pitchers by the bottom of the 12th inning. Neither team had scored since the Carbo home run in the eighth. There seemed to be no end to the drama until Carlton Fisk hooked a ball down the line. "The ball hit the foul pole!"

Clayton did not have the energy in his 74-year-old body to jump this time. His teary eyes sat and watched the wonders of the replay with Boston's catcher using all of his body language and willpower in a way that would forever be synonymous with the dreams of Red Sox nation during that moment.

The telephone rang and Clayton heard Tessa screaming before he could say "hello". "That was the greatest baseball game I have ever seen!"

"This exact moment, sharing it with you, is one of his happiest moments since Emily passed, and one of the best of my life."

After finishing the conversation with Tessa, Clayton told himself, "No matter what, I will die a happy man because I will only have to remember this evening to be happy."

* * *

For game seven, Clayton found his oldest yet favorite Red Sox souvenir. "The hat I got from Buckminster Fuller in 1924. Victor always wanted it. He would have loved to see the Red Sox in the series. He died before the 1967 Series. His death is still a mystery." The hat was very well-worn and not suitable for use in public. The only reason the wool hat had not disintegrated after decades of sweat, rain and dirt was that it had been carefully washed and placed in a plastic bag. As such, Clayton considered it a souvenir. "But I will wear it today."

"Bucky Fuller is still alive and active," Clayton recalled with a smile. The fabled Astrodome in Houston is a legacy to his work. The structure, a geodesic dome, was an incredible environmentally sound structure. Just three years before, Clayton read in the Seattle Times that Buckminster Fuller was to be a guest speaker at Whitworth College in Spokane. "Seeing my old friend after all those years makes me smile every time I think of it."

Just as was the case in the previous six games, the last game of the World Series proved to be a war, although a war of respect. "As much as I want my Red Sox to win, I cannot help but admire the talent and success of the Reds. Carlton Fisk, the Red Sox catcher, was the hero of the moment, but Johnny Bench of the Reds is arguably the greatest catcher of all time. I have a soft spot in my heart for Joe Morgan, their talented second baseman. Dave Concepcion is an icon for the Latin world. And then there is Pete Rose. There is no argument that he is a great player but I flat don't like the son of a bitch and I'm sure he doesn't care. Something about him reminds me of Ty Cobb, another great player I never liked."

Clayton found nothing appealing in the refrigerator and returned to his recliner in the living room. "Breaking the curse of Babe Ruth all comes down to one game." As the game progressed every pitch became magnified in importance. Every out heightened the anticipation, the uncertainty. The conclusion of each inning made the upcoming inning more titanic.

By the end of the sixth inning, Clayton developed mild indigestion. He went to the bathroom to pee, trying also to burp or fart. "I just feel like I need to get rid of some gas to get rid of the heartburn." He took an antacid and went back to his chair in the living room.

In the seventh inning, Clayton found himself swearing at the television about some questionable pitches which were called strikes. "That's not my style," he mused. In the bottom half of the seventh, he laughed to himself when seemingly worse pitches were called strikes against the Reds. "I'm glad no one was here to see me make an ass of myself."

His focus remained on the game during the eighth inning but he changed positions in his chair. "My left arm feels like it is going to sleep." The Reds runner on first took off for second and the batter turned to fake a bunt. He stepped out in front of the plate and Carlton Fisk had to hesitate before making his throw to second base. "That is interference!"

After the television replay, Clayton jumped to his feet. "Dammit, that is interference!"

In the fateful moment, Clayton felt his chest seize up like a momentous cramp. Simultaneously his strength seemed to be pulled from him. "I can't stand up." He tried to get back to his chair but his left leg gave out underneath him. His buckled left knee hit the floor without any balance but his left arm softened his fall. "I'm hurt. My breathing is... Oh, I'm having a heart attack."

Clayton managed to scoot himself with his right arm toward the end table with the telephone. His left arm was not functional although it did not hurt. Grabbing the telephone line, he pulled the telephone onto the floor and to himself. "Operator, this is an emergency. I'm having a heart attack...714 Redwood...I..."

The telephone slipped from his hand and hit the floor, momentarily swaying back and forth until the receiver lost its momentum. A second surge of pain and panic seized his body. His right hand went flat against his chest as though feeling to see if his heart was still there.

Clayton fell flat to the floor again, on his back. He glanced at the television but there was no comprehension on his part. "I wonder how long it will take for an ambulance to reach the house." For a brief moment he struggled with consciousness. "I am not going to die yet," he heard his gasping voice say. He saw his Red Sox hat on the floor. He reached it and held it in his right hand.

Thoughts seemed to fly by quickly but a sensation of comfort came to him. "Tessa." Just as soon as had been possible after Tessa's visit, he had changed his will. "I am glad to have an heir."

Clayton recognized the sound of a siren in the distance. He knew it would be too late. "I cannot believe I did not live to see the end of the curse of the Babe." Then he remembered telling Tessa the night before, "I am going to die happy, no matter what." He smiled.

"Thank you Tessa," were his last words.

CHAPTER FOURTEEN

JINXED, OF CURSE

Los Angeles, California
October 1975

"The curse lives on," Tessa sighed. "Mi cursa es su cursa," she thought, picturing Grandpa Clayton. The game was over. Joe Morgan had driven in the winning run for the Reds. Tessa called her grandfather to console him but the line was busy. After a trip to the bathroom, she called again. "It is still busy. I'll try again after I take a shower."

After drying off, Tessa put on her robe and made some green tea. She tried again to call her grandfather. This time the phone rang but there was no answer. "That is odd. Grandfather should be home." She tried calling perhaps a dozen times throughout the evening. Each time there was no answer.

"Don't worry, there is nothing wrong." She tried to will herself into believing that mantra.

At 4:44 in the morning, Tessa woke up suddenly. "There is something wrong! I can feel it. But it is too early to call." She tossed and turned, trying to convince herself there was nothing she could do at least until daylight. She managed to fall asleep, only to have a fearful dream of falling trees. She reached out to grab a fallen pinecone. She could feel its barbed points. She realized it was a dream and she made herself awaken.

As she made coffee, Tessa thought, "How curious it was to feel the pinecone in my dream. It was so real." She was still reliving the feeling when she called her grandfather. Still there was no answer. Tessa sat and brushed her dirty blonde hair while she contemplated the next time she could call.

Unfortunately the workday was not a busy one for Tessa. "Try not to think about grandfather. He simply was not home when I called." Her first call, when the line was busy, did not seem to fit the pattern. "The logical explanation is that I simply dialed the wrong number."

When Tessa arrived home, she dutifully called her grandfather's number. Again there was no answer. She opened the newspaper and began leafing through it. Within a few minutes her telephone rang, causing her to flinch. A feeling of sudden uneasiness came over her as she reached for the receiver.

"May I speak with Katherine Tessa O'Donnell?"

"This is she."

"My name is Isaac Silverman. I am the attorney for Mr. Clayton O'Donnell. I am sorry to have to bother you but I was instructed to call. Your grandfather passed away yesterday. I am the executor of his estate."

She strained to remember the details from the crushing telephone call. Her grandfather died of a heart attack. He called for an ambulance but it did not arrive in time. "Your grandfather made prior arrangements for transportation to be paid for you to attend the funeral if you so choose."

Tessa hung up the phone in complete sadness and shock. Her mind began to deal with the practical matters ahead of her. She reached for the telephone to call her boss but as she did she recalled her last conversation with her grandfather. "He was so happy." The receiver fell from her hand onto the counter. The symbolism of her tears falling upon the briefly pendulating telephone etched her memory.

* * *

During the flight from LAX in Los Angeles to SeaTac Airport, Tessa's thoughts wandered incessantly about her grandfather. "I hardly knew him yet I'm very thankful for my few memories of him."

Sitting back in her seat after finishing her meal, Tessa reflected, "My mother always discouraged ancestral types of conversations and I have been conditioned not to ask. There were not enough stories I could hear. And if grandfather was repeating a story, I listened gratefully. At the same time, there was so much grandfather wanted to know about me."

Tessa purposely omitted the confession about the circumstances of the death of Teddy, her stepfather. "It is more appropriate for a later time, when we have grown closer," she reasoned privately. Now she wondered, "Should I have told him about it? No, I should not second-guess myself. I had no way of knowing he was going to die."

When Tessa started the engine of her rental car, the radio blasted loudly. She quickly reached for the volume knob, having no interest in the news story about the upcoming University of Washington football game. "Just hearing a sports report brings tears to my eyes. I wish the Red Sox had won the World Series. Did grandfather die during the last game? Did he know the outcome of the game?" She thought about the busy signal when she called him after the game. "His last call was for an ambulance but there is simply no way to know if it was after the game. It makes sense that one of the paramedics hung up the phone, which was why there would have been no answer for the rest of my calls."

Turning onto Pacific Highway South, Tessa guessed there were maybe thirty more minutes of daylight left in the day. "I want to drive by grandfather's house and then have dinner at Salty's before I check into the hotel." The setting sun reflected brightly off the front windows of the home she had so recently visited but the sun seemed to have a sad smile as it set upon Puget Sound.

As much as Tessa dreaded all of the funeral activities the following day, it turned out to be an illuminating experience. "There is so much about my grandfather that I don't know. I am learning from each one of the eulogies," she told Mr. Silverman.

Tessa learned about how difficult the early 1950s were for her grandparents after her own father was killed. She learned about how patient her grandfather was and of her Grandma Emily's deep depression and alcoholism. There were many former employees and students there from the music store, including the present owners of the establishment. Many of those people made remarks about how Clayton made a lasting impression on them beyond the workplace or in learning the piano. Tessa met former neighbors of Clayton from Lake Washington and she learned how they remained friends until his death. Some of those people as well as some of his neighbors at Redondo Beach introduced themselves to her as though they were expecting her.

Apparently Clayton had described her reappearance into his life. One elderly gentleman mentioned something about her grandfather having an interest in strange things, like the crystal skull and the sasquatch. He even said Tessa's grandfather and father claimed to have seen a sasquatch on Mount Si.

"I have so many things echoing through my mind," she observed that night at the hotel. "The story about the crystal skull and sasquatch is pretty strange. Mother told me about the crystal skull but I know very little about it. The sasquatch sighting part is too weird since I also believe I have seen a sasquatch, just before Teddy died. This all reminds me of Teddy."

Twelve years earlier, her mother did not allow Tessa or Randy to go to Teddy's funeral, a small affair. Then there was the bevy of police and psychiatrists questioning both she and her brother as well as the subsequent weeks of psychiatric appointments her mother made them endure.

Loretta had taken them both out of school, moving to California before Christmas. "The house we moved into was left to us by a relative who my mother 'could not remember'," pondered Tessa. There were more psychiatric sessions before the two children enrolled in school in Los Angeles.

"The culture shock was tremendous," Tessa recalled, "moving from a rural area on an Indian reservation to the massive population of southern California. I remember how mom promised us a trip to Disneyland after the psychiatric sessions were finished and before we enrolled in school. That was a great time at the 'happiest place on earth'. The Disney characters seem like family somehow."

After listening to a siren scream past the hotel on the highway, Tessa turned on the television. She nonetheless remained absorbed in her memories. "It took a few months in Los Angeles before mom found a job." Despite knowing virtually nothing about physics, Loretta became a secretary of that particular department at the California Institute of Technology. "I never before could recall my mother actually enjoying a job. Maybe she just did not enjoy her life in general." After nearly 12 years, her mother still worked at Cal Tech.

The day after the funeral Tessa was scheduled to meet with Mr. Silverman at 11 o'clock. "I have been nervous all morning. I just have an uncomfortable feeling. I wonder how many other people will be there?"

During breakfast Tessa thought, "Maybe I am part of some type of spell or curse. That would explain some of the events of my life. Those ideas are always extinguished by my mother. It is simply true that my father died shortly after I was born. And then something happened to my mother's parents. And after all of these years, after mother confessed that my grandfather lives in Seattle, he dies suddenly within weeks of our reunion. And of course there was Teddy and those gruesome memories."

The intensity of her thoughts increased as she dressed for the meeting. "What would my life be like if my father was alive? Getting to know my grandfather convinced me that my father was everything I created in my fantasies and better." Tessa really did not know how to create an image of a genuine father figure except through observing the fathers of her friends. "How different would I have been?" A wave of guilt washed through her again. "If I am cursed, can I ever really experience a truly loving marriage? Just call me 'Jinx'."

At the office of the attorney, Tessa was surprised and actually relieved to be the only one there to meet with him. "My guilt and anxiety are so strong, it might be possible for others to see it."

"Hello Tessa," Mr. Silverman said, shaking her hand and then beckoning her to have a seat. Tessa nodded in agreement and sat back in her chair to listen. She learned about nephews and nieces through his late wife's brother who had passed in 1965. There were sizable sums of money left for them. Next she learned her own mother and brother had been left $10,000 each. "As for you Tessa, your grandfather left you $25,000, and…"

"I don't deserve it," Tessa interrupted, tears welling up in her sparkling hazel green eyes.

"Many people feel like you do at a time like this," Mr. Silverman said with a comforting smile, "and some people feel they did not get enough."

Tessa nodded and wiped her eyes.

"As I said, he left you $25,000, but he also left you the house at Redondo Beach. As such, it will be your responsibility to take care of the personal belongings at the house. You may of course use some of your inheritance to hire people to do that. There is one item that had specific directions. Oddly, he was clutching it when the emergency medics found him. The old Red Sox hat is to be given to the son of Emily's brother. Apparently Emily's brother always wanted to buy the hat from Clayton."

His mention of the Red Sox flooded Tessa's eyes. She left the office in a state of bewilderment. "I never wanted anything from my grandfather. I never considered it."

Having already checked out of her hotel, she had four hours until her flight back to Los Angeles. "I'm going to end this trip the way I started it, with a drive by grandfather's house, except this time I have the keys."

Opening the door cautiously as though she were disturbing something, Tessa stepped inside. She walked through the rooms of the one story dwelling with two bedrooms and two baths, the task of disposing of the personal property of her grandfather passing through her thoughts as an overview. "I want this," she said, taking down a picture of her father in his Army uniform. She quickly scanned the large record album collection and selected three albums; John Coltrane, Oscar Peterson, and the West Side Story soundtrack.

On a lower shelf, Tessa spotted a section of oversized books and some notebooks laying flat. "Look at this. It is a high school annual... my dad's senior year." She took it without opening it and quickly leafed through a couple of journals of her grandfather as well as one older one compiled by her grandmother.

"I will love you forever," she said to her lost family.

With the gathered materials under her arm, she opened the front door to leave. "Goodbye grandpa."

CHAPTER FIFTEEN

REIMAGINING HEREDITY

Los Angeles, California
October 1975

"Can I carry your bag Tessa?" Loretta inquired.

"Thanks, I've got it. I always have lots of energy after sitting on an airplane." They walked through LAX Airport to wait for Tessa's suitcase at the baggage terminal.

"You look tired, or maybe just different. Did everything go alright?"

"I have a ton of thoughts in my head."

"That sounds heavy," said Loretta with a wry smile.

"I get it mom," said Tessa, returning her smile. "There are some things I need to discuss with you. We can talk in the car about some of it."

"I can't put my finger on it but something is definitely different," thought Loretta. "Maybe it is just the wear and tear of this latest life lesson. I feel in my heart the time has come to share other secrets with her but I am afraid to do it. I have feared my confession to her for quite some time. Tessa does seem different. That is a good enough reason to procrastinate telling secrets just awhile longer."

In the car, Tessa first told her mother about the meeting with Mr. Silverman earlier in the day. The notification of the inheritance sums for her mother and brother would be forthcoming in the mail so the story was a total surprise to Loretta.

"What do you plan to do with the house?"

"I need to get it ready to sell I guess," replied Tessa with little conviction.

"Did Mr. Silverman give you any advice on who might be might be able to dispose of the stuff in it?"

Her daughter felt a brief painful pang. "The word 'stuff' is so impersonal. Besides, now it's my 'stuff'. But to answer your question, no he did not. What is the hurry anyway?"

"Owning a home involves responsibilities. You have taxes and insurance to pay, not to mention yard maintenance."

"I know, I know. I just don't want to figure it out today since I have only owned the home for about 11 hours."

They drove in silence for a few minutes before Loretta spoke. "Would you mind if I put my $10,000 towards college for Mark?"

"That is a gracious idea! Mother, I think that is a wonderful idea!"

With that positive change in flavor to the conversation Loretta changed the topic to small talk and gossip. Although such dialogue was not generally her style, Tessa welcomed less serious thoughts to entertain. She encouraged her mother with leading questions and felt good about laughing at the stories. Before she knew it, Loretta pulled into the parking lot at Tessa's apartment.

Locking the door and turning on the living room lights, Tessa slumped into a chair. "What a day, what a week, what a month," she said to the universe. "What a life."

* * *

Getting back to routine was welcomed by Tessa. "I am glad to be busy again but my bookkeeping position at the ice company does not seem as serious to me anymore. That office squabble this afternoon was particularly petty and immature. Leave me out of that crap."

"I can't help but think about my future," Tessa thought as she drove home. "There is no way I will stay on the same job as long as mother has been at Cal Tech. What should I do? I am only 24 years old with a lifetime of journey ahead of me. But the immediate direction of my journey is the grocery store to figure out what to make for dinner."

After purchasing a tuna steak, Tessa decided white wine would be a welcome addition to the meal. As she passed the beer section her eyes met those of a familiar face.

"Tess, how are you?"

It was Gabriel, her former boyfriend for more than two years. It had been more than a year since she last saw him but she still struggled to resist a sudden urge to divulge the events of the past month. The familiar sight of a case of beer under his arm was a sad reminder of her late stepfather Teddy. "I'm fine Gabe, how are you?"

"It is pretty much the same old stuff," he replied, gazing at the physique of his former lover. "Me and Heidi broke up again."

"You will survive it, again," Tessa said with a smile.

"Are you between boyfriends?"

"I do not quite look at it that way but I am not seeing anyone right now."

"Maybe you and I should have some fun together for awhile."

"I suppose you'll want to talk Heidi and me into a threesome," said Tessa, blushing because an elderly woman in the store overheard her comment.

"No, I know you better than that. Besides, if Heidi knew I was anywhere near you, she would get jealous."

"Which means of course that you have hopes of getting back together with her. And that is what you should do. Treat her nice and maybe you two can get back together."

"You have a point." The conversation was short-lived after that. Continuing her shopping, Tessa could not help but feel a depth of loneliness. "What is true love like?" She thought of pictures at her grandfather's house of his grandparents when they were younger. "I wish I could have known them together. I would at least have an example of what true love is supposed to be. It's funny, I have never thought of mom having true love but she did with my real father." Gloomy thoughts invaded her mind. "What if I am a cursed jinx? What if I had a true love and he died?"

Tessa woke up from her daydream. "Forget about that stuff," she thought to herself. "Concentrate on the wine choices."

By Sunday afternoon, Loretta's urge to talk to Tessa about certain specific secrets became obsessive. "There have been so many times when I have had anxiety over these matters but now it is becoming a burden. I have a growing feeling of guilt for not discussing these secrets earlier. Indeed, why did I ever keep these secrets from Tessa?" She knew the answer to her own question. "I simply wanted to bury those memories in a graveyard of denial."

But now she had to face that denial. "Surely Tessa will handle the facts about her grandparents better than I did when I first learned the truth. Tessa has been thrust into a world of maturity now. I can't put it off any longer."

Loretta made the phone call to her daughter. "I was wondering if I could bring Asian food over and have dinner with you tonight. I have a very important matter to discuss with you." They agreed on 6:30.

With the exception of some housecleaning and some early Christmas shopping, Tessa spent most of the weekend reading the journals of her grandparents. By no means were the journals a complete chronological history. "These journals certainly are not to be confused with diaries. There are many very personal entries but there are no rules. They wrote whatever was on their minds. There are large gaps after tragedies. Obviously the death of my father was one of those times and the death of grandmother was another. Grandpa Clayton was a patient man."

She lingered with a photograph of her grandfather playing the piano. "I wish I could have known grandfather as the musician he was in his younger years. I heard him play the upright piano in his house a few times. It was fun but I really did not realize how truly important music was to him. I have learned from the journals how much he enjoyed teaching piano. I remember some of the names of his former students from the funeral."

Tessa came upon a passage about the crystal skull in the journal. "Their fascination with very weird stories amazes me. My grandmother had a keen intellectual interest in the stranger things. I have such a deep sense of regret for never getting to know her."

Because a man at the funeral told her about the sasquatch sighting by her father and grandfather, she was not surprised to read about the incident in the journals. "It is way beyond coincidence that both my father and me had sasquatch sightings at approximately the same ages." The bigfoot phenomenon was gaining considerable popularity in the 1970s but Tessa never volunteered information to anyone. "Los Angeles kids think the sasquatch is some sort of horror monster, if it exists at all." Whenever she heard anyone discuss it, she would always nonchalantly say something like, "I probably would just invite a bigfoot in for some hot chocolate."

There were considerably more entries in the journals about the discussions of the crystal skull between her grandparents. Tessa read a number of these entries before she realized who Anna Mitchell-Hedges was. "It is obvious that my grandmother and Anna Mitchell-Hedges knew each other for quite some time. As of the latest entry, Anna Mitchell-Hedges was still in possession of the crystal skull. I wonder if she is still alive?"

Tessa read journal entries several times, trying to decipher the deeper meanings. "After all, I am in no particular hurry." She savored each entry as though she were trying to imagine herself in their conversations. "I wonder how much of what I am reading would be interesting to my mother? How much should I discuss with my brother? These were his biological grandparents too but it still could be a sensitive subject."

It was not until late in that Sunday afternoon when Tessa pulled herself away from the journals. "I need to take a shower before mother arrives." Still wrapped in her towel, Tessa decided to take just a few minutes to begin a journal of her own before her mother arrived.

"Mother, what is going on that is so significant?" Tessa finished bringing dishes to the table for the take-out Chinese food her mother brought.

"There are a few things," began Loretta, "but the first is that I have been seeing someone."

"Wow, who is it?" As she looked up at her mother she observed how vibrant the 44 year old woman looked.

Loretta finished her bite of vegetable egg foo yung. "This is really good." She looked into her daughter's eyes and noticed the "get on with it" look on her face despite trying a bite of the steamed rice. "He is a professor at Cal Tech. I've known him for several years but he was divorced about a year ago."

"He is a physics professor? How interesting. Do you two communicate very well?"

"It is funny you ask. I have complimented him on not talking down to me many times. He explains things at a level I can understand."

"He probably is a good teacher." Tessa took a big bite of egg foo yung as a subtle way of indicating she wanted her mother to do the talking.

"He seems to be popular with the students," Loretta remarked, taking a drink of tea before continuing. "I love talking about the scientific stuff and for some reason he loves my weirdest questions and viewpoints."

"What is his name?"

Loretta giggled. "Minor detail huh? His name is Nicholas Murray."

"Dr. Nick?" Tessa smiled. "How long have you two been seeing each other?"

"It started innocently a few months ago with lunches and going for walks."

"And now it is not so innocent?"

As if on cue Loretta blushed a shade of scarlet, nearly a match with her sweater. "Well, we are adults."

Her mother changed the conversation back to the types of topics discussed by she and the professor such as advancements in technology, multiple universes, and something new called the "black hole". "Some of the Cal Tech scientists are involved in research of the planet Mars."

"He's looking into your background," Tessa teased.

"Nicholas thinks the crystal skull may somehow be related to Mars, or at least some ancient advanced technology."

"He has seen the crystal skull?"

"No, but he has discussed it with a man named Frank Borland who did extensive testing on it. Nicholas was quite impressed that I had seen it."

"Did you know that my dad's parents were really into that? My Grandmother O'Donnell knew Anna Mitchell–Hedges, who found it."

"Yes, your father and I discussed the skull on a number of occasions. Nicholas feels the skull may actually be a repository of ancient knowledge, if we knew how to crack the code."

"I'm not sure I understand what you mean."

"Do you know about the new game, called a video game?"

"Sure I do. I have played it before. Pong; it is a little strange."

Nicholas explained to me the greater purpose behind that game is mainly to introduce a form of computers to the American public. It is a friendly way to bring computers into the home so people will be less frightened or confused by the new technology," explained Loretta.

"Which has what to do with the crystal skull?"

"Computers will be able to store and retrieve great quantities of information and crystals are a big part of that technology," answered Loretta, who then stood up to begin clearing the table.

Tessa followed her lead and put the leftover food cartons in the refrigerator. "I am happy for you mom and I liked the food but was it really necessary to do this is to tell me about your new boyfriend?"

Loretta shuffled somewhat uneasily, straightening something on one of the kitchen counters that did not need adjustment. "There is more… about your grandparents."

"I have been reading my grandfather's journals all weekend. My Grandmother Emily also kept journals. I should be able to find more of them the next time I go to the house," stated Tessa, somewhat relieved her mother was willing to discuss the matter.

"That is not what I mean," Loretta said almost wistfully. "This is about your other grandparents, my mother and father." She knew she was about to cross a new boundary with her daughter. She had been thinking about the discussion for days and intermittently for years. "There is something else I need to talk to you about. Before I say what I have to say I just want to tell you again that I never held you responsible for Teddy's death. I have told you before, I believe you saved my life. And I am very sorry for all you had to go through after that."

"I know mom. You have told me that many times and I really try not to think about it very much. It is definitely an experience that shaped my life."

"I agree, although I'm not exactly sure what you mean."

Tessa looked at her hands as though she were briefly examining them. "Well, one main thing it shaped was avoiding religion. I mean, the heaven and hell concept seems to be pretty heavily favored against me."

"That is really my fault," her mother stated mournfully. "I should have got us involved in church
again. Certainly God will forgive you. It is because I myself have no chance of salvation that I did not
want to go to church."

From there, Loretta began her confession about her own parents, much of it learned from her father's confession written during the last year of his life. She described to her daughter as much as she knew about her own father's defection from the Soviet Union, his brief time in Canada, and being brought to Washington, DC by the United States government. Loretta told the story of how he was placed in a job as a stunt driver in the movies until his Soviet pursuers spotted him in a film. She outlined his life as a secret government operative and how he did not know that his wife, Tessa's grandmother, was an undercover FBI agent. When she told Tessa about her grandfather Al's job as an animator for the Disney movies, she also remarked, "What a coincidence your regular doodling of Disney characters is. It was always such as strange reminder of everything I hid from everybody." Then she divulged a similarly detailed synopsis of the life of her mother.

At this point Loretta wanted to gather her thoughts and at the same time take a bathroom break. Although she had answered questions as Tessa asked them, she invited her daughter to think of anything in particular she might want to know. When she returned, Tessa handed her a glass of white wine.

"What did they look like?"

"I do have some pictures," Loretta said and left to retrieve a satchel she brought. "I should have given these to you a long time ago," she said, fighting back tears, "but I have been in fear of this talk."

The glasses of wine were consumed rather quickly. Tessa sifted through the photographs over and over again while her mother continued speaking, pausing only to refill the wine glasses. There were very few questions asked. Instead, Tessa felt a growing sense of anxiety. "My ancestral perceptions are like daytime turning into night," she told her mother as she commented on the dual undercover role of her grandfather and the death of her grandmother.

"Your grandfather did not tell me the truth about my mom until about three years after she was killed. I could not handle it at all and I reacted harshly. I left him a note saying I was leaving and I asked that he not try to find me. I headed for Canada but ended up in Colville instead. After I met Teddy, I used him as an excuse to break off relations with your father's parents in Seattle. For years I have truly regretted my actions. I do not expect you to forgive me, just as I will never be forgiven by God."

"There is so much to think about. It will take me a while for all this to sink in."

"I wish I were finished but there is more." She then went on to describe her grandfather's death in 1963, dying in his sleep in a hospital room. There was an inheritance, which was why Loretta moved her family to Los Angeles. "With the inheritance, your grandfather included handwritten memoirs of just over 40 pages." Loretta produced those from her satchel and gave them to her daughter.

"There is yet one more thing to discuss. I know you are going to want to look through those memoirs and what I'm going to say is in there. But I still need to talk to you about it first."

"You have just one more nuclear bomb to drop, huh?" Tessa asked her mother sarcastically.

"Yes, one more to go," conceded Loretta, wiping away tears. "One more bizarre thing. Your grandfather was part of an experiment to create a warrior ape-man for the Russians. It did not affect him physically. The memoirs confessed his relief that myself as well as you were normal human babies."

Loretta stood up and began pacing but momentarily she returned to her seat at the table. "Unfortunately I told that fact to the psychiatric people who were examining you after Teddy's death. That is why they tested you so much, like a guinea pig."

"They thought I might be some kind of killing monster?" Tessa asked in horror.

Loretta finished her wine. "It is hardly fitting to say how sorry I am about all of this. I cannot even say it is a relief to be rid of the burden of the secrets. But it is late and I just want to have a good cry on the drive home," she said, putting on her coat.

Tessa hugged her. "You had tough decisions. You just did what you thought was best."

Loretta touched her daughter's cheek with her fingers. "It should have been better."

* * *

Nearly two weeks after her mother revealed the secrets of her family's background, Tessa noticed a small article in the newspaper about the crystal skull. "It is being displayed at an exhibit in San Diego," she paraphrased. "The exhibit will end tomorrow. The exhibit is being moved to Phoenix, the last scheduled stop on the tour. The owner of the skull, Anna Mitchell- Hedges, will take part in the presentation on the last day."

As soon as she could, Tessa went to the public library to use a Phoenix telephone directory to find phone numbers of motels. It took a few calls to learn which motels were near the exhibit but she eventually made a reservation at the Vagabond Inn. "I'll make the drive across the desert after work on Friday. I know both mom and Randy have weekend plans so I'll make the trip alone."

For some reason that Tessa neither articulated nor justified, she decided to keep her plans private. "My mother would really be interested in the skull exhibit. I'll give her a full description of my experience when I return to Los Angeles."

At the exhibit in Phoenix on Sunday, Tessa arrived before Anna Mitchell-Hedges, the owner of the crystal skull. There were several other people around her while she viewed the exhibit. "Try to simply keep an open mind in the presence of the skull," she coached herself.

Instead she found herself distracted by comments from a couple who came and went. "I wonder if the skull somehow has ancient knowledge of extraterrestrial life? Would the energy of the skull change in the event of a UFO sighting?" In the context of their conversation, the couple implied recent sightings of unidentified flying objects in the desert.

Tessa's mind accelerated dimensionally at the potentiality of such an idea. She stood transfixed,
looking at the crystal skull, losing any connection with others around her. "I have a vision, rather a feeling of a vortex into some separate dimension. There is no real meaning to it. The intensity of other dimensions is being projected to me from the crystal skull."

"Where is the vortex to another dimension? There is no obvious answer. I feel the energy of the skull informing me to search for it." Tessa felt a strong desire to explore a place where answers to ancient mysteries could be found. "Maybe I am a mystery. My newly discovered but unexplored side of me might explain one of my mysteries, as scary as that seems. Maybe solving my own mysteries will help me to solve others. But how can I do that? I want to find out. I need to find a way."

Her expanding thoughts were suddenly interrupted by the voice of the museum director. He was introducing Anna Mitchell-Hedges, which brought Tessa back to the present moment. She looked around, only to discover the 67-year-old owner of the skull looking directly at her with a wry smile. "The skull gives you joy of life. All through my life he has protected me. I call it the Skull of Love."

Tessa momentarily had the urge to speak to Ms. Mitchell-Hedges but she shuffled back into the gathering group and listened to the speaker. "I didn't even know my grandmother. What would I say to her?"

Ms. Mitchell-Hedges described how she found the skull as a 17 year old, the reaction of the local natives, the scientific testing, the various exhibition tours, and brief descriptions of other skulls. After her short speech, Anna Mitchell-Hedges responded to questions from the audience. Occasionally she glanced toward Tessa, perhaps expecting an inquiry. None were forthcoming from Tessa but she did take time to thank the speaker for her speech and shake her hand.

Most of the crowd dispersed after the presentation. Tessa spent roughly another 15 minutes with the skull, hoping for an encore of the previous energy. It did not happen. "I feel a vibration of farewell from the skull, or maybe it is a reflection of my own thoughts."

After leaving the exhibit, the late afternoon drive through the desert back toward Los Angeles was made without the use of her cassette tape player or radio. Tessa's body maintained a certain electric nervous energy but her mind was more calm and resolved. "I feel as if I am preparing for a trip into the unknown. The unfolding path likely will take the remainder of my life. Since I saw the sasquatch when I was twelve I have believed that my life quest would not be alone, but I guess it is. I have determination but I am scared."

Roughly an hour into the drive, Tessa decided to stop and take a short stroll in the desert. "What is my next step?" She discovered a corner of her mind involuntarily producing an image of the crystal skull. She tried to will her heart to become as warm as the desert breeze.

Tessa sat on a highway guard rail, gazing at the stars. Within minutes she became drowsy, having a difficult time keeping her head up. "The crystal skull did nothing but enhance my sense of biological fate. Why me?"

She stood up but then quickly sat back down. "Okay, I'll rest my eyes for just a minute or so." She sat as motionless as she possibly could. "I feel paralyzed and all of the hair on my skin is growing. Do we have to do this now? Those sick psycho scientists who treated me like a guinea pig when I was a kid probably brainwashed me into all of this."

Momentarily Tessa lost her balance on the rail and slumped to the ground. "What happened? I must have dozed off." As she became fully awake, she noticed the morning desert sun baking the skin on her arms. "Why is it morning?"

Returning her vehicle to the highway, Tessa resumed driving toward Los Angeles. "The crystal skull, what a joke! I get so frustrated! I just want to rip the head off something. I'm not supposed to listen to it, or whatever. The only thing I know is that I need to go back to Redondo sometime soon, probably before the next full moon. Why did I miss so much of the night? Why is it morning?"

CHAPTER SIXTEEN

SCRAMBLE OF DESTINY'S EGG

*Redondo Beach, Washington,
December 1975*

The sound of the buzzing alarm clock caused Tessa to flinch out of her slumber and begin groping the night stand to extinguish the sound. "I set the alarm? For 6:33?"

Wordlessly Tessa dressed and began making a light breakfast of toast and cereal. "Am I going somewhere?" she wondered while continuing her task.

After backing the green 1972 Chevrolet Impala out of the garage, Tessa took a moment to peruse the vehicle. "It reminds me of the cars we used in driver's ed class. I can't believe Grandpa Clayton left it to me with the house."

Within ten minutes Tessa was headed north on Interstate 5. "It's December 22nd, the first day of winter." The early rays of morning sunshine broke out as she drove past the Space Needle and Lake Union, where a small plane landed on the water. While manually searching for radio stations on the dial, Tessa laughed. "Grandpa should have ordered FM radio for this car."

"Snohomish County," read Tessa on the road marker after driving for 40 minutes. "I've never been this far north on this freeway." Her trek continued north into the steadily growing brightness of the morning sun. The sight of a state trooper administering a ticket in the midst of the rural landscape forced Tessa out of her daydream. "Why am I supposed to be doing this? Never mind, I'll know."

Tessa took notice of the gas gauge at the Skagit County road marker. "I have plenty of fuel, I guess, if I knew where I was headed. Where am I going?" Still she drove northward, content the events of the day would unfold as they should. "I used to know. I'm supposed to know again when it happens. I feel like there is a program I'm supposed to watch or be in." Ducks landing on flooded farmfields north of Burlington captured her attention. "It won't be long now."

The freeway ascended into the foothills between the Skagit valley and Bellingham and before long Tessa came upon the sudden splendor of Lake Samish. "Wow, a crew team is rowing on the lake. It must be the college team up here. How did I know about a college?" She struggled with her memory until reading "Bellingham Next 7 Exits".

"I take the third exit. That's the one I am supposed to take. Why am I here?"

* * *

Squinting at the midday sun, Mickey thought, "The weather should be good for the drive to Spokane tomorrow. I need to get one more Christmas gift, wrap the presents and pack for the trip." The urge to wrap presents seized him and he continued until a ray of sunshine beaming through the window diminished his desire. "Bright sunshine on the winter solstice. I gotta get out of here."

Mickey dressed for the 45 degree weather and inflated the tires on his bicycle. "The last present I need to buy can fit in my coat pocket. Why drive?" From his apartment in the Fairhaven part of town, he rode along the boulevard by the bay toward downtown Bellingham.

"Thanks to window shopping last week, I know just the scarf I want to get for Aunt Margaret." From the clothing shop on Cornwall Avenue, Mickey cycled to Railroad Avenue to peruse used albums at a head shop. His attention was drawn to a shiny reflection on the counter. "Wow, it's a little skull toy." By clicking the nearly flat plastic piece from side to side, the holographic image appeared to move. "It reminds me of the crystal skull. My parents will get a kick out of this."

"Doesn't it seem like the skull toy is talking, without sound of course?" The indigo blue eyes of the young woman at the counter sparkled in her mild enthusiasm.

"I'll get worried if I hear it speak," joked Mickey as he was leaving the shop, "or growl."

Once outside, Mickey realized he had nothing specific planned. "I feel like going on a long bike ride. I'm going to the reservation. I'd better snag something to eat while I am in town." Looking at his change, Mickey declared, "It looks like I'm getting a burger at Herfy's."

"Hello." Mickey turned toward the voice behind him. "This is for you," an elderly, white haired woman said as she handed him a small slip of paper. Smiling broadly she decreed, "Be well," and departed.

"Thank you." He watched as she disappeared around the corner. "Indigo eyes again, wow. She seemed so happy. Too many elderly people have a permanent scowl. I'm not going to have that kind of frowning face." A tear came to his eye as he remembered his grandfather.

Opening the folded note, he read: God Loves You
It's amazing and incredible but it's as true as can be,
God loves and understands us All and that means You and Me.
God's grace is all sufficient for both the Young and the Old,
For the lonely and the timid, for the brash and for the bold.

God's love knows no exception so never feel excluded,
No matter Who or What you are, your name has been included.
And no matter what your past has been, trust God to understand.
And no matter what your problem is just place it in God's hand.
For in all of our Unlovliness this Great God loves us still,
God has loved us since the world began and what's more,
God Always Will.

"I'll probably never see her again. She is just some sort of angel of the moment." He placed the slip of paper in his wallet. "I think I am supposed to be in this exact spot at this exact time."

From downtown, Mickey's route followed roads on the east and north sides of Bellingham Bay for nearly ten miles until reaching the Lummi Reservation. "Lummi Island seems so close and I've never been there. I should at least figure out where the ferry terminal is."

Fatigue began to take its toll as Mickey reached the southern tip of the reservation. "There is not much sunshine left. I better head back soon."

He stopped riding to contemplate continuing his journey to the ferry terminal. "What is that?"

A sudden bright and lingering trail of light streaked across the sky. "What the hell flies that low like that?"

* * *

"I'm full," Tessa confirmed to herself. "The fish and chips was good but I didn't need all those fries. Maybe I'll just go for a walk and see a little bit of downtown."

During her stroll through the streets of Bellingham, Tessa reviewed plans for the upcoming holidays. "I fly back to Los Angeles in two days. It seems so out of the way to be here. Why am I here again? It seems like I have dreamed some of this before or something."

In a clothing store, Tessa was drawn to a rack of scarves. "Maybe a scarf would be a good Christmas present for mom. I probably should get her at least one present from the great northwest."

Walking a different route back to her car, Tessa stopped to look at posters in a store window. "I can find something better than a poster for Randy. Maybe they'll have something unusual." After entering the shop she walked directly to the counter where small plastic toys were displayed. "A little skull toy. I like this but I want it for myself."

By two o'clock Tessa had returned to her vehicle. "I have a couple of hours of daylight left. I think I'll drive around the bay for awhile. I wonder how you get to those islands?" She was just about to put the key in the locked door when she heard a voice behind her.

"Excuse me, hello, this is for you." A smiling elderly woman held out a slip of paper to her, which Tessa accepted. "Bless you, be well." The lady gave her a warm smile and departed.

Tessa put the slip of paper into her coat pocket, shuffling her purse to the other hand to resume opening the car door. "Thank you!" Her shout prompted the elderly woman to look back with the same warm smile. "What a happy woman," she thought to herself. "Isn't something supposed to happen when I see indigo blue eyes?"

Once inside her car, Tessa scanned the poem she had received. "Like I have any chance with God. It says God loves me no matter what but I don't think it will work for me no matter what. Is there something wrong with me?"

Tessa followed the main streets overlooking Bellingham Bay, noting a sign indicating that both the freeway and the airport were directly east. "I'll find my way back here to head for Seattle."

The leisurely 35 mile per hour speed limit afforded Tessa the opportunity to gaze out at several small boats on the bay. There is something strange around here, some kind of weird energy. "Seeing a Lummi Reservation sign put her at ease. "This is where I am supposed to be!"

A colorful streak of light in the sky interrupted her thoughts. "There it is! It looks like a prism. I'm here." She increased the speed of the vehicle, heading for the unseen trajectory of the falling light. "I feel like I should know what I am looking for. It must have crashed into the water. Is it my imagination? Those people I just passed seemed to be looking in that direction. Are they supposed to come with me? Who's supposed to be there?"

After traversing the southern point of the reservation, Tessa noticed how far the low tide was out. "The water looks so shallow." She continued following the meandering road next to the shoreline in the sparsely populated area. Her car began to decrease in speed almost instinctively. "Did I do that? Of course, who else?"

Down the moderately sloped bank, perhaps 25 feet in elevation but 35 yards away, a large egg shaped object was glowing on the beach. "Look at that! It is almost as big as a Volkswagen Beetle." The egg pulsated with brief prismatic flares which seemed to evaporate in the air.

Tessa parked the Chevrolet. She felt the poem in her pocket as she double checked having her keys and then found an opening between rocks to walk toward the shoreline. "I really am special. That's why I am here, to be special." Her eyes widened as she approached the object. "What a weird time to have that feeling. I feel like every hair on my body is growing."

* * *

Gliding his bicycle to a stop with his eyes fixed upon the slightly glowing egg shaped object, Mickey noticed one other person on the beach. He dismounted, leaned his bike against a rock near the roadway and began walking toward the shoreline. "How can something that looks like an egg fly across the sky?"

"What is it?" Mickey asked the lone woman on the beach. She remained nearly motionless, eyes glued to the object. With no response forthcoming Mickey continued to the object. He reached to touch it.

"Be careful! Are you sure?"

Initially startled by the young woman, Mickey proceeded to feel the exterior of the object. "There are no seams. It almost feels like an egg."

"What does that mean?"

"My dad used to be an aviation mechanic in the service. Nothing is seamless that is made by man. How would you get in?"

"An egg can't fly anyway," responded Tessa.

"Did you see it fly?"

"I thought I did."

A formation of headlights was rapidly advancing from the west. Soon a different group of automobiles appeared to the east.

"Should I touch it?" Tessa inquired while stepping gingerly forward.

"Be careful!" Mickey teased. "Look what happened when I touched it."

His remarks briefly confused Tessa. While feeling the object she answered, "Yes, we wouldn't want anything to happen to us."

Apparently traveling at a high rate of speed, the automobiles coming from each direction arrived almost simultaneously, some screeching their tires as they stopped. A number of men exited the vehicles and began running toward the glowing object. Others removed equipment from the vehicles before joining the men at the beach.

Instinctively Tessa and Mickey stepped out of the way of the advancing men, content to watch the proceedings. "They have no faces," thought Mickey. "They have some sort of face covering that's as black as their clothes."

The men first began touching the egg shaped object but then attempted to use different objects to test its consistency, tapping it and listening with stethoscopes. All of their actions were without orders or comment.

"They can't budge it," Mickey whispered when the men tried to move the object. He glanced up the bank to see if his bicycle was where he left it but his eyes were diverted to movement. "Another witness probably wondering what the hell is going on like me. It looks like a big shadow trying to hide behind the rocks."

The very large shadow stood straight up, revealing substance in the moonlight. "Do you see that?" Mickey whispered.

"See what?"

Before he could point in the appropriate direction, Mickey's astonished eyes momentarily observed the red glow of two eyes before they disappeared. "It, it vanished," he stammered.

"What vanished?" Mildly annoyed, Tessa quickly scanned the area, vainly trying to see something that was gone. "What do you think those men are doing to the...flying egg? It isn't glowing much anymore."

Her words seemed to ignite the interest of two of the men working on the object. Quietly two of the men put their equipment on the ground and began peering up the moonlit beach where two other men emerged from the vehicles.

"They set up security in a hurry," surmised Mickey. "They are probably going to boot us out of here."

Tessa looked on silently in apparent confusion, nervously glancing in varius directions as the security men moved toward them.

"We'll get out of your way," volunteered Mickey. "What is it?"

"Come with us," ordered one of the men.

"Hey, we weren't doing anything except seeing if everyone was okay after that thing fell," objected Mickey.

"I just wanted to look at it," Tessa admitted meekly.

"Please come with us or we will have to remove you by force."

"For what purpose?" Mickey demanded.

"What you have seen requires some debriefing."

"Are we supposed to know what that means?" asked Tessa in an assertive return to clarity.

The armed security sentry pointed toward the elevated roadway and the two civilians began walking in that direction. After reaching the roadway Mickey turned toward his bicycle. "You and your girlfriend need to stick together with us," commanded the man dressed in black.

"She's not my girlfriend. I don't even know her name."

Tessa's head volleyed back and forth while listening to the dialogue. "I'm Tessa!" she suddenly interjected.

Yet another sentry emerged, previously hidden in the shadows of the rocks. Positioned between Mickey and his bicycle, he slowly advanced toward the others. "You are with them."

The rear doors of a gunmetal gray van were opened. Tessa was pushed mildly from behind and she stumbled into Mickey, subsequently causing him to glance backward. "Are we prisoners?"

His question resulted in a shove from a different sentry. Mickey and Tessa obliged silently with suppressed anger and fear. The doors were closed, subjecting the captors momentarily to total darkness. When the driver and passenger doors were opened, a wire fence type barrier was revealed separating the front and back of the van.

"We're headed north," calculated Mickey.

As if waking suddenly, Tessa seemed dazed. "Where am I? Who are you?"

Mickey peered incredulously at Tessa in the darkness, unable to determine her sincerity. "I'm Mickey. Are you okay?"

The guard in the passenger seat glanced back at the prisoners without speaking, causing Tessa to shrink into her seat.

"I'm on my own," thought Mickey. "On my own against who? Everything in my life has taught me to value Mother Earth, but now this egg comes from the heavens, maybe to hatch into a new reality for mankind. Is my life changing? Could this just be a secret instead of a mystery?"

Suddenly, boldly, Tessa inquired, "Where are you taking us?" She began shrinking back into her seat when her question was completely ignored.

A few minutes later the front of the van became illuminated from an exterior source. "We must be near the refinery or the aluminum plant. We are taking the country route to wherever we are going," thought Mickey. "I guess I'll be hitchhiking home. Home from where? What about my bike?"

The unexpected touch of Tessa's hand upon his shoulder brought his consciousness back to the present moment. Still he could not decipher the absent minded expression on her face.

"Are we your prisoners?" Mickey's question was initially unanswered. With increased volume, he asked, "Are we your prisoners?"

"Not for long."

"I don't think we're in Ferndale," whispered Mickey when the van was eventually parked. His suspicions were confirmed when he stepped outside. "We're in Blaine."

"They must not be hiding anything from us, or us from anyone," suggested Tessa.

"Then why are we parked behind a deserted tavern?"

The rear door to the quiet building flew open and two men trotted down the steps. "You got here faster than I thought. Anything we need to know?"

"No details, no names, no traces." Without further comment the two men dressed in black reentered the van and promptly left the scene.

"Where are we?" asked Tessa.

"This little ole bar is where Loretta Lynn got her start," retorted the taller of the two men. "And you are right here with us."

"What sort of 'debriefing' is this?" demanded Mickey.

Both men laughed and the taller one spewed out a stream of tobacco before speaking. "You were just sold into slavery."

"I'm getting out of here," announced Tessa, turning to depart.

The cocking sound of a shotgun halted her progress. "Let's go inside and we'll tell you all about it."

No lights were illuminated inside the building but a light in the parking lot permitted reasonable visibility. Chairs were placed upside down in the old honky-tonk bar. Mickey noticed the upright piano on the small stage as the men led toward the bar area. "Both of you remove your shoes and socks," commanded the taller man, using the shotgun to poke both of them.

"Wait here," the jockey sized villain commanded. His companion stepped backward a couple of paces, maintaining his pose with his weapon in a rehearsed and choreographed move. The floor opened beneath Tessa and Mickey and they fell onto the lower linoleum basement floor. The trap door closed immediately above the scarcely lit room.

"Are you okay?" asked Mickey, quickly climbing to his feet.

Tessa nodded affirmatively and extended her hand for assistance. The two surveyed the room and found the light switch. Walking to the open door Mickey lamented, "The floor is covered with glass from broken bottles. There are blood stains on the floor. These guys need some serious lessons in hospitality."

Several minutes later the two men trooped down the stairway. "Did you have a nice trip to the basement?"

"What do you want from us?" asked Tessa.

"It depends on who we sell you to. My guess would be slavery but we do have some Nazi types who would love to experiment on you medically."

"Why us?" demanded Mickey.

"You must have seen too much of something. We don't ask questions and neither do they."

"Who is they?" returned Mickey.

"My point exactly," smiled the man without the shotgun, revealing rotting teeth. "You saw 'they'."

"You can try to scream or escape if you want. Nobody is around to hear you or help you. You ain't worth much dead but I'll kill you both if need be. If you try to escape the broken glass on your little footsies will really hurt and we'll follow you by your trails of blood."

After the two villainous men left the room and reached the middle of the broken glass, the smaller man turned back toward Tessa and Mickey and flipped up the middle finger of his left hand with a chuckling sneer before rushing to catch his colleague at the stairway.

"We're in a bad way," declared Mickey.

"What's going to happen?"

"We can escape the glass. Getting out of the building will be more difficult."

"What's your plan?" inquired Tessa, staring at the glass.

"The only plan I have requires quick action. Our best chance is to act immediately before they come down to check on us."

"That's not a plan."

"We can hear them walking around upstairs. Watch." Mickey removed his flannel shirt. He then faked a cough while simultaneously making a quick tear in the fabric of the shirt. Mickey slowly ripped the shirt into pieces and gave some of the material to Tessa. "Wrap your feet."

Tessa helplessly watched Mickey accomplish the task but took no action herself.

"Here, let me help. We need to have it real tight on the balls of your feet and on the toes. We are going to walk out of here and across two rooms of broken glass to the cellar window. When we get there I'm going to smash the glass and we will squirm through."

"Are we going to be okay?"

"The bad guys will be down here in a flash when they hear the window break, so we need to be fast." No more words were spoken as Mickey used the last piece of cloth to wrap his hands.

"Watch me, how I walk," commanded Mickey, "then do the same." He left the room without hesitation.

Just before Mickey reached the basement window, Tessa missed a step on the glass. "Ahhh! Ow!" She sank to one knee. Mickey quickly moved to her and covered her mouth. He picked her up bodily and moved to the window.

"Are you ready?" Without waiting for Tessa's response, Mickey smashed the glass with his covered left hand and quickly began removing shards of remaining glass from the frame. The sound of hurried footsteps echoed across the upstairs wooden floor. Using an old trunk for hoisting leverage, Mickey nearly tossed Tessa through the relatively large opening.

"God damn you assholes!" The smaller villain barreled down the stairs but ran in the wrong direction, toward the just vacated room. He was already changing direction when the near toothless man joined the scene.

Mickey jumped up, catching his weight on his wrapped hands, but he was pulled back by his first pursuer. "Not so fast dickhead."

As Mickey's wrapped feet hit the ground, both of his heels were slightly lacerated. His downward momentum resulted in a squatting position. In one continuous motion he reached for a piece of shattered window glass and jammed it into the thigh of the taller captor.

"Oh dammit! You fucking shit!" The pursuer stooped in pain. With a sweeping motion of his left hand, Mickey visciously sliced the villain's neck.

"You bastard!" The smaller enemy was several strides away on a dead run, his logger boots crunching glass on the way.

Realizing his left hand was injured from his successful counterattack, Mickey switched the glass shard to his right hand. From a distance of about five feet he threw the glass in an overhand manner.

"Ah fuck!" The glass flew directly into the left eye of his pursuer and stuck! Mickey watched the man drop to his knees, scream and flop his back onto the broken glass.

"Maybe I should have been a pitcher."

As the villain tried to yank out the piece of glass, it broke, leaving much of it embedded in his eye socket. Momentarily he lost consciousness.

"He's dead. They're both dead," Mickey announced as he emerged from the basement. "I'm going to get our shoes."

Mickey returned wearing his shoes and carrying Tessa's. "Hey wait!" He stood dumbfounded as he watched Tessa sprint toward the road until he was blinded by the darkness. "I've got your shoes!" Mickey moved forward past the glare of the overhead pole light until he could see her moonlit silhouette.

Tessa stopped briefly as if listening to something. She took several more steps before stopping again.

"Tessa!" The timing of Mickey's yell was an unknowing warning. Two shadowy figures quickly emerged from behind two leafless maple trees near the property driveway and leaped at Tessa.

"What the hell? They looked like they were flying with capes." Once fully engulfed in the darkness, Mickey paused to see what had happened with Tessa and her captors. He saw no movement.

There was nothing, no trace of anyone, anything. Mickey moved forward cautiously but tripped on a shoelace that had come untied. "Tessa? They tackled her right here. What? Do they have some kind of invisibility stealth capes?" he joked to the darkness. Mickey's senses became extremely sensitive and he moved his head like a curious cat to detect any sounds or motions.

On the arterial, a large car paused on the dark roadway. A passenger door on the far side of the car opened and subsequently closed several seconds later.

"What was that? Did they take her?" Mickey watched the vehicle speed away, cognizant of his untied shoe. "I need to find my way to the police station." While kneeling to tie his shoe, Mickey detected movement to his left, a darkly clad someone moving in the shadows toward the rear of the tavern. "Who's there?" He instinctively shifted to an athletic, defensive stance. A sound behind him made him turn, unfortunately toward two assailants. He tumbled to the ground under the cover of whatever was draped over him. His struggle was brief as he sensed his consciousness leaving him. "Why who?" Mickey heard himself marvel, "I don't hurt."

No longer able to move, Mickey struggled a few more seconds to hear his assailants. "He's out. You help clean up the glass and the bodies."

As consciousness faded, he wondered, "My body too?"

* * *

Awakening to the darkness, Mickey could not muster any awareness of his physical being. "I can't feel anything. It is like only my mind is alive except I think I'm somehow in motion."

He listened, expecting a thought to talk to him. "Whatever they captured me with must have been drugged. Who are they?" The complete darkness produced a sickly anxiety. "Am I covered with something? Do I still have a body?"

During the ensuing minutes, Mickey was not sure if he was asleep or awake. "Wait, I'm not moving. My senses are begininng to return to me, like novacaine wearing off. I can hear something. What is it?"

Straining his willpower to identify the indistinct sound, Mickey was jolted by a gentle touch. "Who is moving me?"

"A cosmic helper."

Mickey attempted to pinpoint the source of the response but still could only hear the indistinct sound. "I can feel my mind growing stronger. Maybe my brain circuits are waking up." Frustration mounted. "I can't talk. Nothing on my body can move."

A sudden inner warmth calmed him. "I feel like a light with colors is glowing inside me. It's a prism. The crystal skull. What are you doing here?"

"I love you."

Despite the happy glow of his soul, Mickey asked, "Should I wake up now? The crystal skull doesn't talk."

"It isn't the crystal speaking to you."

Mickey's growing awareness recognized the previously unrecognized sound. "It's water, it's waves. I can hear waves but I understand you."

"That's right, waves. We are the good guys. So are you."

"Did you save me?"

"You saved you. It was your love."

The physical sensation of his incapacitation being lifted from his body surprised Mickey. "I'm getting better." His eyes blinked at the starry sky but his peripheral vision was limited. "Who are you? Where are you?"

A huge face leaned into his narrow scope of vision. "You have a strange destiny."

"Was the crystal skull here? I felt it."

"It is your symbol. It will be in your dreams to help you. It will always find you."

"Can I find it?" Mickey's increasing return to three dimensional reality accepted the telepathic mode of communication. "You are a sasquatch. Is this a dream?"

Mickey became aware of the full moon outlining the shape of the huge head peering down at him. The eyes of the being suddenly glowed distinctly and brightly red before vanishing.

"I love you."

* * *

An eagle's call awakened Mickey and his eyes immediately spotted the bird gliding above the beach where he lay. "Thank you friend." He sat up, completely shocked by the local environment.

"My bicycle!" He sprang to his feet and approached his bike, still leaning against a big rock. "I'm not sore," he commented aloud, looking over his body, "and sleeping on a beach isn't like sleeping in a bed."

After a cursory examination of his bicycle, Mickey sat on one of the rocks, viewing the beach. "I wasn't drinking. Why would I pass out? And how come I'm not cold? It's winter. And what happened to my shirt?"

Mickey shrugged off his own questions and instead tried to reconstruct the events leading up to the present moment. "I remember riding to the reservation but I don't remember coming this far. I feel like I have a Watergate brain...a big part of the tape is missing."

After kneeling to dump sand out of his partially cuffed pant leg, Mickey surveyed the road along the beach. "A green Chevrolet. Maybe I'm not alone, and I need to pee."

Walking toward the vehicle, he squinted into its nearby shadows. "Someone's on the ground!"

Within seconds Mickey knelt next to the unconscious, attractive dirty blonde haired woman, her arm under her head. Mickey checked her breathing and looked for blood. "She seems okay. Maybe she passed out too."

The woman mumbled something so Mickey assisted her in sitting up. Her eyes opened but she registered no comprehension of his presence.

"Do you want to be in your car?"

Another mumble was interpreted as a 'yes' and Mickey helped the woman to her feet, stepping sideways with her to avoid the car door. He used his hips to guide her onto the bench seat. "Can you hear me? Are you okay?"

"They want me. They took me."

Mickey stroked the hair out of her tilted face. "Who did?"

"A killing monster?"

"Who is a killing monster?"

"Forget it. I am. Forget it." Her vague consciousness departed her and she slumped forward, her head falling upon the car horn. The sudden volume caused a reflex action backward and then sideways onto the seat.

Mickey moved her left leg out of the way of the car door. Almost unintelligibly the young woman mumbled, "You're the one, the one who touched me."

"I suppose I am."

"Thank you. I'm going to wake up for a few minutes and then I'll be going," she said, but she did not get up off the seat.

Mickey mounted his bicycle and began the ride back to Bellingham. "None of the scenery looks familiar. It was daytime when I rode out here, I think."

While gliding down a small hill, Mickey checked his pockets. "The skull toy!" His mind looked skyward as he tried remembering something important. "Oh my goodness! I'm supposed to drive to Spokane for Christmas."

He placed the skull toy back in his pocket. "Still, there is something else to remember. It seems like I had a bad dream about bad people but I can't remember the dream. Is it something I'm supposed to remember to forget? I hope I still have hair then. My feet hurt and I gotta pee."

CHAPTER SEVENTEEN

OUT OF PRISM FOR BAD BEHAVIOR

After peeling the skin from her right cheek away from the vinyl seat of the car when she awoke, Tessa sat up with the help of the steering wheel. "Where am I?" She squinted through the sunight at the uninhabited, deserted beach.

"My head hurts." Forgetting about her location, she slumped back down on the seat. "I want to sleep some more but I shouldn't."

"Why not?" her thoughts countered aloud.

"You will probably get hungry or cold or sick." Tessa smiled. "I like my dialogue. It's going somewhere and I don't care where."

"But I should. Why am I not cold?" She surveyed her clothing and sat up again to view the interior of the Chevrolet. "What did happen?"

Tessa strained to remember but instead developed an unrelenting thought pattern. "You can't remember." The sound of a boat motor on the calm early winter waters of Lummi Bay caused Tessa to seek the source of the noise. "It was here. Something happened here."

As if someone had thrown a switch, Tessa developed a headache. "You can't remember. I can't remember."

In a moment of fundamental cognition Tessa briefly panicked as she looked for her car keys. "Who has them?" She located them in her coat pocket. "What's this? Oh, the little skull toy." She manipulated the toy before returning it to her pocket. "It reminds me of the crystal skull." Her headache increased in intensity. "Is it punishing me?" She located the toy in her pocket and flung it out the window. "I need to avoid the crystal skull. Will it avoid me?"

"I slept here." She felt the car seat with her hand. "Where is here?" She started the car engine. "I don't remember how I got here but somehow I remember which way to go home. That's a good thing to think about, home." Images of the house she inherited from her grandfather came to mind. "Wow, my headache suddenly went away." She started the engine and began driving. "My feet hurt."

"What did they want with me? Science isn't ready yet. I don't want to know what they want. Who is they?"

Noticing the 35 miles per hour speed limit sign, Tessa sped up cautiously. "Does mother know I'm here? I don't even know I'm here. Where? Someone knows I'm here. There was someone else, someone from my future."

After a couple of miles on the roadway which meandered along the contour of the shoreline, Tessa noticed a cyclist in the distance. The man stopped, laid his bike by the side of the road, and trotted off into the bushes. "Where's he going? Oh, he must have to pee."

Tessa peered into the rear view mirror but immediately closed her eyes. After several seconds she opened them again. "Yes, it is me."

But it wasn't. "How can it be? I look like I did when I was 12 years old, when I killed Teddy." Tessa was startled by her young looking smile in the mirror. "I feel every hair on my body growing."

The Chevrolet increased its speed, causing Tessa to glance at her foot on the accelerator. "I can reach the pedal." The man was nowhere in sight as she approached the clearly visible bicycle along the roadway. "I should know that man. I think maybe I do."

Again the vehicle increased its pace but this time Tessa's eyes remained fixed on the bicycle. The 1972 Chevrolet swerved quickly and purposely, striking the two wheeler with the front right tire, causing it to react violently against the wheel well and passenger door. The bicycle, no match for the massive automobile, was left twisted and inoperable while the car kept going.

"You're the one? Not until the white moose and her albino calf show up, whenever that is."

She laughed. "I'm the one. I am going to be the Queen of Diamonds. At first it was going to be crystal but I want diamonds." Her normal smile in the rearview mirror confirmed her pronouncement, but the grin soon disappeared. "I have to wait 30 years. Why? I don't remember but it is something about my body, maybe menopause. Destiny can be such a curse."

AUTHOR BIOGRAPHY

Gare Martin presently lives in Omak, Washington and is a parent, grandparent and lifelong resident of the state. He has B.A. and M.A. degrees in History from Western Washington University. In many cities, towns, states and provinces, Gare has played harmonica, bass, guitar and vocals, baseball, softball, basketball, football and soccer. He first performed as an acrobat on television at age 8. He also worked 25 years in the real estate industry and is an experienced public speaker and instructor. Why write magic realism science fiction? "I had a possible bigfoot sighting between Mt. Spokane foothills and then in 2003 I spent thousands of dollars to venture to Boston and Cooperstown to break the curse of Babe Ruth. Somehow the stories seemed connected." Gare is a member of the Pacific Northwest Writers Association.

The original idea for the Emagication trilogy was a non-horror sasquatch story, which led to non-traditional situations and solutions. Although the primary characters originate from diverse places, most of the trilogy has a northwest setting. "I am a dedicated researcher of virtually everything unexplainable. Also, some of the strange phenomena that happened to me are sprinkled throughout the trilogy, but you already knew that, didn't you?"

ABOUT THE BOOK: QUANTUM CRYSTAL SKULL

Book I of The Emagication Trilogy

Joseph Stalin's evil experiment to cross-breed humans and apes failed, with one exception. What ever became of that lone escapee to North America? Why is the crystal skull a catalyst for either destiny or fate? Can secrets become self-condemning? Presented as a magic realism cyclical period piece, QUANTUM CRYSTAL SKULL is the first book of THE EMAGICATION TRILOGY. The story is grounded in social history but is shaped by unique perceptions of a crystal skull as well as sightings of sasquatches. What happens when biological mutation has a crystal skull as a catalyst? Ultimately the first book brings the story to the northwest and provides the challenging lines and boundaries for the predicaments of the second book of the trilogy.

Ancestral family prophecy from a Native American shaman grandfather convinces Amanda, the family matriarch in Spokane, that her children or grandchildren will be involved. Will family secrets affect that destiny? Alexiev, the escapee from the Soviet Union, finds freedom to be elusive. He fears his own secret more but he is relieved when his child was born without biological mutation. Instead it surfaces with his estranged grandchild. Clayton and Emily in Boston are the first of the characters to interact with the crystal skull after it was brought to Canada from Central America. They are also grandparents of Tessa, victim of the biological mutation. Mickey, unsure of his role in the family prophecy, has a chance, bizarre incident with Tessa. Or was it chance? This provides the setting for the second book of the trilogy.

SASQUATCH RACES is presented in a different style of magic realism and primarily involves the third generation characters of the first book. A field search with Tessa for bigfoot uncovers shapeshifting humans who transform Mickey involuntarily into a sasquatch. He faces being alone, unprepared for the most basic circumstances, or joining a terrorist group. Who can rally the true sasquatches? How can they help?

EMAGICATION, the third book of the trilogy, was written in yet a third style of magic realism and is interactive with the first two books. Why would Novalogy attempt to control the moon? How does a clone battle his original for his soul? The learning curve for author Glade Mahoney involves two reappearing red stones, time dilations, a psychic sasquatch, a secret native storytelling society and a guided interdimensional incarnation event. He must create the first two books of the trilogy to necessitate "emagication" as a solution.

The entire trilogy is expected to become available during 2016.

CPSIA information can be obtained
at www.ICGtesting.com
Printed in the USA
FSOW02n2245300916
25592FS